LATE BREAKING

Late Breaking

STORIES

K.D. MILLER

BIBLIOASIS
WINDSOR, ONTARIO

Copyright © K.D. Miller, 2018

FIRST EDITION

Library and Archives Canada Cataloguing in Publication

Miller, K. D. (Kathleen Daisy), 1951-, author
        Late breaking / K.D. Miller.

Short stories.
Issued in print and electronic formats.
ISBN 978-1-77196-247-6 (softcover).--ISBN 978-1-77196-248-3 (ebook)

        I. Title.

PS8576.I5392L48 2018   C813'.54   C2018-901730-9
                                                 C2018-901731-7

Edited by Daniel Wells
Copy-edited by Emily Donaldson
Typeset and Designed by Chris Andrechek
Cover image: *Refrigerator*, 1977 by Alex Colville, Copyright A.C. Fine Art Inc.
All interior paintings by Alex Colville, Copyright A.C. Fine Art Inc.

Published with the generous assistance of the Canada Council for the Arts, which last year invested $153 million to bring the arts to Canadians throughout the country, and the financial support of the Government of Canada. Biblioasis also acknowledges the support of the Ontario Arts Council (OAC), an agency of the Government of Ontario, which last year funded 1,709 individual artists and 1,078 organizations in 204 communities across Ontario, for a total of $52.1 million, and the contribution of the Government of Ontario through the Ontario Book Publishing Tax Credit and the Ontario Media Development Corporation.

PRINTED AND BOUND IN CANADA

These stories were inspired by the paintings of Alex Colville

Contents

Kiss With Honda, 1989.

The Last Trumpet

LEN SPARKS HAS STARTED TO look forward to the advice column in the *Sackville Tribune-Post*. Reading about the situations people get themselves into charges him up in the morning. "Idiot!" he will all but snort over his cereal. "How and *why?*" Crackling the paper, shaking his head, while Sister watches him with her worried beagle eyes. "How and *why?*"

This morning, what he reads makes him go so still and quiet that Sister comes close, needing his palm on her head to forestall a whine. A woman has written in about her impending death. Specifically, her burial. She wants to be placed in her late husband's coffin, turned on her side to face him, so that when the last trumpet sounds and they wake to the Resurrection, they will embrace each other with joy and rise together.

Len has to read the letter a second time to be sure the writer is serious. She must be very old, he thinks, then reminds himself that he's eighty-six. But still. Are there people today who actually believe that kind of thing? Take it literally?

The advice columnist's name is Fran, and she gets it right most of the time. With this poor soul she is gentle.

Tactful. She suggests that the woman talk to her pastor, then perhaps discuss the matter with an undertaker. Len feels a stab of pity, imagining each man wondering whether to laugh or cry.

Sister is resting her chin on his knee. He starts in on a good scratch, neck to tail, that makes her close her eyes and sigh deep in her throat. "That's enough now," he says after a minute. "Go lie down. Go." Sister obeys, padding to her wicker bed lined with the cushion whose plaid is dim under a layer of shed hair. Len supposes he should have the thing cleaned. Did Joan ever send it out to be cleaned? He can't remember.

He stirs the coffee he poured before he sat down so it would be cool enough to drink when he got to it after his cereal and canned peaches. He can't stop thinking about that letter. What would it be like to have a rock-solid belief in something like the resurrection of the body? To be able to put aside all logic, quiet all questions and doubts, simply not see images of putrefaction and protruding bone?

He sips his coffee. Puts more milk in from the small pitcher, his shaking hand making it slop a little into the saucer. It used to drive Joan nuts, the way he drank his coffee almost cold. "I can pour it the night before and leave it in the fridge for you if you like," she said more than once.

He'll visit her this afternoon. It's the first of the month. October. Might not be able to do it again till spring. For years after she died, he kept his monthly appointment at her grave regardless of the weather. But the last few winters have been fierce—deep snow and ice storms. Last year he actually got one of those pronged attachments for the tip of his cane. He hates it, the way it resembles the claws of some strange beast.

"I've become a strange beast, Sister," he says aloud. The dog hears her name and raises her head, looking at him hopefully. "No, not yet. Just settle down. We'll go for a you-know-what in a little while." Even now, in her twelfth year, she goes all puppyish if she hears *walk*.

He wonders if she still misses Brother, or even remembers him. Brother was always the more rambunctious of the two, and one day when he was barely a year old he ran into the street and was hit. Len insisted on letting Sister see and sniff the body so that she would understand that Brother was dead. But it didn't seem to work. She took on a puzzled air, poking into every corner of the house, searching the face of each visitor as if to say, "Do *you* know where Brother went?" Or at least, that's how it seemed to Len. Joan was more prosaic. "She's not all that bright. Just give it time. She'll forget he ever existed." She never said so, but Len knew that, of the two, Joan would have preferred to lose Sister. Brother was definitely her dog. Their personalities matched—curious, adventurous, demanding.

The dogs got their names by default. It was how the woman at the kennel referred to them as puppies—Sister and Brother. "Whatever you do," she said, "don't get two males from the same litter. They'll be like Tom and Jerry—egging each other on and wrecking the house. Two females are better, even though they can get a little territorial sometimes. But a sister and a brother? Bingo."

They couldn't decide on names. Fred and Ginger? George and Gracie? Beatrice and Benedict? One day they realized the dogs had decided for themselves, the female turning her head if she heard *Sister*, the male thumping his tail to the sound of *Brother*.

Len folds the last section of the paper. Places it on top of the other sections and squares the pile. Then he stacks his breakfast dishes—plate, saucer, cereal bowl, fruit bowl, coffee cup. Readies himself to get up. He still refuses to bring his cane to the table. The cane is for outside. Its place is in the brass umbrella stand by the front door. The day he'd allow himself to hobble around with it in the kitchen—

He pushes his chair back and gets carefully to his feet, thinking through the distance from table to sink. So far, so good. None of that sickening light-headedness he's had of late, forcing him to sit right back down. Now. Dishes to the counter. Then. Papers to the recycle bin under the sink. Two trips.

Is the stack of dishes rattling more than it did yesterday? Would a tray help? He could maybe assemble his breakfast things the night before on a tray. It's the turning around that's a bugger. Well, he could set his place at the other end of the table. Facing the sink. Six steps. There. Set the pile on the counter with a minimum of clatter and slide. Now do the whole thing over again to get the newspapers into the box. Jesus.

A tray. Does he even have a tray? Joan used to bring drinks out to guests. He tries to picture her. Would she have used a tray for that? She'd never let him help, that was for sure. His job was to entertain, be all chuckly and urbane in the living room. If there was ever a crash and a whispered "Shit!" from the kitchen, he would rise and go, saying, "My lady wife hath need of me." Then, when she hissed at him to just keep out of her way, he would re-emerge, give the company a seraphic smile, and say, "Every day a honeymoon."

Company. Joan did love a party, for all her fussing. Probably loved the fussing too. Mostly couples they'd have over, back in the day. Neighbours. His colleagues from the

12

school. Hers from all her volunteer jobs. A few singles. Men, usually. Joan was a man's woman. No doubt about that.

Len pauses in the middle of gathering up the papers. There was that one guy. Tall. Balding. On the arts festival committee with Joan. Was he the one with the silver Honda? Would he have come to the house? Taken a drink? Shaken Len's hand?

No way to know. And no point dwelling on it now. It's in the past. He's made it to the sink for the second time. The papers are in the box. He'll wash the dishes, sit for a bit, then take Sister for her walk.

*

It's cold for early October. He should have worn his heavier coat. His November coat, as he thinks of it. The windbreaker that got him through September is just light enough this morning to leave him chilled. He could have used gloves, too.

How do animals manage the temperature extremes, he wonders, watching Sister meander and sniff, seeking the perfect place to squat. All this one has is the same short pelt all year round. True, he does tie her coat on her in the winter, and puts booties on her feet for the salt. But still. He doesn't know much about beagles, where they originated, why they were bred to be the way they are. Something to do this afternoon. Google beagles.

Sister has finished, and watches apologetically as Len plants his cane, bracing himself with it to go down on one knee and pick up the mess with the hand already inside the plastic bag. It's all about preparation, he thinks, hoisting himself back up onto his feet.

He stashes the plastic bag in the first waste container he finds, then heads down Bridge to Main. He and Sister always enter the waterfowl park near St. Paul's, where Joan was rector's warden the two years before she was killed. Her funeral was huge. Crowd spilling out the door. People he barely knew coming close to take his hand or squeeze his shoulder and murmur something. None of them the face he kept looking for, in spite of himself. Surely the guy wouldn't have the gall. Or would he? Slip in the back at the last minute. Slip out again just before the end. Take off in his silver Honda.

They pass St. Paul's, then take the path to the board-walk. They're a bit late this morning, so the mist has mostly lifted off the water. Still, there is that point on the near horizon where everything dissolves into grey—no distinction between water and sky. The sight always cheers Len, for some reason.

Cattails knocking against the handrails on either side are already crisping, and most of the songbirds have left. But there's still plenty of chatter and chirp to distract Sister from her sniffing. She woofs at a squawking raven overhead, then gets so fixated on some gum underfoot that Len has to pull her away.

When they come to their usual first resting spot, one of the little lookouts built off to the side and ringed with benches, they find it occupied. A young couple. Both smoking. Both wearing dark glasses on this cold grey morning. As Len passes by, pulling Sister back to his side and already trying to sight the next lookout, he hears the young woman say, "There are other. Issues. Besides. That."

One of *those* conversations, from the sound of it. Remember them? Joan pelting him with words. Him just waiting for it to be over. Do all women do that? Stir things up just when they've gotten settled and calm? Insist there is some *other issue* whose existence was always news to him, yet for which he was somehow always to blame?

He never repaid her in kind. Could have. Could have pointed a finger. Said a few words of his own. Would it have changed anything, if he had? Or would she have found some way to turn it around and as usual blame him?

Sister whines softly at his side and he realizes he's been tightening up on the leash. "Sorry, old girl. Let's have a bit of a rest." They've come to the next lookout which is vacant, thank God. Len sits stiffly down on the bench, feeling pain transfer from his feet to his knees. It never leaves now, just moves around.

The fog has lifted. He can see where the boardwalk zig-zags out into the marsh, then back around to solid ground. The surface of the water is pocked with single raindrops. A muskrat noses open a seam, then submerges again.

This is usually when the simplicity of the place, its birds and animals living so completely in the present, settles him down and cheers him up. But he's morbid this morning. Brooding on things best left buried. Must be the effect of that letter to the advice columnist. Damn fool woman wanting to wake from the dead in her husband's arms. Beats opening your eyes alone inside your own coffin, he supposes. Having to heave against the lid, lift all that weight of dirt, claw your way to the surface in answer to the last trumpet sounding. Except he doubts she sees it that way. Probably imagines things being all lovely and easy and miraculous. Likely hasn't occurred to her that when her husband opens his own eyes and sees his wife again—this time for all eternity—his reaction might be something less than unmitigated joy.

Len hasn't a clue what happens after death, and is not sure he cares. He stayed away from the church for a year after Joan's funeral. Kept telling himself he'd never go back. But in time, he did. And now he's there most Sunday mornings. It's an outing. A chance to see people.

When Joan was alive he only went because she was so involved with the place. She ran it the way she ran the arts festival committee and the library board. Hustled him into his tie and out the door every Sunday morning so as to have time to perch on the kneeler in front of their pew to pray—eyes shut, slightly smiling lips moving. Len himself just sat. He had been raised a Presbyterian, and his parents had looked little and lost at the Anglican mass Joan had insisted on for their wedding.

Joan knew how to insist. It was her gift. How she got things done. They never talked about her habit of praying prior to a Sunday service—what she prayed for, what she believed in. Besides herself, that is. Yes, Joan Sparks definitely believed in Joan Sparks.

A pair of mallards glide past. Perfectly in sync, they upend to feed. Do they mate for life, Len wonders. Something else to look up. Imagine how serene that would be. *This is your mate. There will be no other. So just paddle your feet and don't even think about it.*

But what if one of them dies? When the police came to the door with the news that Joan had been hit by a van while jaywalking across Main, Len's first thought was, *Just like Brother.* His second was, *I never told her. She'll never know that I knew.*

It had been close at times, over the years. Oddly enough, the day he found out, it was easy. Maybe he was in shock. He got through dinner with the usual small talk about work. Had no problem leaving out the part about getting a headache after lunch, asking another teacher to supervise his spare, knocking off early. Walking home as usual, wondering if Joan would be there, or off doing one of her projects. Then, from half a block away, seeing a silver Honda just pulling out of their driveway. Joan on the porch watching it. Suddenly running down the steps. The car pausing. The driver leaning out. Joan bending to kiss him.

Len seemed to know exactly what to do—step quickly back behind a tall hedge and watch as the Honda passed him by, the driver invisible through the sunlit windshield. He felt as if he were in a play, performing a role he had been rehearsing all his life. Next the script directed him to turn and walk to that little cafe around the corner. Sit over one cooling cup of coffee until his usual coming-home time.

That night he lay in the dark beside Joan, aware of the inches between them. Feeling words crowding the back of his throat. *Why? How long—? What does he—?* It had been weeks since she'd wanted him to touch her. But she had always been temperamental that way. And he'd always just ridden it out, relieved and grateful to have her back when she came back.

So that was what he did. And when, in time, she did come back, did slide those few inches to press up against him, all he felt was the usual gratitude and relief. And though he never stopped looking for it, he never saw the silver Honda again.

*

Although beagle-type dogs have existed for 2500 years, the modern breed was developed in Great Britain around the 1830s from several breeds...

Len resisted getting a computer at first. Held out as long as he could against Joan, who started agitating for one in the early nineties.

Beagles are scent hounds, developed primarily for tracking hare, rabbit, deer, and other small game. They have a great sense of smell and tracking instinct that sees them employed as detection dogs for prohibited agricultural imports and food-stuffs in quarantine...

He gave in, of course, thinking that would be the end of it and discovering it was only the beginning. Updates all the time and always the latest gizmo Joan just had to have. Then the desktop/laptop debate, which Len conceded almost before it began. Then, within months of acquiring the machine he is using now and will likely take to the grave, Joan was pricing smartphones, claiming she needed to be free of anything plugged in at home. *Does she mean me?* Len remembers musing at the time.

Joan's phone became a third presence, their electronic child, never asleep, forever interrupting. She claimed it consolidated and streamlined things for her, but it seemed to Len that it complicated her life, harassing and obsessing her. She was focused on it when she stepped off the curb and was hit.

Beagles are intelligent but single-minded, and popular pets because of their size, even temper, and lack of inherited health problems.

What if human beings were bred for specific tasks, the way domesticated animals are? Not for the first time, Len fantasizes some extraterrestrial race, whose intelligence compares to that of Homo sapiens the way his does to Sister's, arriving one day on Earth and taking over. In just a few generations, humans would be sorted into functional breeds—some to do menial work, some to invent or create, others to organize and keep records. Len is aware that he finds something attractive in the notion. Knowing one's role, one's nature, and being unwilling, even unable, to deviate from it.

But what if it had actually happened in his lifetime? Where would he have fit, in the scheme of things? He was fifteen when the Second World War ended. His father had fought in the Great War, and never stopped talking about it. Unlike other boys his age, Len did not chafe at being just too young to join up. He felt secretly relieved, as if he'd gotten off scot-free.

He took a general bachelor's degree and became a high school teacher in Sackville, New Brunswick. He was good enough in the classroom to keep order and impart his subject, which was geography. An inoffensive discipline, neither soft art nor hard science, offering a smorgasbord of topics from tariffs on trade goods to tectonic forces shifting the ground beneath his students' feet.

Somewhat to his surprise, he married a strikingly beautiful woman who got more so with age, her white hair contrasting dramatically with her dark brows. A woman, however, who was not unlike one of those tectonic forces—never resting, never satisfied, incapable of engaging with an individual or a group without pushing them around.

Joan was scornful of Sackville, for all she practically ran its cultural and spiritual life. She was furious with Len for refusing a vice-principalship in Moncton—*A real city, at least! This place is a village!* But Len for once put his foot down and refused to move. He had found his place. Sackville *was* a city, albeit a cosy one, with its historic university and fall fair. It was small enough that he could walk back and forth to work each day. Walk to church each Sunday morning. Afford a big old house with a wraparound porch that never failed to move him when he turned the corner at the end of the day and sighted it. He was used to his life. Even the discomforts of his marriage were accustomed discomforts. He never cheated on Joan. Not for lack of opportunity. A high school teacher in a small place like Sackville gets a certain number of eyes turning his way. But it stopped with the eyes. Sometimes Joan would even have to tell him—*Didn't you see Trish Bromley just throwing herself at you?*—after some gathering or other. All he would remember would be the woman's upturned face, her expression interested. Well, all right. Maybe a bit more than just interested. But such occurrences always left him mystified. He knew he was not unattractive. He just felt so thoroughly married. He had been made to be married. To Joan. He felt safe in his life. Out of harm's way. And there was nothing wrong with that.

He may have spent all his political capital as breadwinner when he refused to move for that promotion. And it's possible Joan was paying him back when she had that affair—if that's what it was—with the guy in the silver Honda. He doesn't know. He never will. It's in the past, he reminds himself, shutting down the computer.

*

The cemetery gates always strike him as a bit pretentious—two big gothic wings wafting him in. But here he is, as usual. First of the month. A little later in the day than he would have liked. The dark comes down early, and they shut the place up at five.

He almost didn't make it out the door. That damned light-headedness again when he tried to get up out of his desk chair. It dropped him right back down with a *whump*. All he could do was sit and wait for the room to stop spinning. He thought about just staying home, leaving the visit till tomorrow or the next day. But no. That would be the start of something. Something he does not want to start.

Sister was so sound asleep that he decided not to wake her for a second walk. She's sleeping more and more these days. He supposes the time is coming. But not just yet. She can still get around. Still likes her food. And she's a presence in the house. Sometimes he'll lower his paper or look away from the TV and see her eyes upon him. He'll wonder how long she has been quietly studying him, and why. Maybe she knows he's all she's got. Maybe she senses that he will one day decide she has lived long enough. *Oh for God's sake, Len,* he can just hear Joan, *she's a dog. They don't think beyond their next bowl of kibble.*

Joan's grave is not far in, but it is up a bit of a rise. Len has to stop half way and catch his breath. When she died, there was actually a sale on cemetery plots and he got a two-for-one deal. He paid a little extra even so, because there was a bench facing where their headstones would be. At the time, he didn't care all that much, but now he's glad of a place to sit during these monthly visits.

He leans on his cane and looks around at the acres of graves. Generations upon generations. Taking up land. Would the day ever come when the needs of the living shredded the last notion of what is sacred? He imagines graveyards being excavated for condominium foundations. Jaws of earth-movers prying up dry and not-so-dry bones. Shards of mahogany. Crisping bouquets. All of it loaded onto trucks trundling up out of the deepening pit, then taking it—

"Hey, you got a light?"

Where did he come from? A boy. Maybe fifteen. Wearing jeans and one of those hoodie things or whatever they're called.

"I'm sorry?"

"I *said*. Do. You. Got. A light."

Rude young—"No. I haven't."

"You sure?"

"Yes, I'm sure," Len says, stumping past. "I don't smoke. And neither should you." Honestly.

The bench is just a few steps around a bend in the cemetery path. When he reaches it he grabs onto the armrest, braces with his cane, and sits gingerly. Even through his heavier coat, the seat is hard and cold.

Joan's headstone is a plain white marble tablet. Name and dates. No *Beloved Wife of* or any other sentiment. He did want to make the right decision. Searched his memory for any hint she might have given about preferring to be cremated. Except Joan didn't hint, and she didn't prefer. If she wanted something, she opened her mouth and—

"You just out takin' a walk or somethin'?"

Damn. He didn't hear the kid following him. Len tightens up on the handle of his cane. Draws a calming breath. "I'm visiting my late wife." He nods toward Joan's grave.

"Oh yeah?" The boy sits down beside him. "How long she been dead?" His face is a pale oval, the eyes dark-lashed, the lips fleshy, curled in a smirk. There is a pink cluster of pimples on his chin.

Len moves his left hand into his lap. He's wearing his good watch—the one he got at retirement. And his wallet—cash and credit card—is in his lapel pocket. But he has his cane. One good crack across the bridge of the nose—

Oh, calm down. The boy hasn't done anything wrong. As a teacher, Len learned to focus on the question asked and filter out any attitude. It usually worked. "As you can see from the date on the stone, my wife passed away eight years ago," he says firmly, then faces front.

"What she die of?"

Is he being baited? The way the young sometimes bait the old? He wants to say, *You'll be like me some day. I know you don't believe it, but it's true. Unless you die young in some damned fool way. Racing a car. Putting some garbage into your veins or up your nose or whatever your type does.* Keeping his voice steady, he says, "It was an accident. She was hit crossing the street. Now if you don't mind, I would like to be quiet."

"Sure. No problem. Quiet as you want."

Len tries to ignore the boy after that, but he must have a slight cold because his breath snuffles. He wants to focus the way he usually does, calling up memories of Joan. Just fifteen minutes or so of acknowledgement. It's what he does. Once a month. He was her husband. She was his wife. All the difficulties and disappointments notwithstanding.

Len sucks up all the integrity in the room. Did Joan ever actually say that? Or can he just imagine her saying it?

No matter. Focus. Try. But his mind throws up a picture of how she—her body—must be now. Why didn't he just go ahead and have her cremated? Scatter the ashes wherever? Except he wouldn't have scattered her, would he? No, he'd have kept her in a box or an urn somewhere in the living room. Ridiculous. Superstitious. Still, he did want her to be in a specific place. That was another odd thought he had right after she died. *At least now I'll know where she is. What she's—*

"You come here a lot?"

Len sighs. "I come here once per month. For just a few minutes. Of quiet reflection."

"You and her married for long?"

"Forty-eight years."

"Wow. All that time. Just you two. What's that like?"

"I'm sorry?"

"Like, didn't you get sick of each other?"

Len says nothing, just looks steadily ahead at Joan's grave, thinking he might as well leave but unwilling to let the boy force him out.

"Like, didn't you fight or nothin'? My folks, they fight all the time."

Maybe, Len thinks resignedly, this could be a teaching moment. "There are always tensions in a marriage," he says. "Especially a long one. But you adjust to each other. And if there is a foundation of respect—"

"You ever give her a little tap?"

"What?"

"You know. Just a swat now and then. Keep her in line."

What kind of home does this boy come from? "Absolutely not." Then, quoting his father, "When a man raises his hand to a woman, he ceases to be a man."

"She pretty good, then?"

"Excuse me?"

"You know."

"I'm sure I don't."

"You get what you want? When you wanted it?"

"Look, I don't know what you're—"

"Or did you have to beg for it?" The boy's adenoidal breath is almost in his ear. "Did you have to say, *Pleease, Honey! Pleease! Pleease?*"

Len plants his cane. Pulls himself to his feet. Feels the blood drain sickeningly from his head. Lands back down. "Oooff!" One slat of the bench bruises his tailbone. His cane clatters to the ground beside him.

"Hey! Geez. You all right?" The boy is crouched in front of him, peering into his face. Grinning. "You know what? You should put your head down. Between your knees. Yeah. That's what you're supposed to do."

And that is what Len does, because the boy puts his hands on his shoulders and pushes him down hard until he is bent double. "I can't breathe!" he squeaks, and the pressure eases a bit.

"Now, you just stay that way," the boy says tenderly. "You hear me?" When Len does not respond, he presses down hard again.

"Yes!" Len even nods—wags his head between his knees. He can see the end of his cane, where it fell. Could he reach it if—

"Good. That's good." A pale hand picks the cane up. Pulls it out of his line of vision. He hears a whoosh of air. Another. Is the boy swinging his cane around? Revving up? Len braces for the impact. He'll be found beaten to death in front of his wife's grave. Because he always visits his wife, doesn't he? Every bloody month. His wife with her prayers and her good works. His wife who cheated on him. Opened her legs. Took him for a bloody—

Whump!

He winces at the sound. Dares to look up. The boy raises the cane. Brings it down again. On Joan's grave.

Whump!

"Bitch!"

Whump!

"Cunt!"

Whump!

Len jerks with every blow. *Right. Wear yourself out. Take it out on her. Give it to her. Give it to her.*

The boy stops and stands, breathing heavily. Len quickly looks down again. Hears the sound of a zipper. A splashing. "Drink it, bitch!"

Drink it, bitch.

A clatter. Running footsteps. Getting fainter.

After a long moment, Len looks up. There, a few feet in front of him on the path, is his cane. No sign of the boy. He listens. Hard. Nothing.

Carefully, he half-rolls off the bench onto his knees. Feels cold gravel through the fabric of his pants. Crawls to his cane. Braces with it. Pulls himself to his feet. Hobbles to Joan's grave and leans on the stone. "I'm sorry," he wheezes. "I'm sorry." He is tired to death. He could lie down right here and now with Joan and fall asleep. But if he does that, Sister will die slowly inside the house of hunger and thirst. She won't howl or bark at a window the way Brother would have. And even if she does, who will hear? No one comes to the door. There's no mail delivery any more, just that bloody community box he has to walk to. He should have asked a neighbor to look in on him every other day or so. But that's how it starts. The exchanged looks. The being talked about. *Poor old Len …*

He's getting his breath back. Patting the headstone now, saying, "All right then? All right." He checks his watch. It's not yet five. If he starts back now, he'll make it to the gates before they lock them.

Once he's home, should he call the authorities? Report the boy? He did get a good look at him. But his mind veers from the thought of a young officer, perhaps even a woman, sitting in his living room and listening to his tale of what happened. What was done to him. And to Joan. Then asking questions. Forcing him to reveal more and more detail. It would be like having to describe a humiliating but deserved punishment.

So the boy will get off scot-free. Maybe Len will even encounter him one day when he's out walking Sister.

Sister. She'll be waking up. Wondering where he is. Making that worried little whine in her throat. He starts toward the gates. Is he actually hungry? What does he have in the house?

He should start getting his groceries delivered. He hasn't been eating well, because he can only carry one bag home at a time from the store and he doesn't want to be seen trundling one of those old-lady bundle buggies. So yes. Delivery. He'll set that up. Tomorrow. Nothing wrong with it, either. Not as if he's getting Meals on bloody Wheels.

And what was he thinking about this morning? Setting his breakfast things out on a tray the night before. At the other end of the table, facing the sink. He must have a tray somewhere. He'll take a look tonight. Pick one up tomorrow from the hardware in town, if necessary.

It's all about preparation, he reminds himself, stumping down the hill. Catching sight of the gates.

January, 1971.

LATE BREAKING — *title of Jill Macklin's novel*

JILL USED TO LIKE BEING interviewed. Once every other year or so, it was flattering. Now that it has become a daily occurrence, it just makes her tired. "So, Jill, *tell* me..." (*No, she wants to say. I'm not going to tell you a damned thing more.*) "Now, *that's* interesting, Jill! Are you saying..." (*I'm saying whatever I just said.*)

Her questioners bulge and pulse with energy. "In your novel, Jill, you *actually*..." (*Yes, you annoying young thing. In my novel I actually depict two older people—older than you believe you yourself will ever be—fucking. Pawing each other. Slobbering all over each others' parts.*) "May I ask if the book is based on anyone you ..." (*May I ask if you have any idea how ridiculous that question is?*)

But Jill does not say that, or any of the other things she wants to say. Instead, she smiles charmingly at the interviewer who could be her child, or even her grandchild, and says, "Well, what else does a writer have besides her own experience? That's not to rule out the power of the imagination, of course. True, I might take some episode from my own life as material. But then I work it. I change it. I fit it to the story at hand." (*Or sometimes I leave it raw and bloody, soaking into the page.*)

"Jill, can we just get back to something you said a moment ago …"

She is starting to understand why people confess to crimes they have not committed. She read somewhere that the promise of a hot meal is enough to break some innocent suspects down. In her case, all it would take would be someone saying, "Jill, here's the deal. If you will simply admit to the whole world that the parts of your novel in which the heroine grovels, pleads, and sacrifices the last shred of her self-respect on the altar of a thoroughly unworthy man are based on fact and that you yourself are the inspiration for that heroine, we'll let you go back to your hotel room, raid the mini-bar and order room service."

The hotels, Jill must admit, almost make up for the airport-security lineups, the podiums she must approach without tripping or dropping her book, the audiences she can't see through the glare of stage lights. For at the end of each day's trials there is the hotel room that is hers yet not hers. Hers the comfort of the enormous, fresh-sheeted bed. Not hers the chore of making that bed in the morning. Hers the miraculous cleanliness and order that restore themselves in her absence. Not hers the job of fishing hairs out of the sink or replacing damp towels with fluffy and dry. Hers the magical mini-bar that grows back the parts of itself that she consumed the day before. And hers, best of all, the tiny bottles of shampoo, the elfin soaps, the doll-sized flasks of lotion and gel and ointment that reappear each day in the bathroom. She makes one set last her stay, hiding it in her sponge bag so the maid will put out fresh supplies she can take with her when she leaves. In her travels so far, she has collected six sets of Lilliputian toiletries: lavender in Halifax, eucalyptus in Montreal, vanilla in Toronto, lemon grass in Winnipeg, tea rose in Saskatoon. Here in Vancouver, she emerges out of the bathroom each morning smelling of mint. She shampoos with mint, scrubs her skin with mint, anoints herself all over with minty white goo. From time to time throughout the day, while she listens to one or another of the nominees read from their works, she will raise a wrist to her nose. She smells like a breath lozenge. An air freshener. An agent of sweetening and cleansing.

*

Jill Macklin is one of four authors nominated for the Olympia Featherstone Award For Fiction. For the past week and a half, they have been flying together across the country, always assigned to the same middle row of the plane, strapped in side by side like babies in car seats. After their first flight, it was tacitly agreed that Philip Phelps and Jill herself would be allowed to sit on the aisles, in deference to their aging bladders. The younger woman, Jaya Ghosh, usually gets up only once per flight, smiling an apology as she squeezes past their knees. The younger man, Jason Rayburn, never has to go, no matter how much he has to drink or how many hours he spends in the air.

At each airport, they have been met by a volunteer holding a sign with OFAFF NOMINEES printed on it, then shuttled in an OFAFF van to their hotel. Depending on the time of day, they have either been allowed to go to bed or have been given one hour to settle in before being picked up by the same van and transported to a lunch, a dinner, a reading, a panel discussion, or yet another onstage interview, followed by questions from the audience.

"I suppose they expect us all to be fast friends by now," Philip rumbled a day ago while they were waiting at the baggage carousel. They had just arrived in Vancouver from Saskatoon. They would have three days on the coast, culminating in the award presentation.

"They're probably imagining this great meeting of minds or something," said Jaya. "Oh, there's my baby!" She bent and reached for her hot pink rolling case with the panda sticker. Jill wondered if she could sense Philip's old eyes resting fondly on her backside.

"Nope. They think we hate each other's guts." This from Jason as he grabbed his camouflage-coloured knapsack. "They figure each of us is plotting how to kill off the rest and get the award by default."

"There we are, Philip," Jill said, pointing to their identical blue cases, which always, eerily, emerged onto the carousel together. Then, as she stepped back to let the old man wrestle both bags over the barrier and onto the floor— something he insisted on doing—she said to Jason, "Do you really think they would give the award to the survivor? If one of us murdered the rest?" A common topic of conversation has been how much money they could each have made by now if they wrote mysteries, or some other genre that actually sells. "Because the winner must have been chosen a while ago, right? Philip, are you *sure* I can't—oh, all right. Anyway, even with three of us dead, couldn't one of the victims still get the award posthumously?" Just then Jaya spotted the OFAFF NOMINEES sign and they all obediently trooped toward it.

They in fact were getting along quite well with each other. Jill's only real fear at the start of the tour had been not about airports or public appearances or questions she would be expected to answer with intelligence and charm. No, it had been that old first-day-of-school fear. Strange faces. A group already formed and closed.

It came from the constant moving during her childhood. By the time her father settled down, she had attended four different schools in six years. Her father came back from the war with medals, then failed at one thing after another before buying the frame shop on James Street in Hamilton. Up till then, every second year or so, there would be that morning of walking beside her mother through strange streets, each step bringing a new teacher and new classmates closer. Her mother—who took charge of every new community, starting book clubs, galvanizing the local little theatre—exhorted Jill to hold her head up and smile, to step forward and introduce herself, to make friends. But Jill stayed small and quiet as the new girl, earning a place for herself in the middle—neither leader nor loner, just helpful and pleasant and friendly enough.

It was a relief to settle down finally in Hamilton, where she worked by her father's side in the frame shop evenings and weekends through high school and university. The day after graduating from McMaster, she was back cutting mats and dusting moulding samples.

"You could teach!" Her mother, as exasperated with her now as she had ever been with her father. "You could travel!"

"I'm fine where I am."

Over the years the frame shop has done more than pay the bills and make it possible for her to write. Most of her friends are former clients—people who brought some cherished image to her to beautify, and left with a sense of having been cherished and beautified themselves. It is her niche. Her knack.

*

At the beginning of their tour, each candidate received an OFAFF swag bag made of royal blue canvas. Each bag contained an OFAFF pen, an OFAFF note pad, a name tag in a plastic case on a silken string, and a letter printed on thick, creamy Olympia Featherstone Foundation letterhead. The letter began by informing them that they had been nominated for the Olympia Featherstone Award For Fiction. (Jaya: "Makes me feel like I'm being accused of something.") It went on to remind them that this was not only an extremely prestigious award, but the one that, of all the literary awards in the country, offered the largest purse. (Jason: "This week, maybe. Until the Biggar gets bigger.") It admonished them to refer to the award both in writing and in speech neither as the Olympia, nor as the Featherstone, nor—horrors—as the *OH*-faff, but always and forever as the Olympia Featherstone Award For Fiction. (Philip: "See how even the bloody preposition is capitalized?")

Jill smiled at each of her colleagues' comments, but made none of her own. She had noticed that, save for the hours they spent in the air or in their hotel rooms, they were never allowed to be alone. In the OFAFF vans, there was the OFAFF driver and volunteer, each potentially cocking an ear to their conversation. At every lunch or dinner given in their honour, they were never seated together, but were each allocated to a different table, where they were studied and questioned by assorted guests. These tended to be municipal politicians, an editor from a local paper or magazine, a high-ranking member of the Library Board, and sometimes even the owner of an independent book store, if any such still existed in that city. And of course, each table would have its assigned Olympia Featherstone Foundation employee seated next to the author. These people, Jill observed, tended to be young women, alarmingly thin, dressed and made up

for maximum sparkle and apparently on the brink of nervous breakdown. They smiled till the cords of their necks
stood out. They laughed too loud and greeted the most banal
comment with "Oh, *yes!*" or "That's so *true!*" And every one
assigned to Jill had apparently not only read her book, but
been deeply moved by it. Similar sparkling young things
were perched at their respective tables beside Philip, Jaya, and
Jason. The prettiest was inevitably put with Philip to endure
his courtly lechery. Every minute or so, Jill observed, each of
the sparklers would nervously check the time. They had to
get their authors fed, toileted, and positioned backstage for
the reading or the panel discussion or the onstage interview
for which an audience was already gathering.

Jill wonders if there have been minor disasters in years
past. Authors drinking too much before a reading—she has
noticed Philip's sparklers monitoring his every raising of
a glass to his lips—or locking themselves in a washroom
cubicle and refusing to come out. She herself is aware of a
lurking desire to sabotage the proceedings. She would never
give in to it, and doubts any of the rest would. But she can
tell they all want to believe Jason when he claims that, if he
wins, he is not going to get up there and say he's humbled
by the award, and that any of the other three would have
been equally deserving. "Nope. I'll say that I won because
I'm the best writer and I wrote the best book. Then I'll grab
the cheque, say, 'So long, suckers!,' and leave."

The cheque. Whether they admit it or not, their banter has
to do with the fact that, in less than forty-eight hours, one of
them will be wealthy, and the other three will be going home.

For years, Cornelius ("Call me Corny") Biggar—
self-proclaimed ornamental sticker king of southern

Ontario—enjoyed an ostensibly friendly rivalry with Olympia Featherstone—old Vancouver forestry money. Each offered a $50,000 annual prize for literary fiction.

Then, three years ago, Corny Biggar called a press conference. He had, he said, decided that "fifty thou was peanuts. And if I was gonna do this culture thing, I'd better man up and *do* it." And so it was that the purse for the Biggar Prize metastasized to $100,000.

Olympia Featherstone, when informed of the development by a secretary who reads the newspapers on her behalf, rose to the challenge. Though she called no press conference, made no statement, she did attend a Board meeting of the Foundation that bears her name. There, she murmured a single directive. Later that year, just before the award presentation, she signed a cheque for double the usual amount.

The following year, Corny Biggar again raised the stakes to $250,000. Once more, Olympia Featherstone matched it.

This year, however, on the second of January, she stunned the cultural community by being pre-emptive. Through a Foundation spokesperson, she announced that the Olympia Featherstone Award For Fiction would henceforth come with a purse of $500,000. Corny Biggar, who for years had been investing heavily in oil, was not available for comment.

Jill cannot imagine suddenly having $500,000. She can't even understand what it would be for. Payment for having written *Late Breaking*? How could she be paid for such a thing? By the page? By the word?

Maybe something karmic is going on and she's being feted and fed and treated like royalty now because the universe wants to apologize for putting her through hell last year. But how could money—even five hundred thousand dollars—possibly pay for a broken heart? And if it is a case of poetic justice, why did she have to break her heart in the first place?

It doesn't even make sense on a simple level. She wrote a book. Dennis Little of Littlepress, based in Stoney Creek, published it. It got good reviews. All true. But she wrote five other books prior to *Late Breaking*, and they all got good reviews too. Critics routinely refer to her prose as *transparent* and to herself as *consistently underrated*. According to one young reviewer who adopted her as a personal cause and ended up having a breakdown, she has been *tragically overlooked*. She has never won a prize, never even been nominated for one. So why did she suddenly show up on the OFAFF radar screen?

Unlike the Biggar Prize, which trumpets both its long and short lists to the press minutes after they are compiled, the Olympia Featherstone Award For Fiction eschews all publicity until one month before presentation. Its vetting process is a secret, and the identity of its apparently high-profile judges something they themselves are contracted to take to the grave. Rumour even has it that there are no judges, that the reclusive Olympia Featherstone vets the candidates herself and either chooses the winner, or, if she decides that no book meets her ever-evolving standards, withholds the prize money for another year.

Something called "the Olympia effect" has been identified. Unlike "the Biggar effect," (BE), which causes book-sale figures to balloon, the OE attacks authors like a psychological virus. It could be the month of constant travel and performance, or the faceless judging process, or the knowledge that at the end of it all you will either have more money than most people ever see, or nothing. Whatever the reason, nominees have been known to quit their day jobs in a manner that makes it impossible to come crawling back, abandon their spouses, drop their friends, and, in one case, enter a monastery. The most common reaction, for winners as well as losers, is to stop writing. But for all that, whether because of the prestige or the size of the purse, no one has ever turned down a nomination for the Olympia Featherstone Award For Fiction.

Jill has decided that in her case, being up for the award is causing some erosion of her character. There is an attitude an author is expected to assume onstage while listening to colleagues read from their works. Alert. Appreciative. Verging at times on rapt. Laughter in the right places. A smile of delight over some clever phrase or original observation. For Jill, this masquerade has gotten increasingly difficult as she and the other nominees have flown together across the country, touching down to read the same passages over and over. Sometimes she is tempted to rummage in her purse while one of the other three is at the microphone, to wrestle a candy out of its crinkly wrapper then roll it loudly round her teeth, to study her shoe, lick her thumb, bend down and rub at a spot on the toe.

She has no doubt the rest are as bored as she is. They have each admitted cheerfully to not having read the others' books and doubting they ever will now, given that they've heard the best bits so many times over.

The protagonist of *Transit Bride* (Arrivé, Montreal), by Jaya Ghosh, is a young East Indian immigrant named

Parmindar who runs away from home to escape an arranged marriage to an elderly relative. The passage Jaya reads depicts Parmindar riding the Métro in the wedding dress she will wear to rags as she slowly comes to realize she is in fact a boy.

Jason Rayburn's self-published e-book, *iMessiah*, portrays a dystopian near future in which protagonist Jesse reaches out through social media to precariously employed millennials, winning their allegiance by assuring them they are not the tech-obsessed selfish brats everyone assumes they are. Meanwhile, Jesse's alter ego, Creed, is leading a political party that, if elected, will have job-hoarding Baby Boomers disenfranchised and forced into Homes. Jason reads the scene where the two young men engage in a battle of tweets.

Philip Phelps's book, *Michael* (Mackenzie & Fraser, Toronto), is the latest version of the book he has been writing and rewriting all his life—a coming-of-age tale set in Cape Breton Island. He reads the scene in which young Michael, longing for a life beyond the fences of the ancestral farm, is persuaded by Liam, the aging, legless woodcarver who is his only friend, to be the first in his family to step onto the mainland and purchase a one-way bus ticket to Toronto.

It has occurred to Jill more than once while listening to the others read that hers is the only protagonist who ends up dead. In *Late Breaking* (Littlepress, Stoney Creek), Meredith takes her first lover at the age of seventy-three. Jill originally made both characters octogenarians, but Dennis Little, who wanted them sixty-five at the oldest, compromised with seventy-three.

(Jill: "I thought seventy was supposed to be the new forty or something."

Dennis: "Sure it is. When it comes to travel and golf and gourmet cooking and anything else you can put on the cover of a magazine for boomers. But not—")

Even her publisher had trouble getting over the idea of wrinkled bodies, greying pubic hair, two *old* people heaving together into mutual climax. So Jill, out of some perversity, always reads the defloration scene, which she managed to make both grisly and funny.

It sprang fully formed into her mind two years ago, when she and Eliot Somers went to bed for the first time. She hadn't had sex in almost a decade, and in the interim seemed to have dried up and shrunk—a case of estrogen-starved atrophy, according to her doctor. She lay there gritting her teeth, listening to Eliot's running commentary—*Interesting. I can feel all kinds of ridges. And your muscles seem to be trying to expel me.* What would it be like, she found herself wondering, if an older woman was a virgin on top of all of this? Would she pass out?

That was the inspiration for *Late Breaking's* Meredith. When her lover goes back to his wife, Meredith loses her mind. She gives away her possessions, donates all her money to a feral cat-rescue mission and in the final scene walks naked through the streets of Hamilton to her death in a snowbank, completely unnoticed by bustling Christmas shoppers.

It is usual for Jill to hear gasps from the audience while she reads, which may explain why she is never slated to go on first or last. The program starts with either the beautiful Jaya Ghosh or the wise-cracking Jason Rayburn. Then Jill goes up to the microphone, after which the audience is given a chance to get another drink. The second half starts with whichever of the young, attractive authors has not already read. Philip Phelps is always last. This allows time for his designated sparkler to get some coffee into him and walk him around a bit outside to sober him up.

The Olympia Featherstone Award For Fiction, unlike the Biggar Prize, which all but calls for bets, has no acknowledged front runner. But there is a feeling in the air that the old man is going to win. He has survived one nomination for the OFAFF before this, and two for the Biggar. At every venue, he has teased his pretty young sparkler by pledging to do "some serious drinking" at the pre-presentation cocktail party, to continue "working at it" through dinner, then to get up onstage and deliver his acceptance speech whether his name is called or not. Whenever he weaves to a microphone to read, he clutches the podium like a drowning man clutching driftwood. He seldom looks at his book, preferring to declaim from memory, his eyes searching the back rows as if for the faces of long-dead friends.

*

Don't, Jill thinks, seconds after waking. But by then it's too late. She has already started the searching, the tender probing for hurt. Yes. There. Still. Not as bad as before. But.

For months, her first thought on waking, her last before shutting off her light, has been of Eliot Somers not there. Not warming her from his side of the bed. Not turning in his sleep and reaching an arm to hook round her and keep her close. At its worst, missing him has been a constant noise in her ears, a smell she cannot expel from her nostrils. *Absence of Eliot.* Now, at least, she can play with that phrase a little. It sounds like something she might have on hand in a spice rack or medicine chest. Cream of tartar. Oil of cloves. Absence of Eliot.

Still in her nightie, she opens her purse and pulls out her phone. She'll just check her messages, then get dressed. This day has been kept free for the nominees—no official meals or readings or interviews or panel discussions—to let them shore up strength for the award presentation the next night.

Nothing from Abdul, not that she was expecting to hear from him. Before she left he told her firmly not to worry, that he could run things and would only get in touch if the frame shop was on fire. Jill often forgets how young Abdul is. His wide-spaced eyes and jowly features, which remind her of a Boston terrier, have something settled and middle-aged about them.

Jill treats herself to mint-scented salts in her bath, then pulls on jeans and the green, fleecy sweatshirt she bought with this trip in mind—something warm yet light enough for late October on the west coast. Once she's finished the granola, fruit, yogurt, and coffee she checked off on the breakfast card the night before, she sets out into the cool mist to walk the Granville Island seawall.

There is a feeling of unreality to this place. The cupped and gentled ocean. The manicured path, its little lookouts and cul-de-sacs with their strategically planted rocks. Everything whispers of wealth. Jill guesses she could afford to live here for what—six months? Doesn't matter. The day would come when, like Meredith, she would have nothing left.

Unless, of course, she wins.

She wishes she could do what Jaya and Jason seem to have done—accept the fact that Philip will likely take the prize. If she did that, she could just relax and enjoy her time here in Vancouver. But for once she can't resign herself to being an also-ran. Something in her, something fierce and demanding, is insisting she win. One morning shortly into the tour—she thinks it might have been in Montreal—it was just there. Like a lump under her skin. Slipping about, dodging her probing fingertips. A sense of entitlement, of life owing her a debt she has every right to call in.

One afternoon two autumns ago, Eliot Somers walked into the frame shop. Abdul was off that day, so Jill waited on him herself.

He had just sold his house and moved into a condominium, he told her, and had decided to cover his kitchen walls with ancestral photographs. He had some formal portraits of his parents and grandparents, even a daguerreotype of his great-grandparents.

Jill spread the pictures out on the big work table. "No siblings?" she ventured to ask, looking them over.

He told her he was an only child. *Like me,* she found herself thinking. She guessed him to be about her age, too. A smallish, compact man in a rust-coloured sweater and charcoal jeans. Still-dark hair cut short, thinning on top. Immaculate fingernails, as if he had just scrubbed them with a brush.

Jill and Abdul sometimes joke about how the job allows them to tell a great deal about a person in a short period of time. As they bring mat and frame samples up close to the art, they and the customer bend toward the effect, almost sharing breath. They can catch a whiff of alcohol. Notice dandruff and sweater balls or cashmere and the scent of fresh shampoo. And of course, they can assess someone's taste by what they choose and what they reject. Jill has learned to pick up on hesitation—an imaginary bill mounting in the customer's mind—if she suggests a second mat overlaying the first in a slightly darker shade, or perhaps a line incised near the edge for texture. Or, as was the case with Eliot, she can sense an openness to suggestion, a willingness to pay for whatever is best for the work.

"I've just retired, and I'm going to be spending more time in the kitchen," he told her. "I've always been a rather pedestrian cook, and I want to get a little more adventurous." He did not babble on about himself the way some do, assuming interest on her part. He offered up details humbly, as if honoured that she would listen. She encouraged him, asking more questions than she normally did.

He had worked for the last thirty-five years for a major charity whose focus was education for disadvantaged girls. "I started out as a stockbroker. But then when my daughter was born, it occurred to me that there had to be more to life than making rich people richer." He smiled—a bashful smile that reminded Jill of someone she couldn't quite place.

She smiled back and handed him the invoice she had just made up. *So*, she thought. *A daughter. No mention of a wife, but—Oh, he'll just go now. A few weeks later, Abdul or I will leave a voicemail saying that his frame order is ready. He'll drop into the shop, pay the balance of the bill, take his photographs, walk out the door, and disappear.*

"I'm a widower." He had closed his fingers over the edge of the invoice, but not taken it. They stood holding it together. "I'm sorry," he said. "You must get people telling you all kinds of things. I don't know why I—"

"No. It's all right. Please don't be sorry. How long has it been?"

"Three years now." His voice was calm. She suspected it was a worked-on, achieved calm.

She held his gaze—pale grey eyes, she noticed—and said, "That's a lot of changes. Losing your wife. Retiring. Now moving." Then she surprised herself. She released her end of the invoice and put her hand out. "I'm Jill Macklin."

He held her hand a second longer than was usual. "Macklin's Frames. So the store is a family business?"

She told him about her father, about learning the job from him. Most people come in knowing exactly what they want, and usually it's the worst thing for the art—a pink mat to match the drapes in the living room, a gold frame to pick out the gold of the chandelier. For years, she listened to her father gently, patiently, respectfully suggesting that it was better to frame to the art, rather than to its surroundings. Then, without a hint of reproach, offering a variety of pink mats, a selection of gold frame samples.

Did she really tell him all that? Yes, and more. About deciding half way through university to be a writer, with the frame shop as her day job. Keeping the business going all through her father's last illness. Then—

Then Eliot Somers asked her if she had plans for dinner that evening.

Again the bashful smile. One week later, when she was tracing a fingertip round the shape his chest and belly hair made, like a capital H, she finally realized who he reminded her of. "Kevin Spacey!"

He chuckled and said he'd heard that before.

Heard it from whom? And how recently? A small, anxious voice in the back of her mind. She told it to be quiet. Began planting a trail of kisses from his nipple, down over his belly, into the springy bush where he was once more beginning to stir.

The sun has broken through the mist. The ferries have been going back and forth for some time. Jill sits down on a park bench to rest for a minute. Checks her messages one more time. Nothing. She can imagine Abdul frowning, telling her to trust him and stop worrying.

Though he never said anything, Jill could tell Abdul was aware of what was going on between her and Eliot. She caught a bemused look from him one morning when she spun around in her desk chair like a schoolgirl because, for the first time, Eliot had signed an email with the word *love*. And that day, months later, when she couldn't help herself, could only sit at her desk with her hands clamped over her mouth, shoulders shaking, trying not to make noise, she took comfort in his wide turned back, his deft handling of calls and customers.

She tucks her phone back into her purse and snaps it shut. She did tell people she would be away. There is no need for this small disappointment, like the pang of a single plucked hair. But every time she boots up her laptop or checks her phone, she still looks for a certain sender name. A subject line reading something like, *Friends?* Or, *Sorry.* Or, *Could we possibly talk?* And whenever she enters the lobby of her building, the sight of a narrow white edge peeking through the metal grille of her mailbox still puts her on alert. Will it be the envelope she self-addressed, stamped, folded, and tucked inside another envelope addressed to him? Will it hold a reply, finally, to the letter she toiled over for weeks?

She stands up. Brushes the back of her jeans and hooks the strap of her purse over her shoulder. The boutiques and galleries will be opening up. She has gifts to buy. She's hoping to find something in ceramic for Abdul, who throws pots in his spare time. She has a set of mugs he made—thin handles and pedestal bases, glazed in dove grey. It intrigues her to think of his thick, brown fingers producing such delicacy. She wants to get something for her friend Harriet, too.

And she's going to look for a gift for herself. Something special to have and to keep. A treat. No. A comfort. Still.

Jill has gone over and over what happened, reciting it to herself as she would a fable or myth. She was loved, then not loved. Eliot was there, then gone. The part of the story that eludes her is the moment just before the *then*.

Up until that moment, Eliot would pull her into a doorway as they walked down the street, needing to kiss and caress her in the middle of a sentence. He read all her books in a single week, practically reciting his favourite passages back to her. He complimented her tiny feet, her tilting, humorous eyes, the way her breasts exactly fit his cupped palm. Every Monday he sent her an email listing the times he would be free that week. She would tell herself not to agree to every suggestion, to hold some of herself back for friends and writing. But then she would capitulate, saying yes and yes and yes.

The sex had gotten so much better—as she joked to Harriet, it couldn't possibly have gotten worse—with the help of an estrogen cream called Oasis. She would start to throb down there the second she opened the door and saw his smile, would stand close to catch a whiff of him as he took off his jacket in the hall. "My God," he said early on. "You really *need* this, don't you?"

Need. She decided it was a compliment. Once more told the small voice to be quiet.

She did a reading in a library with some other local authors. Eliot came and sat in the front row. "I was making love to you the whole time you read," he told her afterwards. Then said that his daughter Mary would probably have enjoyed the event. Suggested that next time maybe Mary could come? And meet Jill? Also—he was thinking that the two of them should go to England, where his parents were from. He had cousins there he was still in touch with.

Yes, she said. *Oh, yes.* To be presented to his family. To be so acknowledged. Well, she deserved as much, surely. Why shouldn't this good thing finally be happening? Why shouldn't she be given exactly what she had almost stopped hoping for?

"It's great that you were open to the experience." Harriet, raising a glass of white wine after Jill first told her about Eliot, tumbling over her words and grinning like a girl. The small voice had warned her against telling anyone, for fear of jinxing things. But she had dismissed that as a silly superstition. And Harriet was right. She had indeed been open. Courageously so. Willing to take a chance on things being different this time.

She had had six previous lovers in her life, the first in university. Each time, being seen naked, being touched intimately, had wakened a craving for more and more touch, deeper and deeper intimacy. She would come to need her lover's attention the way she needed air or water. In time, even when he was with her, holding her, she would get anxious, anticipating his letting go, getting up and leaving. And so of course he would leave. Permanently.

But that wasn't going to happen this time. Not again. Not with Eliot.

She did another reading a few weeks later, in an art gallery. Waited for Eliot to suggest inviting his daughter, then suggested it herself. He looked away. Said something vague about Mary being busy.

She reminded him brightly of his idea of going to England. Maybe they could plan the trip for this summer? When business was slower? And she could safely leave the frame shop in Abdul's hands for a few weeks? He smiled. Changed the subject.

"Just take a step back, Jill." Harriet again. "Give him less importance. Less power. Get busy with your own good life."

But that was just it. Eliot *was* her good life. Her best life. She had been content enough with work, writing, friends. Had made a point of counting her blessings, reminding herself of how much better off she was than many women her age. Then Eliot took her hand in his, and everything became secondary to his touch. Besides, it was easy for Harriet to talk. Her husband drowned years ago in the lake up at their cottage while she was in the kitchen getting their lunch. She was left with happy memories of a long marriage that ended through no fault of her own. It was one thing to be a widow. Another to be—

Dumped. Slowly.

Eliot was too busy (doing what?) to see her as often. He was too tired (from what?) to make love. He had once said he couldn't wait to show her his new place. Now, each time she asked, he put her off, saying it was still too much of a mess from moving in. But hadn't he been moved in for months now?

"I could help. I could flatten the boxes." She hated the way her voice sounded, stretched thin, fake-hearty.

She did try, delicately, cleverly, to get him to talk about the growing distance between them. He ducked the subject, dismissed her worries, denied that anything had changed. And so, appalled at herself, telling herself for God's sake not to do this, she fetched her diary. Showed him the date, weeks ago, of their last love-making. He grimaced. Pushed away the shaking book. Muttered something about pressure.

His daily emails had dwindled to one, and that only in reply to one of her own. Then he stopped even replying. Stopped returning the voicemails she composed in her mind and rehearsed aloud before picking up the phone.

"Are you prepared for how he might answer this?"

Harriet had just finished reading the four-page letter Jill had crafted to be warm but not clingy, upbeat but not flippant, exerting absolutely no pressure, presenting herself as wanting nothing at all save to know what place, if any, she occupied in his heart.

Yes, she said. She had prepared herself for any possible response. Now all she had to do was wait.

Over the next week, two weeks, three, she kept checking the duplicate invoice she had on file in the shop. Yes, she had addressed the envelope correctly. And in any event, she had put her return address on it, so it would have come back to her if it hadn't reached him. A dozen times, she reminded herself of the little joke she had made in the first paragraph about including a stamped, self-addressed envelope. Surely that wouldn't have irritated him. Surely it didn't constitute pressure. Again and again, she convinced herself that a reply to a letter such as she had sent could not be dashed off. It would require thought. Take time. A month, even. Two months. Longer.

How long after she sent her letter did Dennis Little email her? She recalls numbly reading his message about having admired her work for years, considering her underappreciated and wondering if by any chance she had a manuscript on the go that she would consider sending to a tiny start-up in Stoney Creek. What she had was two pages of notes about an elderly woman named Meredith falling in love, having sex, and breaking her heart for the first and last time. With the recklessness that comes of not caring whether one lives or dies, she wrote back to say that yes, she was working on a novel.

She wrote *Late Breaking* in a kind of trance—an almost uninterrupted flow. Given the subject matter and the way she had just dashed it off, she expected Littlepress to reject it. Instead, she received a letter full of compliments and apologies—the latter for the enclosed cheque, whose amount made her smile.

When the reviews started to appear, she could hardly recognize the work they were praising, barely identify with this *author Jill Macklin* person. And when her nomination for the Olympia Featherstone Award For Fiction was announced, all she could think was, *Will Eliot see this in the paper? Will he wonder how I am? Maybe finally answer my letter?*

*

It's the evening of the award ceremony. The whole time she's getting ready in her hotel room, Jill fights an urge to just put on the jeans and sweatshirt she wore yesterday. But then, when she descends to the pre-dinner cocktail reception and sees Philip in his tux, Jaya in her yellow silk sari and even Jason for once in a jacket and tie, she's glad of the filmy blue-green caftan and silver pants Harriet bullied her into buying weeks ago.

It's a grudging, sulky gladness. She is in fact furious. With herself, with all this award nonsense, with everything. She spent most of yesterday roaming the Granville Island market, trying to persuade herself to buy the one thing she wanted—a white ceramic plate with a beautifully articulated raven on it, each black feather picked out in detail. She had no trouble spending money on Harriet, getting her a palette-shaped brooch in copper, or on Abdul—a white bowl with a black feather motif by the same potter who made her plate.

No. Not her plate. Because she didn't buy it after all. And now here she is, all dolled up for the sake of a prize she hasn't a hope in hell of winning. Whenever she tries to work up a little excitement, something in her swats it like a fly and she's left with nothing but pre-emptive jealousy of Philip Phelps.

And oh, the icing on the cake. Here comes one of the designated sparklers, who caught sight of her moping in a corner with her glass of wine, and has been trained to zero in on any author who appears to be even momentarily less than ecstatic.

"I'm fine by myself," she assures the girl before she has a chance to ask how Jill is, or offer to refresh her drink or bring her some more hors d'oeuvres or do anything else that might make her stay on this planet more pleasant. "But poor old Philip over there looks like he could use some company." So the sweet thing floats off in Philip's direction, obviously happy to have a mission. And the old man's face lifts at the sight of her. Soon the two of them are engaged in grinning, flirty conversation.

Later, Jill will wonder if she might have been some kind of accessory. Culpable in some way. But for now, she drains her glass of white wine, finishes off a tiny quiche, and wipes her fingers on a paper napkin. She has one more dinner to get through. Then the award ceremony, where she will smile the smile of the good loser. And waiting for her at the end of it all will be the one thing she can count on. Smooth and cool, then gradually warm and comforting, the fresh sheets on her wide, wonderful hotel-room bed.

lacuna - gap in story

*

The seatbelt sign has just come on. Jill stows her tray, tucks her purse under the seat in front of her and buckles up. She loves flying, and in the last month has done more of it than in her entire life. She especially enjoys take-off—the revving of the engine, the speeding down the runway, then the amazingly delicate lifting into the air. In five hours, she will be in Toronto. Abdul, bless his heart, is meeting her at the airport and driving her home.

It feels odd not to be flanked by the other—no, not candidates. Not any more. Jason is on his way to Saskatoon, Jaya to Montreal. As for Philip—

Toronto? Or Cape Breton Island? Where he was living, or where he was from?

"Gotta hand it to the guy," Jason said just an hour or so ago, once the three of them had found each other in the departure lounge. "He got the girl and the money."

"Jason, have some respect for once!" Alone among the candidates, Jaya had shed tears at the award ceremony the night before. Then, as the audience reacted to the news, she had stripped off her bracelets and pulled out her earrings—a traditional act of honouring the dead, Jill supposed.

"What I can't understand," she went on now, "is what got into that girl. I mean, how could she just throw her career away like that?"

"Maybe she knew old Phil was going to win, so she made him name her in his will before he got his leg over."

"Jason!" She punched his bicep, hard.

Just then Jill's flight was called. "You two should get married," she said as she gathered up her coat and purse, enjoying the astonished look the young people gave first her, then each other.

The plane has levelled off, achieving that illusion of stillness it will maintain for the next several hours. After take-off, flying is a bit of a bore, Jill must admit. A thing for which she should be grateful. After all, what would make it exciting? A sudden silence. Flickering lights. Then that plunge, which she has read can take several minutes. Several minutes of knowing the thing you spend your life trying not to know.

Did Philip have an inkling? And where is he now? Not in the hold, surely. Jill tucks her feet up. Then she puts them flat on the floor again. Silly. The logistics involved—body, box, paperwork—would take more than one night.

She slept well, and still feels remarkably rested and refreshed. Some burden seems to have been lifted from her. *It solves a lot of problems*, she remembers her father once saying about death. But what connection could there be between her light-heartedness this morning and what happened the night before?

Olympia Featherstone had just been introduced, and was about to make one of her rare public appearances to announce the winner and present the cheque. As they all applauded, an OFAFF employee pulled the curtain aside for the old lady. There emerged, slowly, the tip of a cane. Then the polished toe of a custom-made orthopedic shoe. The audience kept applauding, waiting for a knee, a hand, the gleam of silvered hair. Instead, there was a pause. The shoe withdrew. Followed by the cane. The employee holding the curtain appeared to receive some direction from backstage. Then he too slipped out of sight behind the rippling velour.

The applause petered out. A minute passed. Two. Finally another, older OFAFF employee emerged and went to the podium.

"Ladies and gentlemen, there has been … Mr. Philip Phelps is … that is, he would have been … the recipient of this year's Olympia Featherstone Award For Fiction. However … unfortunately … Mr. Phelps met with … Mr. Phelps died. Suddenly. We are deeply saddened. Please—" The audience was beginning to murmur. The employee had to raise his voice. "Please … we ask you to proceed back out to the reception room. Coffee will be served." At this point the younger employee re-emerged and whispered something to the older, who announced, "And dessert. Has also been assembled."

Over coffee and their second dessert of the evening, which everyone was suddenly quite hungry for, the story that no one must ever tell was leaked. Sometime between dinner and the award ceremony, Philip and his sparkler slipped upstairs to his room. From there, the front desk received an hysterical call. Staff found the young woman wrapped in a sheet, and Philip on his back on the bed, a look of profound surprise shaping his stiffening features.

Joy. Is that what this is, Jill wonders, not for the first time. This feeling of lightness she woke up with? She has, of course, felt joy before. But it's been so long that it seems a new thing. Actually, it's more like an absence. Of an absence. Does that count as a presence? She is still aware that Eliot is gone. She just doesn't care anymore. She doesn't care about the award or the money either. Is perfectly happy to be going home with nothing.

No. Not nothing. She opens her purse. Pulls out her wallet. Yes, she did keep that business card. "You can always order it through my website," the potter, a tall Dutch woman, told her the other day when she was deciding for the ninth time not to treat herself to the raven plate. The potter was not much younger than Jill, and seemed to understand her hesitation. "I can ship to anywhere in the world."

Jill decides she will order the plate. It will be fun to imagine it travelling the breadth of the country, arriving at her door miraculously intact. She looks out her tiny window, happy as a child to see that they are flying above the clouds.

Woman on Ramp, 2007.

Harriet
nameless boy as surrogate for son

WITNESS

As soon as Harriet's in, the second she hears the screen door bang shut behind her, she feels an arm come round her neck.

"Ranald?" She can hardly gasp the name. The arm tightens. Something with a point pushes into the small of her back. Breath—smelling of Juicy Fruit gum—blows hot across her cheek.

She turns her head to the right and the pressure on her throat eases. It can't be Ranald. He doesn't chew gum. And not even Ranald would play a trick like this. "What do you want?" she says. Her voice surprises her—low and calm-sounding.

No answer. Just a sharp intake of breath. The arm at her neck is trembling, and she detects a tremor in the hard point digging in just below her back ribs. Is he just a kid? One of the town boys, maybe, who stand in a sullen pack outside the 7-Eleven?

"Tell you what." She tries to sound companionable, to take the tone she used to with Ranald when she had to coax him out of one of his sulks, give him some means of retreat with honour. "You can just let go of me. I won't turn around. I won't look at you. I'll never know who you are. You can get out of here, really fast, and it will be all right. You won't be in any trouble."

Whoever he is, he probably came up here on a dare, and can't—

She's on the floor. On her hands and knees. A second shove, from a foot to her buttock, pushes her flat. She breathes in the dusty smell of the rag rug.

"*Where is it?*" He sounds like he's trying to make his voice deeper and rougher than it is. The foot gouges her buttock. "*Where?*"

"You mean—my money?" Another gouge. "My purse is in the bedroom. On the dresser. I don't have much—"

He grabs her bathing-suit straps. Pulls her up onto her knees. She scrambles to get her feet under her. Then his arm is at her throat again. The pointy thing in her back.

"Go get it! *Move!*" His voice cracks on the last word.

They do a clumsy dance out of the living-dining room, around the corner, past the bathroom. She thinks of something and stops. He shoves her. "Wait." He shoves her again. "No! Wait. Please. There is a mirror on the dresser. I promised I wouldn't look at you. So put your hand over my eyes. Or turn us around and back us into the bedroom. That way you'll know I haven't seen you."

They stand still. She can feel him panting, can smell the Juicy Fruit on his breath. All at once he swings her to the side, shoves her onto the bathroom floor. She slides on the tile, slams her head against the toilet. Sees stars. Hears him going into the bedroom. A clatter. A thump. Then he's pounding past her, back through the cottage, out the door and gone.

Slowly, she sits up. Touches her head where it hit the toilet. No blood, but a goose egg rising. Her knees are red from where they skidded on the rug and the tile. Her elbow hurts. And she's starting to stiffen up all over.

But she's okay. And utterly amazed at herself. The way she remembered that trick of turning her head so she could breathe. When was the Safety for Seniors talk? Last winter. And she almost didn't go. Figured it would just be common sense, nothing new. But she did go, and she did learn something. "If someone comes up behind you and puts their arm across your windpipe," the young police officer told them, "turn your head into the crook of his elbow. That will give you some breathing space." What would have happened if she hadn't heard that bit of advice? She could be unconscious. Brain-damaged. Dead, even. She feels her head again. She should put some ice on that lump. She imagines it sticking straight up like a lump in a cartoon, pointy and bald, pain-stars orbiting round, and starts to giggle.

Is she in shock? Is that why she felt no fear, tried to negotiate with her attacker and even thought to warn him about the mirror? Whenever she has imagined one of Ranald's threatened scenarios coming true, she has seen herself terrified—witless and begging. Maybe the fear will come later. Right now, she feels proud of herself. Deserving of a treat. Ice cream? A gin and tonic before lunch?

Odd how she thought at first it was Ranald, that he had driven up a day early without Patrick, hidden inside the cottage while she was down on the dock and waited for her to come up the ramp. Just so he could grab her from behind and teach her a lesson. *I don't like you up there by yourself.* When did he start standing too close, literally talking down to her, forcing her to peer up at him like a child? And when did he stop calling her Mom? He doesn't call her anything now. Just *you.* Thank God he and Patrick aren't coming till tomorrow. She'll have time to put some ice on her head. Come up with a story. Anything will be better than the truth—that she left the back door unlocked while she was down on the dock and one of the yokels, as he calls them, got in. So did she fall down the back porch steps? Yes. That's plausible. *My injuries are consistent with a fall down the back porch steps,* she thinks, and giggles again.

Her purse. Damn. How will she explain having no purse, no keys, no money? She gets up, limps into the bedroom and there, like an answer, is her purse lying open on the floor. Hanging onto the dresser with one hand, she bends carefully and picks it up. Credit and debit cards. House keys. Only the cash is gone. So yes, her attacker must have been just a kid.

She should be on the phone right now, to alert the authorities. She almost giggles again. *Alert the authorities* sounds so pretentious. What could she tell them? That she was mugged by somebody with Juicy Fruit breath? Even if they managed to catch the kid, it wouldn't make any difference. Boys will always gather outside the 7-Eleven with nothing to do except build up resentment against cottagers like her. Besides. Ranald might get wind of it if she makes a report. She can imagine him badgering an OPP officer, refusing to listen when they try to explain that if his mother did not see the kid's face—

The car. Oh no.

She runs—stumbles—out of the bedroom around to the back door and looks out. There it is. Of course it's still there. She'd have heard him driving away. She'd like to go out and touch it, but tells herself not to be silly. On her way back through the cottage, she does allow herself to check that her car keys are on the mantle where she always puts them when she comes in. Yes. There they are, on their ring with the big plastic daisy.

So there's nothing to be done. She'll just have her lunch. And she'll have ice cream after, not gin and tonic before. Because she's going to have to drive into town to replace her cash. And tomorrow she'll tell Ranald and Patrick that she fell down the steps. Falling down the steps is less blame-worthy than leaving the back door unlocked. Nothing for Ranald to lecture her about. Make her feel childish and stupid about. Yes. That's what she'll do.

Harriet is a painter. Right now she's in the middle of painting the lake as seen through the living room window. She has set her easel back far enough that it's going to be as much about the window frame, curtain, and sill as the water.

Ever since she turned seventy, she has been thinking about doing a self-portrait. She never used to see the point of them, though she liked Rembrandt's renditions of himself through the years. And while she stared into the mirror as much as any girl, her own young face never struck her as remarkable. Good-enough cheekbones. Nose a little long, or maybe it was the short upper lip making it look that way. Wide-spaced hazel eyes—her best feature, she supposed, since it most resembled what she saw in magazines.

She's not sure what Halvor saw in her. *Likely the top of my head*, she used to joke to company, when the talk turned to how they met. He was a tall young Dane whose family had immigrated when he was ten. Her first week at U of T, when he came up to her at a mixer, smiled down from his height and asked her to dance, his accent thrilled her. Her own roots were Scots-English and her family had been in Canada for three generations, so Halvor was exotic. Her very own Viking. She liked his long hands and feet, his bony red face, his pale eyes like chips of blue ice. Above all, she liked his yellow hair that always shocked her when she saw it, as if it wasn't quite real. All the men in her family were dark, like her. Her mother was fair, but nothing like Halvor. "Going to stir up the gene pool with that one," her father, a high-school science teacher, said when she told her parents she was engaged.

Her own hair is white now. If she finds an errant black strand, she pulls it out. She never coloured it, just let it go when it started to turn grey in her thirties, intrigued by the streaks coming in. Changes in her face and body intrigued her, too, over the years. She could never understand other women's dismay over their sags and bulges and lines.

The only time she did not like how she looked—hated it, in fact—was when she was pregnant with Ranald. She wasn't one of those women who glow, who decide they're goddesses or some fool thing. The whole nine months, the nights upon nights she sat up in bed with heartburn, pounding her chest and drinking milk, which she disliked, she felt as if something was being done to her. And her labour was simply appalling. She couldn't believe it. She alternately screamed at Halvor to go away, then screamed for him to come back. Then, when they set Ranald bloody and squirming onto her stomach, the first thing she saw was his hair. Gucky black strands like an old man's comb-over. Maybe if his hair had been yellow, if she had looked and seen a tiny version of Halvor—

"I didn't know one end of the baby from the other," she was finally able to joke to friends, once Ranald was in school and she had some time again. "Halvor had to show me how to feed him, how to change him, everything." She was an only child, but Halvor was the oldest of five. And he loved being a father—would rush home from work to be in time to give Ranald his bath. "These big hands," she would say, "and so gentle."

Until Ranald was born, Harriet had no idea how much she was counting on her and Halvor's life together continuing the way it always had. When Halvor went off in the morning to the civil engineering firm that had recruited him right out of university, she would tidy and scrub. She loved their little apartment in the middle of downtown, would never let a hair remain in a sink or a snarl of dust gather behind a door. Once the housework was done, she would read until it was time to fix the Danish open-faced sandwiches Halvor had taught her to make. They would go to bed after lunch, and she would almost have to push him out the door or else he'd be late back to work. Then in the afternoon she would paint in the sun room, where there was just space for her easel and a cabinet full of brushes and tubes of oils. Most often, she painted the view from their apartment—roofs and treetops and backyards, all through a criss-cross of electrical wires. She had always loved the wrong sides and the backs of things. Her favourite portrait of Halvor was one she did of him from the back. His eyebrow showed, and one sharp cheekbone, the line of his jaw, his neck and part of a naked shoulder. But the focus was that hair, glorious and yellow, still young and bright, right up until the day he died.

She never painted Ranald, though she did do a few sketches of him sleeping when he was little. He would not sit for her, refused to even try, and she was secretly relieved. The idea of being alone with her son for hours in the taut silence that stretches between sitter and portrait artist filled her with a kind of dread.

For years after Ranald was born and they had moved from the apartment to a bungalow just north of the city, she could not paint at all. It wasn't simply lack of time. Everything around her was too spacious and blank—the lawns, the roads, the shopping malls. She felt as if she were getting lost in all that space—thinning out, stretching, becoming as transparent as the sky. Gradually, as Ranald grew and left her alone for longer periods of time, she managed to gather herself back to herself. She found that she could paint her suburban world from inside the house, framed by a window. It was good practice for painting the lake up at the cottage, which at first overwhelmed her with its immensity.

Twice this summer she has started a self-portrait. She has rigged up a mirror beside her easel, blocked in some colour, then scraped the canvas. She worries about committing something hokey like Norman Rockwell's portrait of himself painting himself. But she can't give up on the idea. She has looked through photographs Halvor took of her, thinking she might work from one of them. He's been dead for eleven years, so the oldest she appears in any of them is fifty-nine. There's one of her coming up the ramp, head down, watching her feet. She supposes she could age the figure, thicken the body and whiten the hair.

Lately she's begun to wonder if what she really wants is not to paint herself but to be painted. To be seen. *We will witness to each other's lives.* She and Halvor had that written into their marriage vows.

Lunch. That's why she was heading up the ramp from the dock in the first place. And some food will raise her blood-sugar level. And that might—what? Wake her up? Make her shake? Cry? Maybe she *is* in shock. If it wasn't for her stiffness and bruises, she could believe she dreamed what had just happened.

In the kitchen, she cuts a generous slice of the cold meat loaf she brought with her from the condominium. She checks that the mustard is out on the lazy susan on the dining table, chops up a tomato, puts the chunks in a bowl then adds some sugar snap peas for green. There's a half baguette in the bread box. She puts it on the board with the bread knife and butter bell, chooses an apple from the fruit bowl on the counter, thinks about the three arrowroot cookies sitting in a little dish in the fridge, then remembers ice cream. Her reward for being brave. If that's what this calmness is.

She isn't even angry with Halvor. For years after his death, if something bad happened, she would get furious with him for not being there to help her deal with it. Well, maybe that's the last bit of her grief gone. She's heard of people actually forgetting what their dead spouses looked like, having to use photographs to bring them to mind. That's not happening to her, surely. She could still paint Halvor from memory.

She carries her cobbled-together lunch to the table and sits down. Saws off a slice of baguette and butters it. Patrick gave her the butter bell, after she complained that because she's on her own it takes her forever to work her way through a pound of butter, so her choices are rancid or hard. *There you go, Harriet. All your butter problems solved.* She likes Patrick. He's short and plumpish, a little like her. The two of them can smile directly into each other's eyes while Ranald stands apart and watches. Patrick teaches grade three—*They're just getting interesting at that age, Harriet, turning into real little individuals*—and he acts as a buffer between her and Ranald. *Now, can I trust you two while I go and do the dishes?* Treating the tension between them like a naughty joke, something to shake a finger at.

She crunches a sugar snap, thinking how much Halvor would have liked Patrick. Halvor was the one who first got the news that Ranald was gay. She herself had suspected it for years. She felt guilty about his having gone to his father. Wasn't the mother supposed to be the approachable one?

But right from the first, Ranald had been like a little pebble. She skidded off him. Couldn't get in. Trying to interpret his shrieking, wordless demands exhausted her and scattered her wits. She could hardly get a sentence out to Halvor, and when she tried to return to a painting she had started in her seventh month, it was like staring at some stranger's graffiti.

Even when he went from being a baby to being a little boy, Ranald stayed closed off from her. She would find him hunched over a skinned knee, crying soundlessly, and would have to beg him to let her see it, let her clean it and put a bandage on it. The two of them spent their days living for the moment Halvor walked through the door. Harriet should have been jealous of the way the boy ran to his father, but all she could feel was guilty relief.

So of course he came out to Halvor. It happened when he was in third year, doing a combined major in art history and math. They had sold the bungalow by then and moved into the two-bedroom-plus-den condominium Harriet still lives in, and that Ranald is pressuring her to sell. She remembers trying to paint that afternoon in the south-facing den she had turned into a studio, but not being able to concentrate, too aware that Halvor had been with Ranald in his room for hours with the door shut. Was Ranald having second thoughts about being an architect? Then when the door opened and she saw them standing together—the boy with his father's height, her hair, and a perfect mix of their features—she knew exactly what they had been talking about, what had happened. Ranald's eyes were wet. He came to her and hugged her, awkwardly. She has tried to remember the embrace alone, to forget the small gesture

Halvor made just before it, as if cuing his son to do something he had managed to convince him to do.

Harriet goes to saw off another slice of baguette, then
thinks no. The last time he saw her, Ranald asked pointedly if
she had been gaining weight. Patrick said, "Ranald!" but did
not contradict him. She has thought about asking Patrick to
call her Mom. Would Ranald take it badly? Probably.

She shakes her head, putting the bread knife down. She
did her job, all the mother things, as well as she could. She
walked Ranald to school, holding his wrist, since he would
not open his hand to hers. She hosted birthday parties with
balloons and paper streamers and themed cakes—cowboys,
pirates, space rangers. She made Halloween costumes and
stuck drawings onto the fridge door and took pictures at
every milestone event. But all three of them knew it was a
waiting game for her. Just a matter of getting through, doing
her time, till she could get back to her brushes and paint.
"I was a fake mother, Halvor," she says, chewing a chunk of
tomato. It's the first time she's talked to him today. "Totally
bogus." *Harriet, you did your best.* When she imagines him
answering her his accent is as thick as it was when they first
met. *And the boy survived. He's as happy as he's going to be. So.*

She's pretty sure that's what he would say, the attitude he
would take. He didn't seem to mind having to be a parent
and a half. And the two men loved each other—no doubt
about that. She remembers them bent over the blueprints
of this cottage—Ranald the young architect answering the
questions of Halvor the engineer. The happiest she ever saw
Ranald was when he and his father were supervising the
construction.

"I still get a laugh out of the ramp," Halvor chuckled to her
in bed that Friday night after they had driven up to the cottage

to spend the weekend by themselves. It was the last night of his life. "He's got his old parents in wheelchairs already."

He drowned the next morning. He had gone for the swim he always took while she fixed lunch for the two of them. She got interested in a talk show on the radio and didn't notice for a while that he had been in the water longer than usual. The autopsy showed signs of a heart attack.

Harriet forks a bit of meat loaf. Dips it in mustard. Feels a twinge in her elbow and wonders what her attacker is spending her money on right now. She can just hear Ranald: *He's probably divvying the cash among his friends, having a big old laugh about how easy it was. And he'll be back. But he'll bring his friends with him. They'll take baseball bats to the windows, get in and trash the place. And God help you if you're here when they come.*

"Keep your hopes up, Ranald."

The tone of her voice shocks her—not just the fact that she has spoken aloud. She's been talking to Halvor for years, but never to Ranald. Would she ever say something like that to his face, something flat and hard like a slap, when he gets going about how utterly helpless she is? Maybe. It would upset Patrick. But for once she can imagine herself doing it.

She's always been so careful around her son. There's never been a big blow-up between them, she's seen to that. For the first year after Halvor drowned, Ranald could hardly look at her. Hoping to siphon off some of his rage, she made a point of telling him that she blamed herself for his father's death, that she couldn't stop wondering whether Halvor had called for her. He never swam far out. If the radio hadn't been on, might she have heard him?

As the years passed, she and Ranald achieved a kind of sullen peace. The question they both knew he was silently asking in those early days—*why couldn't it have been you in the water instead of him*—was never given voice. She wonders sometimes if he ever voiced it to Patrick. She can imagine Patrick listening calmly, then forgiving and comforting Ranald as he would one of his grade threes.

Harriet finishes her apple and decides she doesn't really want ice cream after all. Instead, maybe when she gets back from town she'll treat herself to a gin and tonic. She carries her lunch dishes into the kitchen, puts them on the counter and squirts dish detergent into the sink. Then decides the cleaning up can wait. And she doesn't really have to go to town right now either, does she? She could she leave it till tomorrow morning.

So what *does* she want to do? She stands still in the middle of the kitchen, feeling vague, distracted. Maybe a nap?

Curled up on the bed, still in her bathing suit, she stares at the wall where the first painting she ever did of the lake is hung. For a year after Halvor drowned, she didn't paint at all. Then when she did finally pick up her brushes she took the lake as her subject. This first one shows the end of the dock in the foreground—the spot where Halvor would have entered the water. It's not terribly good. The waves are too opaque. She's gotten better over the years at capturing their translucence and movement. But she never paints the lake alone. Always, there is something solid—a bit of the dock, the frame of the window—as a counterpoint to the water. Context. Something to ground it.

She turns onto her back. Sighs. This nap isn't going to happen. She gets up and pads barefoot into the living room. There, propped on her easel, is her half-finished painting of the lake as seen through the window. It's going to be good. One of her best. But it needs something. It's too neat. Predictable. She picks up a brush. Puts it down. Studies the tubes of paint she selected, the coloured stains on her scraped palette. Finds herself, oddly, thinking about her car keys. The plastic daisy on the key chain. Should she add them in, maybe have them sitting on the windowsill? Would that give the painting some oddness, a bit of an edge?

This is getting silly. She needs to get her act together. Do those dishes. Then drive into town and get some money.

She changes out of her bathing suit into shorts, a T-shirt and sandals. Washes and dries the lunch dishes. Goes and gets her car keys. Scoops them up. Turns toward the door. Stops. Turns back. Stands looking at the arrangement of objects on the mantle.

Something is wrong. Something is missing. She didn't notice before, at least not consciously, because she was so relieved that the keys were still there. But now she takes inventory. There's that piece of driftwood shaped like a horse's head that she and Halvor found. The mason jars of rocks and shells they collected over the years. Framed photographs. Her and Halvor on the deck raising champagne glasses to the newly finished cottage. Ranald and Patrick in their white tuxedos, paddling their canoe up to the dock where the wedding guests waited. And in the middle, a long, shiny space free of dust.

The wooden bookmark. That's what's gone.

Ranald whittled the bookmark for her the summer he went to art camp. He was twelve. When they picked him up to take him home at the end of the month, he held it out to her, eyes averted, mouth grim. He had shaved an oblong of pine thin at one end. At the thick end, he had shaped a raven—caught the hulking posture of the bird, and with just a few nicks suggested ruffled feathers.

She knows where the bookmark is. The narrow end is what she felt poking her in the back.

"How *dare* you!" She can hardly get the words out, her jaw is so tight with rage. Rising. Filling her up to her hair roots. "How *dare* you!" She grips her car keys. Stomps to the back door. Yanks it open. Slams it shut behind her and locks it. She can feel her blood pulsing as she starts the car. Righteous wrath. That's what this is. And it feels good. Feels good even just to say it. "Righteous wrath!"

She wasn't sure she liked the bookmark at first. But she tried, loyally, to use it. The thin end wasn't thin enough. It bent the covers of her books and kept falling out. So she tried opening letters with it, but the edge was too dull. Finally she said brightly to the young Ranald, "I want people to *see* this. I'm going to display it on the mantle in the living room." Ranald said nothing, his face as closed to her as it ever was. And in bed that night, Halvor made one of his rare criticisms. "You should have told him what the problem was. That way, he could have fixed it. Or he could have made you a new one. A better one."

It was one of the few times she got really angry with Halvor—a deep, sulky, childish anger that hung between them for more than a week. It would have been so easy to make things right—agree with her husband and tell her son the truth. And maybe, she realizes now in the car on the way to town, if Halvor had said *why don't you* instead of *you should have*, she might have approached Ranald. Had that conversation. But she never did. The bookmark, still useless, stayed on the living room mantle. Years later, when the cottage was built, she brought it up and displayed it there.

She drives straight to the 7-Eleven. And there they are, slumped against the wall in their hoodies like crows on a wire. She pulls into the parking lot. Brakes hard. Gets out and slams the car door behind her. Marches straight toward the line of boys, thinking, *Righteous wrath*. Crackling with it.

Their lips curl at the sight of her, then sag as she keeps coming. When she doesn't stop, they glance at each other and melt away, back behind the wall, down the alley. All but the one in the middle. The one who recognizes her. He stands as if impaled by her approach, his eyes frozen on hers.

She plants herself in front of him. Glares up. The boy's lip and chin are a rubble of pimples and stray black hairs. What is he—fifteen? She leans in and takes a whiff. Juicy Fruit.

She puts her hand out. "Give it back."

He blinks. Slumps. Reaches into the pocket of his hoodie jacket and pulls out some crumpled bills.

"No. Not the money. You can keep that. But you're going to earn it." She keeps her hand out.

More slowly, he reaches under the bottom of his jacket. His jeans pocket. A secret place, hidden from his gang. He pulls out the bookmark. Holds it toward her.

"Handle first!"

He turns it and she takes it from him. Holds it up in front of his face. "My son made this. For me. When he was younger than you. Look at me!" The eyes jump back to hers. "He made it! Do you understand what I'm saying to you? You can *make* things!" Oh, she could grab him by the shoulders, big as he is, and shake the living daylights out of him. She could haul back and slap him silly.

"Turn around." He does. "Pull your hood down." His hands shake. His hair at the back is a greasy mullet. "Put it back up." He does. And yes. There it is. Exactly what she needs.

"All right. You can turn around again. Look at me. I'm a painter. I need you to pose for me with your hood up. I'll paint you from the back. It's hard work. You have to stand still for long stretches until I say you can take a break. That's how you'll earn the money you took from me. And if it takes longer than this afternoon, I'll pay you more. Come to my place in an hour. You know where it is."

Back in the cottage she retrieves Halvor's photograph of her coming up the ramp and tapes it to the top of her easel. The angle is going to be tricky. Everything as seen through the hidden eyes of the hooded figure that will occupy the foreground. The window will be centered. Through it, a bit of the lake will show. And off to one side, in the bottom corner of the window frame, she will paint herself. The way he saw her.

That's important. She has to capture the aloneness. The unawareness of being watched. Waited for. It's not just a question of adding years. She has to look at this woman and see someone she no longer is. Get past the familiar. Paint what is already strange and gone.

It's easier to imagine the boy. Sent there by his gang to get money. Distracted by the bookmark. Looking at it and seeing a dagger. A raven totem. Picking it up. Turning and holding it to the light. Catching sight of her coming up the ramp.

With a few strokes, she outlines the woman ascending. And in the foreground, the hooded figure waiting. Watching.

She paints. It would be so easy to lose track of time. But she keeps an ear cocked for the sound of the back door opening.

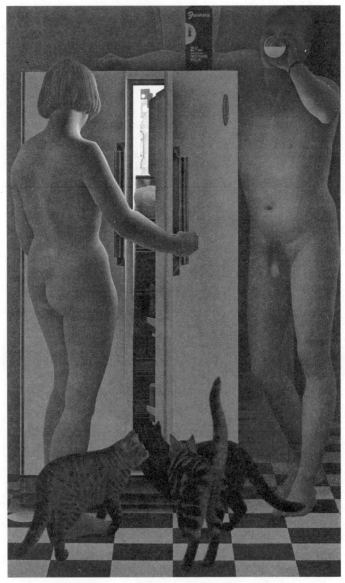

Refrigerator, 1977.

OLLY OLLY OXEN FREE

I WAS PLAYING JACKS. TRYING to. The ball kept getting away from me. I was almost crying when all of a sudden there was a hand. Palm up. And a voice. "Here. Give it to me."

One bounce of the ball. Two. By the third bounce, she had scooped up all the jacks. "These are mine now," she said, putting them in her pocket. "I just won them, so they belong to me. That's the rule."

Maude was very fond of rules. I thought they were real, grown-up rules that she knew about because she was three months and five days older. Also smarter. And prettier. As she liked to remind me.

My mother tried to talk some sense into me. "Don't always do what Maude tells you to," she said. "She's no better than you. Find somebody else to be friends with. Somebody who doesn't boss you around."

But my mother did not understand that someone like Maude can come along and just scoop you up. Scoop up your whole life. Put it in their pocket. Make it theirs.

*

When Miranda moved into the co-op, her insurance rates fell by six dollars a month. The reason for this, she was told, was the proximity of her new domicile to a police station. Though she welcomed the saving, the rationale puzzled her. Did the insurers think having police nearby would deter would-be burglars and murderers? Or was it about reduced response time? Provided, of course, she was alive and able to call 911?

Whenever she walks past the police station on her way to the supermarket or the cleaners or the library, she slows her steps, sometimes coming to a full stop. An onlooker might think she was momentarily confused, even lost. But Miranda knows exactly what she's doing. She's weighing the pros and cons of pulling open the door, approaching the front desk and saying to whoever is behind it, *I need to speak with someone. About something I believe I did.*

She's not afraid of the consequences. After all this time, there might not even be any. *You were a child, Miss Shankland,* she can imagine someone in authority saying. *Eight years old. Frightened. Confused. Maybe you're still a bit confused, in fact? About exactly what happened all those years ago?*

No. She is not. She resumes walking—a little more briskly than before—past the police station on her way to the supermarket or the cleaners or the library. The only thing that confuses her is why she keeps doing this to herself.

*

Fiona is watching Leo eat his breakfast. She has some information she should convey to him—information she has been caressing mentally the way she would caress a smooth stone hidden in her pocket. Some mornings, when she watches Leo first butter his toast, then tear it into bite-sized pieces, then eat those pieces one by one with butter-shiny fingers, she feels very close to pulling that stone out and throwing it at him.

She knows she is supposed to tell him what's bothering her. She's read the relationship books. Instead of fingering her smooth little stone, she should pull it out of her pocket and show it to him. That's how a marriage works. And she can tell he knows something's up. She comes home to sparkling surfaces, fluffed sofa cushions and exquisitely cooked dinners. He follows her around with the look of a chastened child who wants to make things right again. So yes, she should tell him. Put him out of his misery. And she would, too, if she wasn't enjoying his misery so much.

It wasn't always like this. There was a time when she loved the vinegary smell of his feet, the tickle of his pubic hair nudging her cheek and the salt of his cum at the back of her throat. She loved his mane of brown hair, too—yes, she married a Leo with a mane—and the cruel little sculpted goatee, darker brown, that ringed his mouth and bobbed when he talked.

But most of all, she loved his voice—rolling and sonorous and big—everything an author's voice should be. Leo had a way of pausing mid-sentence, mouth a little open, head cocked as if listening, as if waiting to be given the perfect phrase, the only possible word.

In those days, Fiona used to dream of him publishing his novel and being her book club's guest of honour. She imagined him standing tall in one of the group's immaculate living rooms, pinching the crystal stem of a wine glass between his thick fingers, beaming and booming down on the other women's upturned faces. Such a modest little dream. But cherished. Necessary, too. What else has kept her going for nine years? What else has pulled her out of bed all the mornings of all the weeks, then pushed her out the door onto the subway, then out onto the sidewalk for three blocks in the heat and the rain and the snow, then up the steps and through the door to her job at The Cred?

It frightens her to think that the dream might never come true. Does every marriage reach this point, and either break in two or just carry on for the sake of carrying on? Most of the women in her book club are married. Maybe she could ask them. After all, criticizing your husband to the shrieking delight of the other wives is de rigueur at the meetings.

But she's not exactly friends with any of those women. They never have runs in their pantyhose. Their skirts never trail threads or their blouses come untucked. Most of them are professionals—two lawyers, a doctor, a psychotherapist, an architect. They talk loud, their voices sharp. When they all get going at once, then explode into laughter, Fiona thinks she might hate them.

Of course, there is Miranda. The quiet one. Older than all the rest. Nice enough. Retired from that creepy job she had for ages. Fiona can see herself talking to her. But what would be the point? It would be like confiding in a nun. She would have to assume that whole areas of reality were off limits.

Leo is licking his fingers. Sucking, actually. Sucking the butter off each finger in turn. Fiona watches him. Mentally caresses her stone.

*

Leo is at his desk, ostensibly thumbing through his much-annotated manuscript, but in fact listening for the sound of Fiona leaving the apartment for the day. There. Hall closet door opening. Closing. Front door open. Closed. Click of the deadbolt. Steps fading down the hall. Ping of the elevator.

She's gone. The sudden, all-over relief never fails to amaze him. It's like the hit of a drug. Now the day is his alone, till six o'clock. He can spread out into the rest of the apartment. Relax in the big reclining chair in the master bedroom that used to be his study before he was uprooted and moved into this matchbox. Listen to music. Even go to the movies if he likes, provided he's home in time to have the place immaculate and a good supper table-ready the minute Fiona comes back through the door.

Years ago he would have felt free to mention seeing a movie, would even have discussed it while they ate together. "A writer," he told Fiona early in their marriage, "is someone on whom nothing is lost." Years ago, though, he could conveniently forget that he was not in fact voicing his own thoughts but quoting Henry James. And it was so easy to convince not just Fiona but himself, too, that any book he might read, any music he might hear, any movie or play he might take in, was grist for the mill.

In those days, he actually believed that the same was true of restaurant meals. After all, fictional characters do eat, don't they? So did he not have to educate himself as to the flavours, aromas, and textures of as great a variety of cuisines as possible? And were a well-stocked bar and wine rack not just as necessary, for precisely the same reason?

Then there were the demands imposed upon him by The Writing Life, of which actual writing was only a part. It used to make such perfect sense to keep himself at the ready for public readings and interviews. That none such had so far been lined up was, he assured himself and Fiona, of no consequence. Fame, when it comes, comes like a thief in the night. So his hair products and skin toners had to be of the highest quality, and his goatee given the attention, twice a week, of a professional barber whose hot towels were like a sauna from the neck up.

Jesus Christ. The money he spent. The bullshit he spent it on.

Feeling as if he's picking at a too-fresh scab, he opens his bottom desk drawer and pulls out the letter from *Scribbler*. A form letter. They actually sent him a form rejection letter. Not even a scrawled initial at the bottom. As if they had never published him. As if he hadn't worked for them. Won first prize in their literary contest just—

Eleven years ago.

Did Fiona read the letter before leaving it on his desk? The flap was open. But maybe it was never properly sealed in the first place. And surely she wouldn't read his mail. Except she's changed of late. A lot. And he first noticed the change— he checks the date on the letter. Yes. Two weeks ago.

"You're taking a course in haiku?" he remembers her asking. "Aren't they those itty bitty poems?"

She had never before questioned his need to self-edu-cate. Over the years he has enrolled in writing courses at the local university, writing workshops taught in community centres and church basements throughout the city, writing mentorships conducted online.

"Seventeen syllables," he corrected her. She had paused in the middle of writing the cheque that would pay for the course. "A highly compressed form. Very difficult."

"But you're writing a novel."

That had given Leo pause, too, when he was filling out the application. But he had reminded himself, as he reminded Fiona now, of what he had heard from one workshop teacher after another, namely that all writing was essentially writing, thus it followed that any writing of any kind at all—

"Yeah. Okay. I get it." Fiona had signed the cheque and handed it to him.

And just last week, she had questioned the value of his Daily Writing Practice. "You wrote about your toenails? You spent half an hour writing about your toenails? Is it at least going to be part of your novel, what you wrote?"

Why was she undermining his confidence this way? He invoked the compost-heap image that had always convinced her before. He explained, again, why keeping a jam jar on his desk filled with slips of paper on which he had scribbled single words or phrases—*toenails, pebble in shoe, martini, bus transfer*—then pulling one of those slips out of the jar every day and writing on the topic nonstop for a set number of minutes (he kept a kitchen timer beside the jar) could generate reams of material that might not be precisely pertinent to the project at hand, but could, in the fullness of time—

"Okay. Right. Compost."

It had all come to a head on Monday. Fiona had called one of her household meetings. Leo dreaded these, but presented himself at the dining-room table to listen humbly, respectfully, as his wife elucidated the state of their finances. She was, after all, an expert in household debt, having for years nudged boxes of Kleenex across her desk at The Credit Counselling Centre toward clients who wept while she took scissors to their plastic.

Leo did not weep when she circled a date on the kitchen calendar six months hence. Nor did he protest when she stipulated that by that date, he would not only have finished the novel he had been working on for almost a decade but would have at least a glimmer of a publishing contract. Or an interested agent. Something. Otherwise, he would get a job.

It could have been worse, he admitted to himself when it was over. Fiona could have demanded, finally, to be shown the manuscript which he keeps locked in his desk drawer and has never shared with her. ("Does an artist display a painting before the final brushstroke has been applied? Does a composer allow a piece to be played whose last note has yet to be—") She could have measured the half-inch thickness of his opus between finger and thumb. Hefted its total of eighty-seven pages on her palm.

Leo spends his days now in a state of fear. He is afraid of the hollowing in his stomach that tells him morning is over and it's time for lunch. He is afraid of the shadows lengthening along his study floor, reminding him that the afternoon has ended and Fiona will soon be home. He is afraid of his desk calendar, whose squares he imagines marked off in black X's advancing upon the day when he will have to start searching for a job.

A job. At thirty-three. With a BA in philosophy and English.

*

I heard them coming, heard them calling our names. I didn't move or call back to them, just let them get nearer and nearer. Because they were It. They were the seekers now. And for once,

I was the one who got to hide. So if they found me, they found me. And if they didn't, they didn't. That was the rule.

It was starting to get dark. With my auburn hair and yellow sweater, I blended in with the leaves. There was a freak snowstorm later that night. I'd have frozen to death if they hadn't spotted me. Once I was home, I looked out my bedroom window, watching the snow coming down and down. Like a warm white blanket. Covering our footprints. Keeping our secret.

They went on searching the woods for weeks. Police. Civilians. Dogs. Nothing. Not a thread of Maude's clothing. Not a hair of her head.

Miranda is sixty-five now, and has lived in the co-op for three years. On the day she turned sixty-two, when she was still in the house where she grew up, she came home from work to find the message light on the phone blinking. She stood still for a moment, taking her customary deep breaths. Smoothing down that slight ruffle of alarm brought on by anything unexpected—a brisk knock on the door in the evening, or an envelope whose hand-written return address she doesn't recognize. She can't remember a time when she did not react this way to any surprise, big or small. Of course, she can't remember much before the age of eight, when a headline in the local paper dubbed her *the found girl*.

Miranda has learned only a few lessons in her life, but she has learned them very thoroughly. First, she has learned that to be found is to be forgotten. To be still missing, on the other hand, is to be forever kept in mind. As little as five years ago, she came across an article about Maude. There was that same black-and-white photograph. Those same eyes that had looked out from every front page across the country. *The lost girl*. And as usual, her companion was mentioned. But for the first time, the companion's name was not.

The second lesson Miranda has taken to heart is that the best way to hide is in plain sight. If you wish people not to notice you, simply position yourself in their line of vision and do nothing worthy of note. She never missed a day of school, never distinguished herself as either gifted or slow. "Miranda Shankland?" any one of her teachers might have said of her. "Oh. Yes. I remember now. Nice girl. No trouble. Never a problem. Wish more of them could have been like her. But why do you ask?"

Her classmates might also have needed a moment to call her to mind. A girl who was neither a leader nor an outcast. Neither clamoured for nor rejected by captains choosing teams. A nice girl who would lend you her eraser with a smile, but never link arms with you on the way home from school.

Miranda seemed to understand from an early age that some things were simply not for her. Or she was not for them. She engaged in no adolescent rebellion, no fights with her parents. Nor did her parents encourage her to think in terms of marriage and family. Having once almost lost their daughter, they were just as happy to keep her at home. In high school, boys danced with her the way they would with their big sister and confided in her about other girls. Grown men started slightly when she entered a room, as if afraid she could read impure thoughts. At work, when a joke circulated about a spinster postmistress whose headstone read *Returned Unopened*, she obliged her colleagues by pretending not to overhear. And when her periods stopped in her forty-fifth year, she felt no regret.

"The house will always be yours, Miranda," her mother said to her at the reception after her father's funeral. No doubt Mrs. Shankland thought of this as the last and greatest gift from a parent devoted to keeping her child safely in the nest. But Miranda did have a practical side. She had taken a job, after all. And she had known for years that the house was a drafty, leaky white elephant whose taxes and upkeep would bite ever more deeply into her salary and her mother's widow's pension.

So the week after her mother finally died, she went to the library and used one of its computers to research housing co-ops in the city. An article in the paper had called them affordable housing for the disappearing middle class. She applied for units in three such, then, once the interviews were over, accepted a place on the waiting list of the one that was farthest from her present address.

Three years later, she came home from work to see the message light on her phone blinking. Her name had risen to the top of the list, and a unit was available. Would she be interested in viewing it?

"Places always look bigger once you get your furniture into them," the building manager said apologetically, taking Miranda's silence for disappointment. But she was not disappointed. Far from it. There was something almost thrilling about the emptiness of the rooms she was being shown, the bareness of the walls. She had lived all her life with her dead parents' heavy mahogany furniture and ornately framed florals. Here, the light pouring through the undraped windows gave a shine to the pale hardwood floors that made her want to run and slide in her socks like a child. Though she had never been that kind of child.

"I'll take it."

The next day, she gave notice at the Melville Staines Funeral Home, where she had started as the youngest receptionist ever employed there and, over four decades, become the oldest. Felicity Staines, daughter of the late Melville who had hired Miranda all those years ago, accepted her resignation with a show of regret that Miranda assumed was masking relief. And if she was right, the feeling was mutual.

With the death of old Mr. Staines, the place was no longer the sanctuary it had been for Miranda from the minute she stepped through its doors forty years ago for her job interview. Here, she had sensed, was a place where no one, whatever their authority, could burst through those doors and tromp in loud boots up to her desk and point a finger. And the guests, as she was taught to call them, could neither recognize nor remember nor bear witness through their sewn lips. Under Felicity Staines, however, the place was being thrown wide open to the world, the guests all but invited to get up and sing and dance.

Felicity's mother died when she was two, and her father never remarried. The girl had her father's height and pallor, and somehow gave the impression that she had never really needed a mother, having calved off Melville Staines like an iceberg. When she was introduced to the staff of the Home at the age of six, she regarded Miranda gravely across the reception desk for a moment, then said, "Were you ever a little girl?"

In middle school, Felicity started dropping in to the Home to do her homework. She claimed the place was quieter than the library. Besides, her father could give her a ride home at the end of the day.

Miranda did not dislike the girl, who was no trouble. But something about her put her on edge. Though Felicity was not overly familiar, her presence made Miranda want to take a step back, as if to preserve her personal space. The girl gave the impression of knowing the older woman more thoroughly than she possibly could or should.

When Felicity finished high school and announced her plans to study thanatology, Miranda felt a niggle of dread. The dread became certainty when she apprenticed under her father, then settled into resignation when she took over the place after Melville Staines' death.

Miranda did what she could to salvage some of the funeral home's dignity. She had supported and maintained that dignity for forty years with every detail of her deportment and person. The short, simple haircut. The muted colours of the skirted suits she wore all year round. The way she had let her own colours—auburn hair, blushing complexion—fade naturally with time. Above all, her manner of speaking—measured and hushed, as if she hovered perpetually on the threshold of sacred space.

But she was up against the force of fashion. Felicity embraced the latest trends in the funeral industry—everything from the ceramic skull she kept on her desk ("Respect for grief need not be synonymous with denial of the realities of death") to her espousal of biodegradable caskets for unembalmed corpses ("It's time our profession embraced the environment it has been abusing.") She dyed her hair midnight blue, dressed in gothic weeds, and laughed loud. She referred to the embalmer and his assistant as the boys in the basement and called Miranda by her first name. The day the staff-meeting agenda included a serious discussion of contracting with a tattoo artist to offer ash tatts, whose ink was mixed with a pinch of a loved one's cremains, Miranda had trouble eating her lunch.

It was time to go. She would have preferred to perform her duties as usual on her last day then slip out the door without ceremony. However, she tried to be a good sport about the coffin-shaped cake with *RIP Miranda Shankland* scripted in purple icing. And she actually allowed Felicity Staines to embrace her at the door. The younger woman's eyes were damp when Miranda pulled away. And one last time, there was that strangely knowing look.

Once she moved into the co-op, Miranda began to change. The changes had a driven feeling to them, as if they were not quite voluntary. Sometimes, catching sight of her reflection in a store window, she would think, *Who is that?*

She grew her hair out, just enough to let it frame her face, and asked her hairdresser to cover the grey with a paler shade of the original auburn. She gave away her dull suits and began to costume herself in pinks and reds, yellows and greens.

She brought none of the dark old furniture with her from her parents' house. Everything, she was suddenly convinced, had to be brand new and entirely different. Light woods. Pale fabrics. Chrome and glass. When the last piece was delivered and put in place, her apartment looked like the apartment of a stranger.

She dusts and sweeps and polishes every day, feeling compelled to keep the place forever guest-ready. Not that she has any guests. But she catches herself starting conversations with neighbours in the elevator and laundry room. She has signed up to answer the co-op office phone two mornings a week, to water the plants on the terrace and to keep the donated books in order on the shelves in the lounge. She has even ventured out into her new neighbourhood, inquiring at the local library about book clubs. When a librarian gave her the name and number of a woman who ran such a club and lived nearby, she went home and picked up the phone.

It's all so strange. Is she turning into a different person? Most disconcerting is her new habit of walking past the police station. It would be so easy to go another route when she's out running errands. Why does she practically have to pull herself away from the station door? What is she daring herself to do?

*

Fiona had always hated her name. Fiona McFee. Fifi, as she was called all through school. When she was in her third year of university, she met Leo Van de Veld and mentally claimed his name as hers.

Fiona Van de Veld.

Leo was a recent graduate who had stood out on campus because of his height and his reputation as an aspiring writer. In his final year his short story, "The Verging Virgin," had come first in *Scribbler's* literary contest. Fiona remembered reading about it in the campus newspaper, which interviewed him. *The Scribbler people are urging me to develop the story into a novel,* he was quoted as saying.

Hello, I'm Fiona Van de Veld. Why, yes. My husband is the novelist Leo Van de Veld.

They met at a party in one of the residences. Leo had been asked back to campus to present that year's *Scribbler* prize. In the weeks that followed, as they became lovers, Fiona imagined a new life to go with the new name.

I'm so glad you enjoyed his latest book. I'll be sure to pass your compliment on to him.

She never confided any of this to her housemates. She knew it made her look ridiculously old-fashioned. But she didn't care. She was living in a communal house full of girls and cats. The first night Leo stayed over, they sneaked naked together out to the kitchen for a midnight snack. In the white light of the opened fridge, as Leo drank Fiona's share and more of the milk, the cats came and twined around their legs. One of them propped her front paws on Leo's thigh and sniffed delicately at his penis.

"What if somebody gets out of bed and finds us?" Fiona whispered, shivering. The shrug of Leo's bare, beautiful shoulder thrilled her. This was it. The extraordinary thing she had always known was going to happen—had to happen—to Fiona McFee. Her B-plus average, her okay looks, her being neither a loner nor especially popular—it all added up to an ordinariness that felt like a mistake. The wrong skin. So that night, once they went back to bed and Leo Van de Veld gasped out a marriage proposal seconds before ejaculating, she worked in a quick "Yes!"

Once officially Fiona Van de Veld, she had a mission. She would be Leo's muse, his amanuensis, his facilitator and chatelaine. She would inflate a delicate bubble of peace and solitude for him to inhabit, and would fiercely guard its fragile walls. On a more practical level, she would work full-time at a job she hated but which paid enough for the two-bedroom apartment they needed if Leo was to have a room of his own.

Every morning for the first three years of her marriage, Fiona would stand for a moment in the doorway of the master bedroom Leo had claimed as his study. It only made sense to cram their marital bed into the smaller room, and their clothes into its inadequate closet. A big man needed a big desk. Also a big window through which to gaze as he took his necessary breaks in his big reclining chair. So as not to disturb him as he hunched over his papers and dictionary and thesaurus, she would mouth, *Goodbye, my love. Write well.* Then she would turn and tiptoe away to put on her shoes and her coat and go to work.

During the second three years, Fiona would still pause in the doorway of Leo's study every morning. But now she would remind him that they needed milk and bread, and that he mustn't forget to pick up her blue jacket from the cleaner's. She had started to have a few expectations. Well, why not? A little take, to balance all the give.

These last three years, Fiona has insisted on some changes. Leo's desk is now in the smaller bedroom. There isn't enough space in there for his reclining chair, and anyway nothing much to gaze at through the smaller window. Their once joint bank account is now in her name only, and Leo given a weekly cash allowance. She has delegated almost all the housework and cooking to him. And she has started asking questions about what he does all day.

The women in her book club have told her she's doing the right thing and should be proud of sticking up for herself, getting some payback for all the support she's given him. But the truth is, she hated kicking him out of the bigger room. Handing him his money for the week each Monday morning makes her feel like a ball-breaker. And though she's the breadwinner, she feels guilty about doing nothing around the house.

Not nearly as guilty as she feels about the letter, though. And not just the fact that she read it. There's also the way she has turned it into that little stone of resentment she caresses and caresses. She wishes she could go back in time two weeks, to the moment she saw *Scribbler's* return address on an envelope whose flap was not glued down.

Picking up the mail when she comes home from work and delivering anything with just Leo's name on it to his desk is one of the few amanuensis tasks she has hung onto. She so wants to be the bearer of the good news she still tries to believe will come—must come—some day soon.

So the open flap was like an omen. Surely, after all her labours all these years, she had the right to be the first to learn the good news. Maybe some book publisher contacted *Scribbler* because they wanted to get in touch with Leo. They had been going through back issues of the magazine, had found his winning story and—

Or maybe *Scribbler* wanted Leo back as an editor. Paid, this time. Part of his prize had been a chance to intern. So this might be—

The letter was open in her hands. She read it. Once. Twice. Then again. There simply had to be more to it. More words on the page. Better words.

It was a form letter, rejecting Leo's latest submission … *not without merit; however it does not meet our needs at this time.* The one and only magazine that had ever published anything by her husband was now sending him form rejection letters.

Her hands shook so badly she could hardly refold the single sheet of paper and get it back inside the envelope. Nine years. Nine years at the Cred. By now it should be adding up to something. She should be accompanying

Leo on book tours. Listening to him being interviewed on radio. Reading his reviews. But all it's likely to add up to now is another nine years at the Cred.

How much of a damned fool has she been? Does she really want to know? Leo keeps his novel manuscript locked up, but she knows where he hides the key. She wishes she didn't. She is so afraid that one night she will slide out of bed while he snores on. Tiptoe into the smaller bedroom. Sneak the manuscript out of its hiding place. Turn on the light. Start to read.

*

Leo has taken to wandering the neighbourhood for hours each day, ducking into stores and businesses on some pretext, but actually just observing people doing jobs. Soon, he knows, he will be one of them—a person doing a job. If he can get used to the idea, habituate himself to it a bit each day, maybe some of the terror will abate.

Aside from that editorial internship of his student days, Leo has never worked. His parents—a low-paid United Church minister and a housewife—managed somehow to send him to university without his having to pitch in with after-school and summer jobs. They regarded school as his job. And Leo, they devoutly believed, would prove to be exceptional. "We're just waiting," he overheard his father say to a parishioner who had congratulated him on his son's *Scribbler* win, mention of which had been made in the parish newsletter. "And watching. And praying."

They were still waiting and watching and praying when Leo finished his degree and moved back home. Just until he had had a chance to rest from his academic labours, he assured them. And until he found himself.

What he found was Fiona McFee. And what he saw in her eyes was all the hope and expectation that had just started to fade from the parental gaze being turned on him every morning at the breakfast table.

Given the number of courses and workshops he's taken over the years, he probably knows enough about writing, in theory, to teach it. But a potential student would only have to Google his name to discover that theory is all he possesses. That, and eighty-seven heavily annotated manuscript pages. *Weighed in the balance.* The judgement he has avoided pronouncing on himself all this time with his Daily Writing Practice and his pursuit of The Writing Life now whispers in the back of his mind, its diction Biblical. *And found wanting.*

He is going to have to get a job. He is going to have to do the thing he most fears—be the big, overeducated oaf who has to be shown how to do every little thing.

This afternoon he sidled into a shoe store and pretended to be looking at a rack of loafers and deck shoes while in fact cocking an ear to an argument two employees were having behind the cash counter. The older one—Leo supposed he was the boss—was berating the younger one for having allowed some woman to return a pair of shoes she claimed never to have worn. "There's gravel embedded in the soles! Look!" The older man sprayed something from a bottle on the bottom of a shoe and rubbed it with a cloth. "And there's—holy shit, is that gum?"

"She said she only—"

"She said she said she said. Jesus. Bring up the sku and make it an exchange."

"But there was no—"

"I said, bring up the sku."

Bring up the sku, Leo thought, still pretending to examine a pair of navy dockers. *I would have to learn to bring up the sku. Whatever that is. And I would be on my feet all day. But with my back the way it is, I can't—*

"May I help you?" It was the boss. A short man with a greasy comb-over. Leo looked down at him in horror, imagining having to address him as sir.

"Just looking, thanks." Then he stumbled out the door onto the street.

*

We had shared a candy back and forth that day. Our fingers were sticky from it. Maude said that since I had had the candy last and had gotten to swallow it, she got to hide first. That was the rule for the day. It always was, one way or another. Maude always got to hide first. And second. And third. It was just as well, because I could not hide from Maude. I had tried, but I always gave myself away by moving or coughing. That was one reason I was forever It. The other reason was that I could not bring myself to find Maude. I usually knew where she was hiding. But I wanted her to win. So I would walk past her and pretend not to see her. It was worth it to hear her carol, Olly olly oxenfree! and to see her, all flushed and happy, ready to hide again.

I clung to the rock, counting over and over to one hundred. The seekers had to pry my arms away from it, yelling, "We found one of them! We found one of them!" Wrapping me in a blanket. Passing me from one embrace to the next.

But soon the embraces became questions. "Did you see anything? Did you hear anything? Was anyone there?"

I could have answered. I could feel the answers on my tongue, just like the candy I had shared with Maude. I went over and over them, feeling their shape. But I just looked down and made my mouth a straight line.

When she worked at the funeral home Miranda saw men cry all the time. They aren't very good at it, she decided early on. They hold back and hold back, then explode in a wet, spluttering mess that is likely far more humiliating than it would have been to simply let the tears flow in the first place.

Leo keeps gasping out apologies, his thick fingers digging into his red forehead. He is sitting in the middle of Miranda's new couch, managing to make it look small. His elbow and knee have stopped bleeding, thanks to all the crumpled Kleenexes dotting the coffee table. Once he settles down, Miranda will help him apply the antiseptic and Band-aids she fetched from her medicine cabinet.

She had been setting out to pick up her spring coat from the dry cleaner's. It was mid-April and as usual she was getting her lighter clothes in order. Just in time, too, because a freak heatwave had the city digging out its shorts and T-shirts weeks early. She had just stepped onto the sidewalk outside the co-op when a large, vaguely familiar man coming toward her met her eyes.

She froze. Was it—

No. It was just—

Right then the man tripped on a crack in the sidewalk and landed in a sprawl at her feet. She went and helped him up. "Leo? You're Leo, aren't you? I'm Miranda. From Fiona's book club."

The last meeting had been held at the Van de Velds' apartment. Leo had greeted the group and chatted briefly before retreating to his study. *To work on my novel.* She remembers him making a point of telling them that. She also remembers Fiona not exactly rolling her eyes, but looking as if she had just stopped herself from doing so.

Fiona intrigues her. She's a bit scuffed and worn-looking compared to the rest. And she has a secret. Yes. Miranda knows the signs.

Now Leo plucks another Kleenex from the box on the coffee table, wipes his face with it, and blows his nose. His hands are huge. Miranda imagines them stroking the length of Fiona's body, one pausing to cup a breast, the other sliding lower to prise open and enter.

"Sorry," he says one last time. "I'm so clumsy. And this always happens whenever I fall down. I'm told it's just shock. Your blood-sugar level drops, apparently, when you fall. It affects some people more than others. That's all. But still. It's embarrassing. Crying like a kid."

"Here." Miranda tilts the opened bottle of antiseptic into a wadded Kleenex, which she presses to the raw scrape on Leo's elbow. He draws a sharp breath. She applies a band-aid. "You do your knee," she says, pushing the Kleenex box and bottle toward him. "I'll make us some tea." She gathers up the bloody tissues and takes them into the kitchen.

While she waits for the kettle to boil, she is very aware of Leo's presence in her living room. Her first guest. And a man. The only other man who has ever been here is the super, once or twice, to fix things. Has she ever touched a man before this? She wanted to clean and bandage his knee, too. But the thought of being that close to the fleshy thigh below the hem of his shorts, the hairy calf—

She knows that the next time she reaches down to her own wetness, she will be thinking of Leo. What if she took her clothes off here in the kitchen and emerged naked, carrying the tea tray?

The things that go through a person's mind. The kettle boils. Cookies. A cookie would get Leo's blood-sugar level back up. And she has that unopened package she felt oddly compelled to buy the last time she shopped for groceries.

"You're being so kind to me," he says when she puts the tray with the pot and mugs and a plate of chocolate-coated digestives in front of him.

"Where were you going when—"

"When I fell flat on my face in front of you? I wasn't going anywhere. I was running away. From a shoe store."

Miranda says nothing. She pours tea into a mug and passes it to Leo. She's a good listener. It may be the best thing she does. And she has guessed that Leo is one of those men who like to tell a woman all about themselves. She met a few of them at the Melville Staines Funeral Home. After depleting her Kleenex box and telling her the story of their lives, sometimes they would ask her to have dinner with them. This with their wives encoffined in the next room. Always, she would smile and change the subject.

Leo has been talking all this time. About his parents. His marriage. Now he is summing up. "I'm a failed writer with a useless degree. I've wasted nine years on a book that nobody's going to read. I've just been rejected by the one magazine that's ever accepted me. And if I don't get a job selling shoes or some damned thing, my wife's going to throw me out on the street."

Miranda does not say, *What would be so bad about selling shoes?* Another lesson she has learned is that everyone wants to be extraordinary. Be careful what you wish for, she would like to tell them. I became *the found girl* at the age of eight.

And that was quite extraordinary enough. How would you like to see your parents' faces twist into imagined grief every time they meet your eyes? To hear your Sunday School teacher tell the class to bow their heads while she thanks God aloud for your safe return? To suspect the motive behind each new apparent friendship, waiting for morbid curiosity to assert itself? ("You must have seen *something*. *Something* must have happened to you.") To know that it was already all over—that you had ascended the peak of experience, had seen all you would ever see, knew all you were going to know, and now the rest of your life would be one long descent?

Leo slurps tea and takes a cookie from the plate. "Anyway, that's the story of Leo. So what's the story of Miranda?" He asks the question so casually. Probably expects her to look at her lap and say, "Oh, I don't really have a story. There's nothing special about me."

Sometimes, if she was working late in the funeral home and had to turn out the lights and lock up after the last visitation was over, she would go into one of the rooms. She would pull a chair close to the casket, sit down and thank that particular guest for being the one. It didn't happen often—just every few years. There would be something about the curve of an eyebrow, or a certain grace to a pair of folded hands that would invite her to tell her story. When she was finished, she would say thank you again, turn out the light, and leave.

It's the only thing about the Melville Staines Funeral Home that she misses. But here now is a living man willing to listen. And suddenly it all makes sense. Moving into this co-op, in this particular neighbourhood. Growing her hair. Choosing brighter colours. Keeping her apartment immaculate. Joining the book club. Even buying the choco-late-covered cookie Leo is biting down on. Then setting out today to go to the cleaner's at the precise moment that he would be coming along, stepping ever closer to that crack in the pavement.

"If I tell you my story," Miranda begins, "will you do something for me?"

He shrugs. "Sure."

She smiles. Then she takes his hand, brushes cookie crumbs off the fingers, and presses the palm down over her left nipple. "Promise."

*

Fiona sits at Leo's desk, looking at the file that contains his manuscript. For once, he wasn't there when she got home from work. The bed was still unmade, the breakfast dishes still piled dirty on the counter and no sign of supper.

Her hands shook when she retrieved the key and fitted it into the locked drawer. She has the strangest feeling of being part of a fairy tale. The princess has entered the forbidden place and now holds the forbidden object in her hands. She is convinced that once she starts to read the manuscript, huge wheels will start to turn. A single word will suffice to put them in motion. Maybe she should make a wish first. Let the powers that be know, at least, which way she wants those wheels to roll. She can't go on fingering her little stone of contempt. She wants to throw it away.

She makes a wish. She thinks back to that night in the communal house when she and Leo stood naked in the kitchen, raiding the refrigerator while the cats swarmed round, tickling their calves with their whiskery breath. She was so full of hope that night. Faith. Excitement. Joy. She wishes to feel that way again. Be that way again.

She opens the file and starts to read.

*

When Leo gets home he is not surprised to find Fiona sitting at his desk in the study. His manuscript is in front of her, and she is reading the final page. He always knew this would happen. And it seems particularly right that it happen now.

All the way home, he kept telling himself that he should be appalled at his own behaviour, should seek out some punishment, maybe even turn himself in. Except there was no crime. Miranda had been very clear about wanting him to keep going, even when it was obvious she was in pain. And he hadn't so much wanted to as felt that he must. As if he were playing some role that had been written for him. Afterwards, knowing full well that he had deflowered one woman and cheated on another, he searched himself for guilt and found none.

Fiona has turned the final page of his manuscript. She swings round slowly in his desk chair and looks at him for a long time. Her eyes are strangely young. There is something in her gaze that he remembers seeing long ago, but not for years. Awe? And maybe a little fear? Well, her reading his manuscript is a betrayal. So now they have betrayed each other.

He's starting to get hard. One of his pubic hairs snags on his underwear. Is it caught on a crust of blood? He did wash himself off in Miranda's bathroom.

Fiona lets him pull her down onto the floor. Raise her skirt. Shove her underpants down over her hips. He unzips himself. Pops out like a Jack-in-the-box. A little raw from Miranda's tightness. But Fiona is so wet. So ready. They do it once on the study floor, then stumble together in a simian hunch to the bedroom, where she sprawls face down on the bed and he takes her from behind.

Through the whole afternoon and into the evening they doze and wake and fuck. At midnight they're fully awake and ravenous and go naked into the kitchen to eat.

"Remember the cats?" she says, watching him drink milk. "In that house?"

"Jesus, yeah. How many were there?"

Those are the first coherent words they have spoken in hours. Leo hasn't asked her what she thinks of his novel. It doesn't matter any more. He's going to finish it, whether she likes it or not. He realized that while he was listening to Miranda's crazy story. Which couldn't possibly be true. Even though she obviously believes it.

Fiona has gotten her wish. She is filled with an immense gladness that she thinks has to do with what she read that afternoon. In fact, it is owing to the tiniest of breachings taking place deep inside her body.

*

It was so important to the grown-ups that I be innocent. All those big people, looking down at me. I knew, somehow, that I could destroy them with one word of the truth.

The truth was, I had cheated. For once. I was supposed to stay by the big rock and count to one hundred. I always had, all the times Maude and I had played. But just that once, I stopped at fifty. I don't know why. Maybe something had happened that day. Maybe Maude had annoyed me. Or maybe I just made one of those sudden leaps a growing child can make. Whatever the reason, all at once I decided I couldn't stand to hear Maude crowing Olly olly oxenfree. Not then. Not ever again. So I cheated. Broke a rule. Stopped counting at fifty and tiptoed through the woods the way Maude had gone.

It took a long time. The sun was dipping below the tree tops by the time I found her, and I was starting to wonder if I had made her up, like a story. But then there she was. Lying on the ground. Very pale. Very still. And so small, without her clothes. I knelt down and touched her face. Cold. How could this little person have scooped up all my jacks? How could she have bossed me around? With her child's body—flat, then rounded at the belly? And her little cleft pubis, like a pensive mouth?

There was blood.

Sometimes I remember the blood seeping out from under the back of Maude's head. In this memory, my hands are gritty and scratched as if from a rough, heavy stone.

Other times I remember the blood seeping out from between Maude's thighs. In that memory, my hands are clean.

When Leo leaves, Miranda stands naked in front of her full-length mirror. She can't remember the last time she looked at herself this way. The biggest change has been to her face. From the neck down, though, she could be—fifty? Younger? She's kept herself small and trim, so her breasts are just a little lower than they ever were. Her triangle of pubic hair is grey, though. Could it be coloured like the hair on her head, she wonders, with a package of dye from the drugstore? But then wouldn't she have to keep touching it up, with more dye and Q-tips? What would be the point of that? Who else besides her would ever see?

The whole time, she had known Leo was thinking about his wife. And that had seemed strangely all right. As if some plan were being enacted.

There is a small pair of scissors in the medicine cabinet in the bathroom. Once she has snipped off the blood-matted curls and flushed them down the toilet, what is left lies tight and flat like a pelt. She soaps herself and works carefully with her razor. And there they are. The strange little vertical lips she remembers. The air is cold on them, despite the warm day.

In the bath, the water soothes her newly naked skin and penetrates to the soreness inside her. It is over. She has told her story to a living soul. Will the man come for her now? She reaches again for the scissors. Let him.

It was the shoes I saw first. Brogues. Though I didn't know that word then. I've given it to the shoes since. Brown brogues. Standing in the leaves just inches from where Maude lay. Had they just now walked through the leaves? I hadn't heard any crackle. Or had they been standing there the whole time, and I was only seeing them now? Like in one of those puzzles that are a picture inside a picture. A gnarled tree trunk that becomes a face if you look at it long enough. There were brown corduroy trousers growing up out of the shoes. A woolen sweater. Nubbly tweed jacket. Cap. And under it the man's face—all in shadow at first, with the setting sun behind him. But I could tell he was looking at me.

Slowly, he squatted down. I heard his knees crack. He was looking straight into my eyes, and he was very, very serious. He shook his head and said in that hushed, shocked voice that adults save for bad children, "What have you done?"

I have cheated at hide and seek, I thought. My mouth was too dry to say the words aloud. I have broken a rule of the game.

He shook his head, as if he could hear my thoughts, and repeated, "What have you done?"

I have been angry with my friend, I thought. *All this time. I have been angry with her for taking my jacks and not giving them back.*

Again the head shake. "What have you done?"

I have hated my friend.

No, still not enough. "What have you done?"

I have wished dead the one I loved.

I started to cry then. The man just let me. No comfort. No hand on my shoulder. Not even a clicking tongue.

"Well," he said when I had run out of tears, "what are you going to do now?"

I don't know.

"But how are you going to look after things? How are you going to do what needs to be done here?"

I don't know.

He shook his head and stood up again. He was very tall, taller than before, and his face was in darker shadow. He sighed—that disgusted, pettish sigh adults come out with when a child has spilled something or wet themselves.

"All right," he said at last. "I guess I'll have to look after things. I guess I'll have to do what needs to be done here. This once." He pointed his finger at me. "But you, young lady, are going to turn around and go back to where you should have been and do what you should have been doing."

I'm sorry.

"Well, I should hope so."

As I turned away, I heard his last words. "Don't you ever come back here. And don't you ever tell anyone what happened. I'll know if you do. And I'll find you. Wherever you are."

The whole time I was walking back to the stone to resume counting to one hundred from fifty, I kept listening for the man's footsteps in the leaves. But all I could hear were my own.

The only other phone number the co-op's building manager has on file for Miranda Shankland is that of the Melville Staines Funeral Home. So it is Felicity Staines who drains the crimson bathwater and says tenderly, "Oh Miranda" before loading and delivering the remains to the crematorium in the basement of the Home.

For the memorial service, Felicity recruits the boys in the basement to transform the Home's largest guest room into an enchanted forest. Patches of gnarled bark on styrofoam trees become faces if you look at them long enough. There are hollow trunks to hide in and papier-mâché rocks to hide behind. Some tree stumps have games of jacks and snakes-and-ladders set on them. The bewildered attendees—a few of Miranda's co-op neighbours, the members of the book club and Leo—are invited to go hide-and-seek in the forest or sit and play games while *The Teddy Bears' Picnic* plays over and over in the background.

Felicity Staines watches them indulgently as, starting with Leo and Fiona, they comply. Fiona is off work that day because of some nausea that cleared up by late morning. She still does not know she is pregnant, just as Leo does not know that he will finish his book in less than six months and sell it to Dennis Little of Littlepress, based in Stoney Creek. *Olly Olly Oxen Free* will be a critical hit and a runner-up for both the Biggar Prize and the Olympia Featherstone Award For Fiction. Though it will win neither, the book will lend Leo Van de Veld enough credibility to land a creative-writing teaching position in a local community college. He will discover that he likes teaching. That he's good at it. That he takes pride in going out the door each morning after kissing Fiona and the baby goodbye.

But all this is in the future. Right now Leo taps his foot to *If you go out in the woods today...* while Fiona bounces a rubber ball and scoops up all his jacks.

Their daughter, Leonora Van de Veld-McFee, will grow up to be a world-renowned criminologist, specializing in abducted children. Given her parents' slight connection with Miranda Shankland, she will have a lifelong fascination with Maude's cold case, and will always wish she could have interviewed *the found girl*.

And where is *the found girl*? Specifically, her ashes?

Behind Felicity Staines' aubergine-lipsticked smile is the memory of mixing them into the paint on the tree trunks, into the paste in the papier-mâché rocks. And behind that is an older memory of lurking, as a child, behind a curtain in one of her father's guest rooms. Listening to Miranda tell her story.

Mr. Wood in April, 1960.

Octopus Heart

HAS ELIOT EVER SAID ANYTHING about wanting to go to the aquarium? When he unfolds the open ticket Bill Merton has just given him as a belated birthday gift, all he can manage at first is an interested-sounding "Oh!"

He and Bill meet once a month for lunch at the Rendezvous. They worked together for thirty-five years in the finance department of *Girls First!* and retired within weeks of each other. At both retirement parties they pledged to stay in touch. Then a full year went by before Eliot booted up one morning and saw an email from Bill.

He left it a couple of days before replying. Sure, he had always liked Bill. They had had an unspoken solidarity as male employees of a charity devoted to the education and welfare of underprivileged girls. Sometimes, if they met in the men's after an AGM, they would grin and greet each other as Token Merton and Token Somers. But he's not sure he wants to be reminded of the place. He never dropped back into the office for a visit the way he saw so many retirees do over the years. He'd be right in the middle of something but would have to leave it to go greet Old Whoever, then stand in a politely smiling circle, asking the requisite questions about how they were enjoying retirement and pretending interest in the usual replies about how it's the greatest thing ever. (*So what are you doing back here—gloating?*)

But this was Bill. And it had been a year. They would hardly be talking shop. So he did reply, and one thing led to another, and now they do lunch once a month at the Rendezvous. It's a good enough place, right near the subway, equidistant from their condominiums. They have a running joke about ordering the same thing every time—Bill the steak frites, Eliot the moules frites. But hell. It's what they want. And it's their pension they toiled away for all those years.

Their conversation follows a pattern too. Anything new? What are you reading? Did you catch that game? See that movie? And can you believe what some celebrity or politician has just said or done? They don't get personal. Or not often. Eliot knows Bill is childless and divorced, his ex-wife married now to another woman. Bill knows Eliot's wife doesn't recognize him any more when he visits her, and his daughter hasn't spoken to him in years. At some point each would have offered up his particulars, and the other mumbled, *Sorry to hear that.*

Eliot doesn't remember when they started acknowledging each other's birthdays. One of them would have let slip that he had turned seventy or whatever that last month, so the other would have insisted on picking up the lunch tab. So the birthday boy would have demanded to know his host's birth date, in order to return the favour. Then at some point one of them would have maybe handed a paperback book to the other—nothing expensive and certainly not wrapped—just something he thought the other might get a kick out of. And so at the next birthday lunch there would have been another modest gift handed across the table.

Which is how Eliot has come to be looking at a printout of a ticket—just folded, not tucked inside a card—that will admit him to the aquarium once any time this year.

"You've gotta go." Bill has just finished describing his own visit, how his niece and her husband asked him to go along with them, last time they were in Toronto. His cheeks are flushed, and Eliot knows that's as much about the invitation as the outing. "Trust me. Even if you don't give a damn about fish. You won't believe what you're seeing."

The ticket has almost expired by the time Eliot uses it. He finally goes because he has to get out, has to clear his head. The aquarium will be a whole new thing. No associations. And he doubts he'll bump into anyone he knows.

He cancelled the Rendezvous lunch for this month— October—claiming a bout of the flu but in fact wanting to avoid Bill's questioning looks. Though he's not hurting nearly as much these days, his walk is still not quite right and he has to be careful sitting down. Not that Bill would actually ask. But he himself might be tempted to unload. The whole thing has left him kind of unstable. And if he got emotional, neither of them would know where to look.

It took him weeks to make an appointment with the specialist his GP was urging him to see. *It's not going to get better, Eliot. It's only going to get worse.* Even more frightening than the symptoms—the bleeding, and that hard spike of tissue that protruded agonizingly whenever he moved his bowels—was the thought of what the diagnosis might be. But when he finally did see the specialist, the man shrugged and said, *Sounds like a rectal fissure. Very common. We can fix that right here and now.*

Not cancer after all? Surgery all of a sudden? It left him without defences. He blubbered "Get out! Get out!" during the speculum probe and the needle. And afterwards, waiting on the curb for a cab, feeling the freezing already giving way, he searched the faces of strangers for kindness. Comfort.

He didn't sleep that night, migrating back and forth between his bathtub and his bed, where he could only hunker on his knees, rubbing his crotch in fruitless self-soothing and gobbling pain pills like candy. Toward dawn he fell into a doze and dreamed about Jill for the first time in years. She was perched at the end of the bed, shaking her head and saying, *I tried to tell you, Eliot. I did try to tell you.* He was paralyzed in the dream, and the bed was a hospital bed. Jill had been called in as a kind of therapist. Patiently, methodically, she placed her palms on him here and there. Whatever she touched began to tingle back to life.

It was just a dream, Eliot told himself in the morning as he hobbled to the kitchen to make a pot of tea. (Coffee, with all its acids, had been forbidden for a month, along with spicy foods.) And how long had it been since he had had any contact with Jill Macklin? Five years? He still had the handwritten letter she sent him when he stopped returning her calls and emails. Once or twice he had tried to pen an answer, but each time the sight of the self-addressed, stamped envelope she had included with a little joke about facilitating had made him crumple the page he had begun and put her letter back in his dresser drawer under his socks.

... whatever I may have said or done that would explain ... no desire to possess or control ... merely asking for a word from you ... closure ... enable me to move on ...

Pointless, reading and rereading Jill's letter. But it's what he does now. Takes three baths a day—getting in and out of the tub is still a small torture—cooks himself bland food and reads a letter he can practically recite from memory.

... abrupt and bewildering change in your behaviour ...

One of Eliot's childhood memories is of asking his father what love was. He would have been maybe eight years old. They didn't talk much about feelings in his family. You were expected to be polite and pleasant. If for some reason you couldn't manage that, you were expected to go to your room or take a walk or do something else until you could.

But Eliot had started to notice that all the songs on the radio and most of the stories in the storybooks had love as their subject, as the big thing to win at all costs. So he wanted to know what it was.

His father lowered his newspaper and looked at him for a moment. Then he said, "Love is what your mother and I feel for you, Eliot. And what you feel for us. Isn't that right?"

Eliot could tell that it was very important to nod and say yes. He was starting to understand that he was different from others. He would make a friend, and everything would be fine for a while. But then the friend would get angry with him. Something would have happened, and Eliot would have failed to say or do the thing anyone else apparently would have said or done.

As he grew, he watched others for clues as to how to pass for anyone else. He cultivated a surface affability, an apparent warmth. Friendships with girls were easiest, he discovered, because girls came equipped with so many feelings. They could fill in the gaps. For a while, at least.

For a few months, Jill Macklin's elfin face upturned to his, her eyes full of expectation, made him wonder if he might finally have changed, become a bit more like other people. Cautiously, as if conducting an experiment, he told her he loved her. What he actually said was, "I think I might be falling in love with you." And that was true enough. He did feel a stirring, when he said the words. So perhaps—

He had nothing to compare it to. With his wife Caroline, what he had fallen into was marriage. She had been an old-fashioned girl, warm and vivacious, eager to be a wife and mother. He never actually proposed to her. One day he realized that their conversations had begun to feature the phrase *when we're married*. He saw no reason to object.

It actually worked out well for him. Gave him an appearance of normality. Caroline, along with their daughter Mary, filled up the house with their feelings—their likes and dislikes, hopes and disappointments, tantrums and celebrations. It was like a force field, all but pushing him out the door each day to work.

But then Mary left for university. Looking back, he would sometimes try to attribute the changes in Caroline to the dementia that later claimed her. But he knew that was just an excuse. For the first time in their marriage, she was asking him to help her fill up the house. Demanding evidence of his feelings for her. For anything. The more needy she became—for precisely what he could not give her—the more he distanced himself. Closed in on himself.

Now the same thing was happening with Jill. Whatever possessed him to tell her he was a widower? And why did he have to bring Mary into it? *My daughter Mary.* So casual-sounding. As if they were in touch. Skyped once a week. As if she had never screamed at him that there was something wrong with him, that he wasn't human. Now Jill was asking about Caroline—when and how she had died. And wanting to meet Mary.

He watched himself withdrawing. Becoming cold and critical. He wanted to stop, wanted to put his kind and caring mask
back on, to see that girlish joy come back into Jill's face. He
would wake up in the dark hours appalled at what he was doing
to her. Go back to sleep vowing to apologize and tell her the
truth the next day. But then, awake in the light, he would feel
that cold unwillingness grip him again. After all, what could he
tell her? *I haven't seen my daughter in years because she hates me.*
My wife is in an institution. She sits in a diaper all day, staring out a
window. Her expression only changes when she turns and sees that it's
me again. That man she doesn't know, but manages to despise. So he
would convince himself Jill was to blame for being so damned
nosy. Then take a perverse pleasure in listening to her voicemails.
Reading her emails. Pressing ERASE. Pressing DELETE.

… cannot understand how you could treat someone you
professed to love with such …

He puts the letter back in his sock drawer. What would
be the point of answering it now? Her address might have
changed. But even if she's in the same place in Hamilton,
he's settled in Toronto for good. Hardly worlds apart, but—

If he could just stop fantasizing about telling her what
happened in that specialist's office. The most ignominious
parts that he wishes he could forget but instead goes over
and over in his mind. She once knew his body—had seen
and caressed every inch of it. She could listen, with shared
pain, to what had been done to that body.

Dear Jill. If you're actually reading this, I can only thank
you for even opening a letter from me. It's more than I deserve.
Nor can I expect you to

Stop. What is he thinking? After all this time. Writing to
someone who probably wants nothing to do with him. To
tell her he had rectal surgery. He's obviously more shaken

up than he thought he was. His judgement's off. He needs to let some time pass.

And it's not as if he'll never talk to Bill about the whole episode. Next month, once his stitches have finished dissolving, he'll tell him over lunch. Make a joke of it. *Yeah, it was a pain in the ass. But the bottom line is, it's behind me.*

In the meantime, he'll go to the aquarium. Have that to change the subject with.

There are school kids everywhere—running, whooping, shrieking. Barely kept together in their classes by teachers who aren't long out of school themselves. Eliot hopes he doesn't look creepy—a solitary older man gazing into display tanks over the bobbing heads of children.

One tank is a tall, round silo practically the area of his condo and full of broad-leafed kelp growing up and up. Two storeys? Three? Every kind of fish is darting in and out the strands, flashing their neon colours. Eliot doesn't bother with the illustrated legend identifying the species. He's happy just to watch the fish themselves doing their thing. Do they communicate with each other? Can they see him? Other tanks hold golden carp the size of his coffee table. Electric eels as thick as his thigh.

Look, Daddy! He's hiding under the rock!

Sweetie, don't slap on the glass, please. Just look at the fishies.

Everywhere he turns, he sees Mary. As a baby, reaching for a fish eye as wide as her hand. As a child, squealing and pointing. As a teenager, struggling to keep her cool against an uprush of wonder.

As far as Eliot knows, Mary is still teaching kindergarten at that school in Sackville. She had such fond memories of doing her BA at Mount Allison that she went back to Sackville once she was finished her teacher training and took a job there.

The last good time the three of them had as a family was in Sackville, come to think of it. He and Caroline stayed over in the spare bedroom of the bungalow Mary was renting. She showed them all around the place so proudly. The school where she would start her teaching career. The classroom all decorated and ready, weeks before her first students would come and sit down in the tiny chairs. The waterfowl park just steps from her street, where she would walk and gather her thoughts each morning before heading to work. She introduced them to her neighbour, Len Sparks, himself a retired teacher who had become something of a mentor.

At the airport in Moncton, she and Caroline held each other in a long, tearful embrace that Eliot, embarrassed, had to gently disentangle because the plane was boarding. The two had always been so close, more like sisters than mother and daughter. No wonder Caroline seemed lost at home these days. Her loneliness was like a gaping hole in the house. The beseeching looks she threw him when he was trying to read or watch TV made him dread coming home at the end of the day. He worked longer hours. Increased Caroline's housing allowance and urged her to go shopping for something nice for herself. Maybe join a book club?

Yes, he missed Mary too. In his way. Truth to tell, her absence, the fact of her being grown up and educated and self-supporting was something of a relief. The first time he held her, her head cradled in his palm and her feet not reaching the crook of his elbow, he felt a kind of panic. It was one thing to play the part of a husband. Another to— If anyone was going to reveal him to the world as the hollow man he knew he was, it would be this tiny creature.

He switched careers. He couldn't go on stock-brokering for a bank. That wasn't good enough. When *Girls First!* advertised for an investment officer, he applied and got it. Thirty-five years spent working to help underprivileged girls. All for the sake of appearing good in the eyes of his own girl. Whom he has not seen or heard from since he had to put her mother in the place where she is.

There's a crowd of what look like grade threes around the octopus tank. This one is lit more dimly than the others, and there is a sign on it—PLEASE—NO FLASH. Eliot gets as close as he thinks prudent. Even so, the kids' teacher, a young man, gives him a look.

The octopus has wrapped itself around the miniature mountain that almost fills one end of its tank. Eliot can just make out the slits of its closed eyes beneath the bulbous sack that he knows is not a head, for all it looks like a head.

"This is Ella," a young woman wearing a T-shirt with the aquarium's insignia on it is saying to the class. "She's two years old, which makes her middle-aged. Kind of like your grandmothers?" The kids laugh. "Ella likes to curl up around her rock, but—oh, there she goes!" The octopus has detached itself and is spreading its tentacles, sucker-side up. Eliot feels an odd stab in his groin. Revulsion? Except he can't look away. The creature floats to the base of the rock, where it folds in on itself like the fingers of a hand. Then it uncurls one tentacle after another to pull itself back up.

The children have been coming out with *Aw!* and *Ew!* One little girl covers her eyes, shuddering. *Mary wouldn't have done that*, Eliot thinks. Mary always looked straight at things, even through tears. A broken toy. A dead robin. Then straight at him if he couldn't fix whatever it was or bring it back to life.

"Ella's a real star," the guide is saying. "She loves to put on a show. Okay. Let's move along now and say hello to the crustaceans."

Eliot lingers outside the octopus tank. It is shaped like an hourglass lying on its side. The near globe contains the miniature mountain. Leading from that is a shockingly narrow passage opening onto the far globe, which is empty. *Can you really squeeze through that skinny tube?* The octopus is once more wrapped around the rock. *Well, you don't have any bones, do you? So I guess—* One yellow eye opens and looks right at Eliot. The iris is a sideways black slit curved into a crescent that makes the expression merry and knowing.

Again, Eliot feels that strange stab of—what? It's surely not sexual. But it is a connection. *I want to know you too.*

"Didja see the hammerhead shark? How about that giant sea turtle?"

Eliot nods and nods over his moules frites. He hasn't had a chance to tell Bill about his surgery, and doubts now that he'll bother. He's all healed up. And anyway, Bill can't get enough of his impressions of the aquarium. The jellyfish like floating parachutes. The electric-blue lobster tiptoeing about, balancing claws before, tail behind. And of course the climax of the whole tour—the winding underwater glide through the plexiglass tube. Staring into the midnight eye of a shark. Looking up to see a stingray the size of an area rug undulating past.

He's not sure he should tell Bill about the octopus. Bill's great, but he has his limits. He wouldn't want to hear about how close Eliot came to buying that big, stuffed toy octopus for just under seventy-five bucks in the gift shop. How he planned to say, *For my granddaughter* to the cashier. Then had the sense to ask himself what he would do with the thing once he got it home. Sleep with it? Wake in the night to see its bulbous silhouette perched on his chest? Jesus. Kind of thing he might once have laughed about with Jill, but not—

"I really got a kick out of that octopus. And I've been reading up on them." Sure. He can tell Bill about the book he did end up buying in the gift shop—*Octopus Heart*, by Clarissa Pettingill. "Octopuses—and it's not octopi, by the way—they do have a brain, but it's sort of distributed between their eight arms. And each arm specializes in something—one's for grasping, another one's for getting food to the mouth. And they can smell and taste with their suckers. And kind of see through their skin, not just with their eyes. They're incredible." He dips the last of his French fries into his mussel broth.

Octopuses have remarkable facial recognition too, he remembers reading. They seem to appreciate people as individuals, and form opinions about them. Welcome some and squirt brine at others.

Would Ella remember him if he went back? That knowing, humorous look she gave him. Would she—

"Uh, earth to Somers."

"Sorry, Bill." He searches through his mussel shells for any morsels he might have overlooked. "I was just thinking about how everybody in the aquarium leaves everybody else alone. I mean, I didn't see the sharks eating any of the smaller fish."

"Yeah, well, they're living the life of Riley in there. No need to hunt and kill if you're getting fed every day."

"Good argument for the guaranteed annual income," Eliot says, grinning. He knows that will get Bill going. Bill describes himself as politically to the right of Genghis Kahn.

The female octopus lays eggs once in her short life. She braids them into strings as they emerge, using her own secretion as glue to attach them to the roof and sides of her den.

Eliot is rereading *Octopus Heart*. He's been back to the aquarium twice to see Ella, too, choosing different days and times in hopes that the staff don't start recognizing him. Ella does, though. He's convinced of that. The last time, she detached herself from her little mountain and came right up close to the glass just to give him that merry, familiar look of hers—*Hello again, Eliot.*

He knows it's crazy. But whenever he lets Ella look at him, his muscles relax in a way they haven't in—longer than he can remember. He feels as if Ella is seeing through him, into the space inside him. That she knows exactly what it's like to be Eliot Somers.

What's it like to be you, he wonders back at her. Is your life as simple as it looks? Do you have family that you miss? What about mating? Is there any pleasure in it for you, or just pressure and release? Are you lonely in that tank all by yourself?

She tends her eggs without ceasing, he reads now, *cleaning them of algae, defending them from predators. Typically, she neglects herself during this gestation period, never leaving her eggs to hunt for food, even in captivity refusing to feed. It is not unusual for a mother octopus to succumb to starvation just as her babies are hatching and starting their lives.*

Eliot glances around furtively, even though he knows damned well he's alone at home. Jesus. When was the last time he teared up?

He goes into the kitchen to refill his coffee. He still can't get used to doing small things, like hauling himself up out of his recliner with absolutely no pain. All he has left of that episode is a slightly delicious itch when he moves his bowels.

Healing. How does it happen? Well, it needs some kind of intervention first, he supposes, pouring milk into his coffee. If he hadn't seen that specialist and had that surgery, things would just have gotten worse. Maybe infected. He could have ended up with a colostomy bag. Imagine trying to talk around that with Bill Merton in the Rendezvous.

He sips his coffee, looking at the framed photographs of his ancestors that once again hang on the walls of his kitchen. His new kitchen, as he still thinks of it, though it's been years since he sold the condo in Hamilton and moved to Toronto.

It was such an easy decision to make, that last move. For one thing, there was nobody to talk him out of it. Mary wasn't answering his emails. And Caroline—Mary would probably have accused him of deserting her. But he promised himself he would still visit. It was an easy drive, from Toronto to Hamilton. Hell, he'd commuted back and forth to *Girls First!* for thirty-five years.

That letter from Jill was what finally kick-started the move. The fact that she knew his Hamilton address. Could walk to it.

Jill. First time he's thought about her today. And he doesn't automatically think of her every time he sees the photographs in the kitchen any more, either. Is she starting to put him out of her mind too? She was in tears the last time he saw her, and one or two times before that. He still winces when he thinks of her showing him her diary.

Do you see, Eliot? It's been weeks! Not just a little while, as you keep saying. Weeks since we made love. You were so affectionate. And then suddenly, for no reason—

He deleted all their long email strings. Removed Jill from his contacts. All he has left is that letter. Why did he even pack it?

By the time Eliot met Jill, he had retired from his job, put his wife into an institution, alienated his daughter, sold his house, and moved into his first condominium. It all happened in the course of one summer, leaving him too exhausted to unpack.

He lived in a domestic landscape of sealed cardboard boxes and blank walls, waking each morning to drink his coffee and eat his cereal out of the same cup and bowl, which he then rinsed and set to dry on a single tea towel draped over an otherwise bare kitchen counter. For lunch and dinner, he either ordered in or ate out, until his stomach rebelled and he realized to his embarrassment that he had a nodding acquaintance with every waiter in the neighbourhood.

So one day he forced himself to unpack his kitchen stuff. Bathroom the next day—he had been getting by with one towel, a bar of soap, his stick of deodorant, and a razor. Bedroom and living room followed, until finally only the boxes containing framed art and photo albums were left. He hung the art, mostly posters for plays and concerts, in the living room and bedroom. Then he got the idea of decorating the kitchen with framed photographs of his parents and grandparents. He even had a few daguerreotypes of his great-grandparents.

It didn't occur to him until he was on his way to Macklin's Framing on James Street that all the photographs in the zippered leather case tucked under his arm were of dead people. Not one was of Caroline or Mary. He felt a small, cold thrill, as if he were getting away with something.

In the frame shop, he allowed himself to enjoy watching Jill Macklin work. Her small hands lining each photograph up so deftly on the work table. Her greying bob of hair that swung forward whenever she brought a mat sample flush to a corner. And that girlish biting of her lower lip—*This one? No, maybe this one?*—when she was teaming frame with mat.

It was so pleasant to be in the company of a woman who looked at him with clear, gentle eyes. Who seemed— who *was* interested in what he had to say about retiring and moving and wanting to hang old family pictures in his kitchen.

The store was empty. Jill's assistant was off that day. It was just the two of them. "I'm a widower," Eliot heard himself say. And as soon as he said it, as soon as the expression in Jill Macklin's eyes softened, became concerned and caring—for *him*—what he had just said became true. And so he asked her out to dinner.

Eliot goes back into the living room with his coffee. Settles into his chair. Picks up *Octopus Heart.* Tries to read. Can't concentrate. Puts the book aside.

When was the last time he drove to Hamilton to see Caroline? He should try to keep track somehow. Or make a decision—say, second Tuesday of the month. Then stick to it. For some reason.

Soon after they got home from visiting Mary in Sackville, Caroline's symptoms began to show. It took a while for them to become alarming. It was a running joke in their marriage that her job was to forget where her car keys were so he could do his job, which was to remind her of where she always put them. But the day came when she seemed not to know what the keys were for. He found her sitting behind the wheel, looking back and forth from the objects in her hand to the dash. He knew then that he could no longer dismiss her confusion as flakiness. She must have known too. When he gently suggested she put the key in the ignition, she snapped, "I can *do* it!" Then got out of the car and wandered back into the house.

"I can *do* it" became her mantra. She growled it at him when he tried to brush the tangles out of her hair or apply deodorant to her armpits. Only by lying, telling her that Mary was coming for a visit, could he persuade her to put on clean clothes. When their daughter actually did arrive from Sackville during the school holidays, Caroline would soften and smile, holding her arms out to her, making something resembling conversation.

"Did she say anything about me?" Eliot asked Mary once when he had left her and her mother alone together for a while.

"No. Why?"

"Well, early on, she was convinced I was having an affair with Ceely Thomas." A woman in Caroline's book club. Which she had joined at his suggestion, then abruptly quit, about the time she forgot what to do with her car keys. She claimed it was because she couldn't stand the sight of Ceely any more. Couldn't stand having to imagine what she and Eliot had been up to.

"Well? Were you?"

"Was I what?"

"Having an affair."

"*Mary!*"

What Mary saw when she visited was a mother tender and victimized. She never saw Caroline fighting Eliot in the shower when he tried to wash her hair, going at his eyes with fingernails crooked like talons. Things came to a head when he refused to trundle Caroline down to the States for some treatment Mary had read about on the internet. Some doctor the AMA was denouncing as a fraud had posted before-and-after videos of people whose dementia he had miraculously cured. For a fee that would have beggared Eliot.

"Mary. Honey. You have an education. Consider the source, for God's sake. Those are actors in those videos. This man should be in jail."

She looked at him then the way Caroline had been looking at him for almost a year.

Early on, there had still been good days, when Caroline was her old, reasonable self. But these had become so rare that when they occurred he couldn't trust them. Couldn't relax. It was almost a relief when a good day would end, and the next morning he would wake to an empty bed. Come downstairs to find his wife staring out the kitchen window, a bitter twist to her mouth. Turning eyes on him that were cold and accusing.

"You don't love my mother, do you?" Mary finally said.

"Of course I do." The lie rang like a bell between them.

"This isn't Ella."

The octopus in the tank is smaller, and has a rougher, darker hide. And when it opens one eye there is no recognition in its gaze.

"That's right, sir. Good for you. This is Oscar." It's the same young female guide who was there on his first visit, when he first saw Ella over the heads of all those kids.

"Where's Ella?"

"Ella's just taking a little break. But Oscar's a real ham. If you'll—"

"Is she all right?" He shouldn't have interrupted. Or sounded so gruff. The girl has stopped smiling. "I'm sorry," he says. "I just kind of—got to know Ella." *And she got to know me.* "I've been reading up about octopuses. They interest me."

The girl's face relaxes. "Oh. Well. Then I guess I can tell you that Ella showed signs of being ready to spawn. So we—"

"Oh no!"

"She's fine. Nothing to worry about. We just moved her—"

"Has she laid eggs yet?"

"Well, yes she has. And she's just great with them. She—"

"No, she's not just great. She can't be. She's going to die. And you know that. They lay eggs and then they starve to death."

"Sir, could I ask you to lower your voice, please?" Heads are turning. Parents are starting to pull at their children's hands.

"Look, I don't want to give you any trouble. But I'm not a kid. And I'm not some ignoramus. So don't tell me Ella's fine and she's just great when we both know she's—"

"Hi. Everything okay here?"

Oh, Christ. The security guard. The girl must have signalled to him. They must think he's some kind of nut.

"Would you like to take a seat over here, sir? I could get you some water if you like. Sir? Sir?"

He has turned and headed for the men's room. Once inside, he locks himself in a cubicle and leans his fists against the wall. Leans his forehead against his fists.

"Everything okay?" Bill. In the Rendezvous. Pausing in the middle of cutting his steak.

Eliot jerks his head up from where he's been staring at his untouched mussels. He knows what the natural, normal thing to say is. *Sorry, Bill. Guess I didn't sleep so well last night. Hey, did you catch that game—*

"I had something wrong with me. A few months ago. Turned out to be nothing. But for a while there I thought I was going to die."

He stops talking. Waits for Bill to say, *Sorry to hear that* so they can safely change the subject. The silence tightens between them.

He's not going to cry, damn it. He does enough of that at home. He'll be doing dishes or watching TV, and the tears will just start to leak. As if he's filled to the brim with them and they have to spill over. Today he squeezed half a bottle of drops into his eyes to get rid of the red before setting out to have lunch with Bill.

Is he having some kind of a breakdown? He can't stop thinking about Ella tending to her eggs. Slowly starving to death. Maybe that's why he's doing a few strange things of his own.

Last week he drove to Hamilton to see Caroline. Kissed the cheek she tried to turn away from him. Smiled into her glare. Sat beside her for an hour, resting his hand palm up on the armrest of her chair. Just so she could see it. Know it was there for the taking.

Yesterday he started yet another reply to Jill's letter.

… what I did to you, Jill. It was not so much a matter of changing as reverting to type. It's hard to explain, but …

That's as far as he got. But for once he didn't crumple up the attempt and toss it.

And this morning he scrolled down a list of public schools in Sackville. Recognized the name of Mary's. Clicked on FACULTY. And there she was. His girl. Still teaching kindergarten.

He hasn't broken the silence yet. Finally, Bill says, "Sorry to hear that. Had a bit of a scare myself. Couple of years ago."

"Yeah? What about?"

"Prostate."

"Yikes."

"Yeah. Well. I'm okay now. Just not the man I was."

"Who is?"

Should he tell Bill what else he did this morning? How he bought a plane ticket to Moncton and booked a cab from there to Sackville? How he's planning to be in Mary's classroom when she arrives fresh from her walk through the waterfowl park? Looking up at her from one of those tiny chairs?

French Cross, 1988.

Higgs Boson

Is it the way they walk? That deliberate placing of each hoof. Like printing. Or planting. Marion could stand and watch horses walking all day. Circling round and round in the paddock. These last few minutes after her lesson. It's almost as good as riding, watching others ride.

"Had enough?" Steve. Wanting to go.

In the car she says, "I think I'm starting to get the hang of the rising trot."

"Yeah, you weren't bouncing around so much this time."

"It's funny. I get it. Then I lose it. Soon as I start to think about it."

"So don't think about it."

She smiles, looking at his profile. His hands on the wheel. *Don't think about it* is his mantra.

"Patrick's coming for lunch tomorrow."

"Oh yeah? Is he bringing—"

"No," she says quickly. "Ranald's away on a job." Out of the corner of her eye she sees his shoulders relax. He doesn't like their son's husband. Has trouble even saying his name. It probably doesn't help, her jumping in and saying it for him.

They're home. Steve keeps the engine running as she unbuckles her seat belt. "You okay if I go in to work for a couple of hours?"

She lets out a sigh. She could say, *No. I'm not okay with that. It's a gorgeous Saturday afternoon. We could sit out in the back with iced tea and talk, for God's sake.* Or she could say, *That'll reduce your stress and lower your blood pressure the way you've been told to do, won't it?* But she just opens the passenger door and says, "Supper at six."

"How about I pick up some wine?"

"You do that. Something good and expensive."

She goes in the side door, humming *I will hold the world together in my arms.* She wrote folk songs when she was in university. Sang them in her wavering soprano, accompanying herself on the guitar. She only knew about four chords, but that kept her tunes within her limited range. Now all that remains is this one musical phrase, one bit of lyric that she breathes to herself now and then. *I will hold the world together in my arms.*

Marion is almost afraid of how important her horseback-riding lesson has become. It reminds her of when she was a child and Christmas just days away. She would torment herself, imagining her disappointment if she woke up on the morning and discovered there was no such thing as Christmas, never had been, that it was all a dream. Silly. But she'll be getting groceries and suddenly the cart she's pushing will be a long, mane-tufted neck. A bobbing head. Two alert ears swivelling to every sound. And she'll feel that big, warm body under her again, sway to that rhythm of working muscle and bone, smell that smell of leather and sweat.

Patrick and Ranald gave her a package of ten lessons for her sixtieth birthday. *Basic Equitation for Beginners.* They had tucked the pamphlet inside her card. *Students will learn to saddle and bridle their mount, to command a walk, sitting trot, rising trot, and canter. At the instructor's discretion, their final lesson will be an independent solo trail ride.* "Come on, Mom," Patrick said when she protested. "You've been wanting to do this forever." All right. She guessed she had, even though she'd never actually said so. But whenever she caught sight of mounted police or horses in a field, she would say, "Oh, look at those lovely big boys!" Patrick must have heard the yearning in her voice. Seen it in her eyes.

Up till then, her first and only ride had been ten years ago, in Bermuda, of all places. She and Steve had finally made the trip because they'd run out of excuses not to. Patrick had his master's in education and was through his teacher training. He had moved in with Ranald and had a job lined up for the fall. Her and Steve's twenty-fifth anniversary was looming. So there was no more avoiding that Bermuda honeymoon they had promised themselves back when they were students and believed nothing could stop them. Before she got pregnant and he went to work in his father's construction company to support his all-of-a-sudden family.

They stayed at a resort consisting of a string of little housekeeping cottages. The ceramic plaque mounted beside the door identified theirs as Spindrift. It had a date palm growing on its tiny front lawn, and a patio where the two of them had their breakfasts, Marion turned to face the turquoise water and perfect sky, Steve focussed on his Blackberry.

Every morning, while Steve slept on, Marion slipped out of bed and took a walk by herself to the ferry dock and back. She would stay a few minutes leaning on the railing, looking down into the water and, if nobody else was around, crying. Grieving for her twenty-five-years-ago self. How that girl would have cherished Spindrift. She would have been so proud of the tiny kitchenette, heating up soup for them both, making grilled-cheese sandwiches, daring to broil bacon one morning in the grubby toaster oven.

Now, everything was a mockery. The chameleon on the wall she would have delighted in pointing out to Steve. The raven at low tide she would have told him about—the way it anchored a periwinkle with one foot while spearing out the meat with its beak. Worst was the king-sized bed that dominated Spindrift's main room. It was big enough to let Steve keep his distance, turned on his side with his back to her. One cold night—Bermuda surprised them with how chilly it could get—she whispered, "Steve. Please. Hold me. I'm freezing." There was a long pause. She knew he was awake. Then, when he turned wordlessly in the dark and put his arms around her, his hands were curled into fists.

They had been warned to bring umbrellas and waterproof jackets, but day after day was sunny and clear. Another mockery, like the light conversation they managed to keep up. Marion let Steve choose what they were going to do each day, listening while he read aloud from pamphlets about crystal caves and pink-sand beaches. And horseback riding.

"Hey. There's a Morning Splash ride. On the beach. You get to take the horse into the water."

"Sounds like fun," Marion said brightly, her mouth dry. She had never been on a horse in her life, and the thought scared her. But she was trying to be a good sport by day, in hopes that the nights might turn into something less awful. So maybe if she made this effort. Took this risk.

The awfulness had started long before Bermuda. Since Patrick had moved out, the house had been echoing between the two of them. They hadn't touched each other in—weeks? Almost two months. The more delicately and tenderly she tried to get him to talk about it, the more he dodged her. It was just the job, he said. Stressing him out. Construction *always* tanked when there was a recession. She *knew* that. So why couldn't she just *remember* it? And why did their scrambled eggs always have to be so wet? And why couldn't she learn to do stuff on the computer without always having to ask him for help? And would she please stop worrying? Her worrying was driving him nuts.

The riding stable they went to in Bermuda was called Spicelands. The young woman in charge introduced herself as Trace. Her skin was the colour of café au lait and her accent that strange Bermudian mix—somewhere between Caribbean and Cockney.

Marion heard the horse she was going to ride before she saw him. A hollow clopping on wood. Then there he was, nodding his big head in time with his steps as Trace led him out.

"This is Frank."

"Hello, Frank," she said to the wall-eyed gaze. The lids blinked slowly, like blinds going down, then up. She raised a hand. Dropped it.

"Go ahead. Pat his nose. Get to know him."

A nose more than a foot long. Hard under the hair. Another blink from eyes eight inches apart. "You have freckles," she said, feeling foolish but needing to say something. "Like a Dalmatian."

"He's an Appaloosa. They're all marked like that. Okay. Step up onto the block. Grab the horn. Put your left foot in the stirrup. Now pull yourself up and swing your right leg over. Hey, that's good. You got a nice, natural seat. Good posture. You ridden before?"

"Never." She had been so worried about getting up into the saddle. While Trace was checking the level of the stirrups, she said, "He's not—I mean, he's beautiful. But when I imagined how the horse would look—"

"Some people don't want him. They don't want a polka-dot horse for their first ride. But Frank's great. Nice, easy, calm big boy."

Big was right. Bigger than Steve's horse, a brown-and-white patchwork named Gypsy. But it made sense. Trace had asked them both their height when they were filling out the disclaimer forms, and Steve was half a head shorter than her. Patrick too. They were so alike, her boys. Physically, at least. Both stocky, inclined to plumpness if they weren't careful. Steve especially, now that he was less out on the building sites and more behind his desk.

She shook her head. Her mind was such a labyrinth of Steve and Patrick, Patrick and Steve. She was in Bermuda. On a horse, for God's sake.

Steve was putting Gypsy through some paces, making her go and stop and turn in circles. He had told Trace twice that he used to ride when he was a boy. Then he had refused to wear a helmet. "If you need one of those things, you don't know what you're doing." *Steve, that's stupid,* Marion had wanted to say. *That's like saying, if you need to buckle up, you don't know how to drive.* She had expected Trace to insist, but all she said was, "That is your choice, sir." Well, they had signed those disclaimers. If Steve was thrown and hit his head on something and came out of it a vegetable, it would be his own damned fault.

Had she actually thought that? So calmly and coldly?

Yes. She had.

Lunch on Sunday when Patrick comes is cold poached salmon with dill sauce and asparagus salad, out on the deck. It's a drowsy late-August afternoon. The garden is just past its peak and the willow's branches hang heavy and still.

"Sit *down*, Mom," Patrick says as she gets up to take their plates in and bring out dessert. "This is like the old days—just the three of us."

She has been thinking the same thing, glad of it mainly for Steve's sake. Sometimes she lets herself wonder what it would have been like if they had had a daughter. She knows Steve loves Patrick. And Patrick was always a real little boy—rambunctious and adventurous. But would that line be there between Steve's eyebrows if he was listening to his daughter talk about her architect husband's latest contract? Speculating about the new class of grade threes she herself was going to be teaching in a little more than a week?

You're going to have to tell your father.

Patrick had come out to her in confidence months before he told Steve. But Steve must have had his suspicions. For years, the story he and Marion had been telling each other was that their son was so bent on his studies he had no time for relationships. Girls would just get in the way. Now Patrick was starting his master's and getting serious about Ranald. Marion wanted to meet him. Not on the sly. She wanted to have him over for dinner. Meet Harriet, his mother.

Dad. Listen. The way you feel about Mom? That's how I feel about Ranald.

She and Patrick actually rehearsed—role-played, with her as Steve. She helped him choose a time for the talk. Mondays were not good. A Friday might ruin everybody's weekend. Tuesdays and Wednesdays tended to be complicated. A Thursday, then. She thought about making one of Steve's favourite dinners, then realized how obvious that would be, how infuriating in retrospect.

On the designated Thursday, as soon as the three of them were sat down together in the living room, Steve said, "I know what this is about." Marion had perched herself beside Patrick on the couch. Steve was across from the two of them in his armchair. The worst possible arrangement, she realized too late. Steve was calm in a way she recognized. The same look, the same posture he had had all those years ago when she told him she was pregnant and intended to keep the baby. Then as now, she could practically read his mind. *Not what I was planning. But it is what it is.*

He stayed calm. There was no outburst. Nothing ugly. But at one point he did say, "Okay. Okay. Look. I'm all for equal rights. You and—this guy. You want to get married? You want family benefit packages? Fine. You can have all that. Just don't ask me to—I can't—When it comes down to it. Two men. I just. Don't get it. And I never will."

Dessert out on the deck is peach cobbler with vanilla ice cream. "Your mother's fattening me up for the kill," Steve says, picking up his fork the second she puts the plate in front of him.

She kisses the top of his head. "Just more of you to love." Then, to Patrick, "And we don't eat like this every day." She joked once to Harriet about having to pimp Steve's vegetables to get him to eat them. "And he'll only eat fruit if I slice it up," she said.

The three of them eat silently, the only sounds the clink of forks and the chirping of birds from the cedars at the edge of the garden. Not for the first time, Marion wonders what exactly it is that has gathered them around this table. Keeps Ranald and Patrick together in their condominium, and in a few hours will couple her and Steve in their bed. What name to give it. *Love* is too vague. *Water under the bridge* is only part of it.

A few years ago, when the Higgs boson was in the news and people were calling it the God particle, she thought she might have the answer. So she asked Ranald, with his math background, if he would explain it to her. She could have asked Steve, but she was always looking for ways to engage with this remote young man who loved her son.

"You mean it's kind of like—glue?" she asked after listening hard to him for half an hour.

Ranald closed his eyes, summoning patience. Marion smiled. Even Harriet called Ranald difficult. He didn't have

Patrick's sweetness. He was a bit like Steve, come to think of it, which was likely why the two of them didn't get along.

"Think of the adhesive property of glue," Ranald finally said. "Now think of something that makes that adhesiveness possible. That's what the Higgs boson does."

"Okay. So. Without it? Everything would just fall apart?"

Ranald smiled thinly. "Without it, *apart* would have no meaning. Because *together* would have no meaning."

Marion could tell that something about that notion actually intrigued her son-in-law. *Thank God you found Patrick,* she thought. *Maybe he'll keep you human.*

Steve and Patrick are scraping their dessert plates in unison. "More?" Steve says, picking his up and holding it out Oliver Twist-style.

"Nope." She stacks his plate onto hers and Patrick's. "You're back on the wagon."

In the kitchen she makes coffee, fills the dishwasher and listens through the screen to her son and husband chatting. Just as the coffee is dripping its last, the chatting stops. Silence. She freezes, suddenly convinced that if she goes to the window she'll see empty chairs. No crumpled napkins. No half-filled glasses. *Not there. Never there. All a dream.*

These last ten years of peace in her household. The rekindled warmth between her and Steve. Sometimes it feels like something she has stolen. Something she has no right to, and will have to give back.

Then she hears Patrick murmur something and Steve cough. Silly. So silly. But isn't there some old notion that the gods are jealous and will snatch away whatever you love too much?

Don't think about it.

At Spicelands in Bermuda, while they waited on their horses for Trace to saddle up, Steve let Gypsy graze. "She said not to let them eat," Marion whispered. When Frank had reached down toward a tuft of grass, she had pulled his head back up, steadily and firmly, the way Trace had shown them. "You're just like a kid, aren't you?" she had murmured, patting the speckled neck. "Seeing what you can get away with."

Steve snorted. "I'll lay down the law once we get going."

Except he didn't. He couldn't seem to. He lagged behind Marion and Trace while Gypsy went as slow as she liked, grazing on anything in sight. Trace kept twisting around in her saddle. "Shorten your reins, sir!"

"She's got the bit between her teeth." Steve called. "There's nothing I can do."

Marion recognized his tone. She heard it a lot these days. More than once she had wanted to sit him down and say, *Steve, I know you wanted to be an engineer. But you run a construction company. And you've done well. And I know your son is gay. But he's still your son. He's still Patrick.*

It was impossible to make somebody else's peace for them. Marion knew that. But she felt she had to try. And she was so tired of trying.

Ride away, don't say goodbye, just ride on. For the first time in years she was composing a song in her head. Maybe the rocking rhythm as they rode along had inspired her. The trail took them through forest, alongside farmers' fields, even across a highway that had a caution sign with a black silhouette of a horse and rider. *That's me,* she thought proudly, like a child. *I'm riding a horse. A real, live horse.* Frank's ears were a speckled frame to look through. She breathed in the dark animal smell of him, and the surrounding smells of sage, rosemary, and the nearing sea.

Just before they got to the beach, Trace called a halt. Steve was still several lengths behind. She twisted around in the saddle, smiled into Marion's eyes and said, "You're doing great. But Gypsy's being a bad girl today. So I'm going to swap horses with your husband. Gypsy'll behave for Big Momma. You and Frank okay here for a minute?"

"We'll be fine."

She watched as Trace trotted back to where Steve was and explained the plan to him. She could hear Steve blustering on about how Gypsy must have gotten the bit between her teeth, yeah, she's got the bit between her teeth, that's why he can't do anything, it's the bit—

Oh, shut the fuck up, Steve. She'd had it. Worst week of her life, this so-called late honeymoon. The cold, loveless nights. The stupid small talk filling the days.

Then came that moment when Steve was saddled up on Trace's horse, but Trace hadn't yet mounted Gypsy. Marion thought, *What if*— She knew how to steer Frank, and how to make him go. How fast would he go for her? How far could she get?

The three of them are finishing their coffee out on the deck. The shadows in the backyard are lengthening. Marion can smell fall in the air.

"How are the riding lessons coming, Mom?"

"Oh, didn't your father tell you? I'm trying out for the Olympic equestrian team next week."

The truth is, the anticipation of her lesson is a lot better than the reality. She's in a class of four. The other three all rode as girls and caught the rhythm of the rising trot right away. But except for a few paces when things smooth out and she's riding with the horse instead of just on it, Marion keeps bump-bumping up and down in the saddle.

They haven't been allowed out of the paddock yet. Their teacher, a short Quebecois named Roger (Ro-zhay) rides with them, twisting around to see how they're doing. Sometimes he guides his horse in to the centre and halts there to watch them go by, calling out things like, "Heels *down,* Mari-*on!*" He doesn't single her out any more than any of the rest. She's sure of that. But she worries about holding the class up. Last week on her way out of the stable after unsaddling, she overheard one of the women complaining to another about being stuck in the paddock, and still not going faster than a trot. The woman broke off talking and smiled when she saw Marion. Were they all being held back because of her?

"Elbows *in,* Mari-*on!*"

The worst thing is having to ride a different horse every week. She knows that's part of the training, learning to deal with a variety of mounts. But each time she finds herself looking around for Frank's speckled coat. It doesn't feel like ten years ago. Would Frank still be alive? How long do horses live? She has the oddest notion that if she could get up on his back again and go off on the trail, just the two of them alone, Frank could make a rider of her.

As Trace led them down to the beach for their promised morning splash, all three horses perked up, snuffing the salt air. "They love this," she said, turning to Marion and grinning.

Gypsy was behaving perfectly for her, and Buddy, the horse she had been riding, was giving Steve no trouble. Steve clicked his tongue and nudged Buddy with his heels, manoeuvring to be first into the water.

"You two want me to take your picture?"

Marion handed Trace her camera, then urged Frank close to Buddy, who was splashing water up onto his belly with his front hooves. "Okay, everybody," Trace said, focusing. "Show me your teeth!"

At that very second, Buddy belly-flopped straight down into the water.

Marion couldn't figure out at first what had happened. Steve just disappeared, as if through a trap door. Then she looked down and saw him hip-deep in the water, still on his horse.

"Stay on! Sir, just stay on! Do not dismount!"

Buddy stood back up. Steve was soaked. "Shit!" he said.

Trace rode up to Buddy and swatted him on the nose. "You are in trouble! You know better than to do that!" Buddy's ears wilted and he hung his head. "Sir? You okay?"

"Just. Wet."

Marion's mouth had been open the whole time. Then, to her horror, she started to laugh—a loud, braying, snorting laugh that she had never heard herself come out with before.

She tried to stop, but couldn't. Steve looked away and concentrated on pressing saltwater out of his jeans. Trace moved Gypsy near to Frank, reached and put her hand on Marion's wrist. "It's gonna be okay," she said softly. That was when Marion realized she had stopped laughing and had started to cry. "It's gonna be just fine."

Frank stood calmly through all the noise, radiating warmth. He turned his head once to look back at her with one slow-blinking eye. While she was trying to settle down, Marion wondered what horses made of the strange, fraught creatures that sat on them and made them go and stop and turn around for no good reason.

At her sixth lesson, all at once, she gets it. And keeps it. She raises and lowers herself in the saddle in perfect rhythm with the trot, riding so smoothly that her horse might be water, or air.

"Vair-y *good*, Mari-*on!*"

Roger moves the whole class ahead, showing them how to command a canter. Marion loves it from the first, grinning as she tightens her grip and sees the paddock fence posts moving round her in a rocking spin.

"Hey, you were galloping today," Steve says in the car.

"Well, it's called a canter. But it's a slow gallop. And we're all going out on the trail next week." She's flushed and happy. In the stable, the other women applauded her and called her the star. Maybe she'll have them back to the house for drinks and snacks after their final lesson. Invite Roger, too. One thing's for sure—she's going to sign up for the advanced class when this package is done. Start learning to jump.

At home she looks at riding habits online. The wide-shouldered jacket, tight cream trousers and tall boots would look terrific on her slender height. Steve comes up behind her, sees what's on the screen and kisses her neck.

Whispers that the sight of a woman all kitted out to ride turns him on.

Afterwards, while Steve dozes, she lies looking at the ceiling and imagining what it would be like to have her own horse. They could probably afford it. And she could board it at Roger's stable. Maybe Roger would help her pick one out. She hasn't a clue how to buy a horse. All she knows is that she wants an Appaloosa. And she's going to name him Frank.

That trip to Bermuda ten years ago was never to be repeated. Marion could feel the two of them making that tacit decision, like silently building a wall, while they packed for home in Spindrift. On the return flight, while Steve dozed, Marion concentrated on the view out the window. Clouds. Ocean. Then the eastern states. She felt an almost painful tenderness for the tiny houses and thread-like roads. Communities. Clustering in the face of all that immensity.

Once home, they settled into a cold war. What kept things balanced was the need to plan for the wedding. Patrick and Ranald greeted them on their return with the announcement of their engagement. It was already late spring, and they wanted to be married before Patrick started teaching in the fall.

For the next several months, a *just you wait* energy thrummed between the two of them that was oddly sexual. They bickered. Squared off politically, Steve taking increasingly right-wing stances, Marion leaning more and more to the left. Things got dangerous once when they were discussing Patrick's preference for teaching grade three. "Interesting that they would let him near kids that young," Steve said. And even though she knew what he meant and what he did not mean, she tore into him. The truth was, she had been thinking the same thing. Not that there was anything wrong with Patrick teaching little ones. But there were enough people who would assume there was.

Their future in-laws afforded them another battleground, each championing the one the other didn't like. They hosted a barbecue early on to celebrate the engagement and start making plans for the wedding. Ranald hardly spoke except to turn a cool eye on their Tudor-style house and call it *cosy*. ("He's an architect. He has leading-edge taste," Marion said afterwards when Steve wondered out loud who the hell Ranald thought he was.) Harriet arrived late, wearing what appeared to be a smock and with a splash of green paint on her left wrist. ("Hey, give her a break. She's an artist." This from Steve when Marion remarked that Ranald's mother could have made more of an effort.)

Though Harriet offered her cottage in Muskoka as a venue for the wedding, she made it clear that that would be the extent of her hostessing. ("I don't do hospitality.") So all the meetings had to happen at Marion and Steve's. One afternoon Marion was in the basement fishing a bag of dinner rolls out of the freezer when she thought, *I'm not sure I can stand these people who are going to be part of my family.* She felt a sudden, sharp need to say that to Steve. She knew he was thinking the same thing. And she so wanted to lie beside him in bed, having a big old clutching, grabbing laugh about it all.

He was upstairs in his den. *Just go. Talk to him.* But then she thought of all the approaches she had made, all the conversations she had tried to start, and went tight and hard. She stomped upstairs to the kitchen and started making yet another dinner for five.

It was the night after the wedding. Steve was in bed flipping channels on the big hotel-room TV. Marion was in the bathroom taking off her makeup. After the ceremony they had stayed as long as they could at the reception, dancing with everybody except each other on the dock Ranald and Patrick had built out of fresh pine. Then they had driven in silence back to the hotel in Huntsville, where they were staying the night.

Marion took longer than usual creaming her face. Should she tell Steve that she was proud of him? He had been Patrick's best man. He had stood tall with Harriet as the boys in their white tuxedos paddled their canoe up to the dock, Patrick in the stern because he had the stronger stroke. He had listened attentively when the two mothers did the readings—Marion's from St. Paul's *If I speak with the tongues of men and angels but have not love,* and Harriet's the Shakespearian sonnet *Let me not to the marriage of true minds admit impediments.* He had handed over the rings on cue. He had not looked away during the kiss.

Marion tissued off excess cream. Yes. She will be fair. Civilized. She will tell Steve he had made her proud. She turned the bathroom light off and went into the bedroom. Saw him propped up on the big hotel pillows, aiming the remote at the TV. He did not look at her. She thought, *When was the last time he said anything even vaguely complimentary to me?*

She got into bed and looked at the screen. It was some news show. Someone was interviewing two young women.

So this is it. My marriage is going to end. In a hotel room in Huntsville.

"What's this about?" She kept her voice neutral.

"Date rape. These two say it happened to them."

"Well, if they say it did, then it probably did."

"Oh, give me a break."

"Why do you say that?"

"'Cause I'm sick and tired of hearing all this crap I'm supposed to take at face value, and if I don't I'm some kind of bigoted asshole. That's why. I mean, these damn fool girls. The way they dress. The way they act. The way they drink. And they probably enjoy it at the time, but then they sober up the next day and decide they've been raped and come back and point a finger and wreck some young guy's life."

Oh, the things she could have said. *Our son has just gotten married. I didn't get myself pregnant. My parents would have helped me raise Patrick on my own. You didn't have to be a martyr, quitting school and going to work. I did not wreck your life.*

Instead, she told him a story. About something that had happened in university before she met him.

Steve had been her first lover. She knew that was important to him. So she told him about sitting on the floor one night with a guy in his residence room. Playing Scrabble, for God's sake. Scrabble. He gets up, she thinks to get another beer. But he's come round to her side and he's opened his fly. He grabs the back of her hair. Presses her face in hard. She has to open her mouth if she's going to breathe. And the whole time, she's thinking, I *guess* this is all right. I *guess* this is all right. Because she had liked him. And she had thought it was quirky and sweet, his

149

wanting to play Scrabble with her. And she had been hoping he would kiss her.

When it's over he zips himself up. Sits back down. Starts moving his Scrabble pieces around, making a word. She gets up and leaves.

When she tells her roommate, her roommate says stuff like that just happens sometimes and she should forget about it. And that makes sense. It's how they think back then. And after all, she did go to his room, didn't she? And it could have been worse. At least she's still a virgin.

Marion kept her eyes on Steve's the whole time she was telling him. Watched his jaw sag. It was appalling, what she was doing. The lie she was telling.

"Jesus Christ." Steve looked as if he might cry. "Why didn't you bite the bastard?" Exactly what she had asked her roommate. Who was the one it had happened to. The one she herself had advised to forget about it.

"You think I haven't asked myself that? I just wanted to survive, Steve. So I normalized. That's what we do. No matter what insanity is going on, we normalize it."

They looked at each other for a long minute, knowing that this was it. Steve looked away first. Changed the channel. They ended up watching a documentary about the Amazon river. When it was over they turned out their lights and slept back to back, the way they had in Bermuda.

At home, Steve had an upset stomach for two days. Marion would catch him staring into space. Over and over, she had to stop herself from going to him and confessing that it had happened to her roommate. That she had lied about the whole thing.

In bed finally, she put her hand on his turned back and said, "It's all right. I'm all right. It's in the past. I have you now. And you're the best guy there is."

After a long moment he said, "I just want to beat the shit out of him. And I don't even know where he is. Wouldn't know him if I fell over him." He rolled onto his back and looked at her. "Would you know him? If you saw him?"

"No. I can't picture his face." And that was the truth. She had never seen it in the first place.

They didn't make love that night. But she sensed that they would. Soon. Whatever had kept them apart was softening. She could feel it.

I have held the world together in my arms. Strangely, in her gladness, she kept picturing Trace smiling at her, giving her a thumbs-up. And beside her, Frank dipping his big head, blinking his wide-spaced eyes.

In the years since, Marion has sometimes wondered how Trace is doing, if she's still working at Spicelands. She has wished she had written to thank her. For being there when she herself was thousands of miles away from home and convinced her world was coming apart. For looking at her and seeing all there was to see. Then for telling her, accurately as it turned out, that everything was going to be just fine.

The riding class has been going out on the trail, keeping two lengths apart while Roger moves up and down the line on his own horse, encouraging and correcting each of them in turn.

"Canter now! All canter!"

They canter, trot, and walk together at Roger's command. They learn to duck overhanging branches, to lean back and brace against the stirrups when the trail dips, to tip their weight forward onto the horse's shoulders for the uphill stretches.

Marion yearns to ride off on her own, to be alone with her mount, to go as fast or as slow as she wants. At home, she rereads the *Basic Equitation for Beginners* pamphlet. *At the instructor's discretion...* Will she be allowed that final solo ride? What if Roger lets the other three go off on their own but makes her stay with him? She was the slowest to catch on. But she's done so well since. She doesn't voice her worries to Steve. She knows what he'll say. *Don't think about it.*

Sure enough, during their ninth lesson Roger calls a halt at the spot where the trail forks in several directions. Here, he tells them, is where they might take off next week on their first solo rides.

Might. Is he just being a good teacher, keeping them on their toes? Or is he trying to cushion their disappointment? Her disappointment?

"Trot now! All trot!"

He's at the head of the line. She's at the end. She does not follow. Keeps her horse still, watching the others disappear around a turn.

Through the haze of the painkillers, she can hear Roger talking to Steve. He sounds upset, his English more fractured than usual. "The horse is animal vair-y *timide.* Anything spook him. Plastic bag in wind. Bee fly too close to the eye. And when he spook, he run."

It's like remembering a dream. That moment when everything started whizzing past and she couldn't even feel the horse under her, it was all so fast and so smooth, and what was holding her on? What was keeping her in the sad-dle? She gave up sawing at the reins and threw her arms around the big neck, pleading with the animal to stop. But it veered to the side and she kept going straight ahead, fly-ing through the air. And then—

"Your wife—Mari-on—she is not ready for the solo ride. She is too ... *gentille.* She does not make enough of the ... *controle.*"

Then Steve is beside her in the ambulance and they're moving. This is all her fault. And she knows why. All the good times, all their happiness these last ten years. A sham. Based on a lie. That she told.

"I shouldn't have—" Her mouth is sticky and dry.

"Shhhh."

"It wasn't true. What I told you. I didn't—"

"Honey, don't try to talk."

"The scrabble game. That guy. In university. It wasn't me. It was—"

One of the paramedics adjusts her IV, and she falls asleep.

She has a concussion and a broken shoulder. Though she can walk, she has to wear an arm sling and is so stiff and sore that for a week she can't dress or wash. She cries the first time Steve has to help her on and off the toilet.

"I was always—"

"Always what, Honey?"

"Always such a—fucking—*lady!*" She explodes with a simultaneous laugh and fart, which gets Steve going.

"Yeah, you always were," he says, dabbing his eyes on his sleeve. "Even when you were pushing out Patrick. You were trying to be nice about it."

"I just hated—I mean, I was glad you were there—but I hated you seeing me like that. I was afraid you'd never want to come back."

"You kidding? That next six weeks? Never jerked off so much in my life. Kept telling myself I was an asshole to even think about it. But when you were nursing Patrick? Gave me a hard-on every time I saw you pop your nipple into his mouth. I envied the little guy."

"I thought it bothered you. You always turned away."

"Oh, it bothered me, all right."

The way they're talking these days. It must be the enforced intimacy. Steve flushes the toilet and manages to drag her underpants and slacks back up under her.

"I guess I won't be riding again for a while."

"Not at that stable, anyway. I managed to convince Roger that we wouldn't sue or anything like that. But I don't think he wants to see you again."

"It was dumb, what I did. Going off on my own."

"Sure was."

"How mad are you?"

"Offhand, I'd say I'm fucking furious. Okay. Put your good arm around my neck. On the count of—"

"How mad are you about the other thing?"

"What other thing?"

"The thing I tried to tell you in the ambulance. About how I was lying. Ten years ago. In the hotel after the wedding. When I told you I'd been date-raped. It didn't happen to me. It happened to my roommate."

Steve is quiet for a long time, looking at the shower curtain. Then he faces her and says, "Something you should know about yourself is that you're a lousy liar."

She stares at him.

"Look. You think I wasn't unhappy back then too? Should have been the best year of my life. Bermuda. Our kid getting married. You think I didn't want something to just—I don't know—blow all that lousy crap between us out of the water? I haven't a clue why you told me that story. I don't know why I let you get away with it. But it worked. So let's just not—"

"—think about it," she finished.

"Right. Now put your good arm around my neck. On the count of three. One. Two..."

Child Skipping, 1958.

Lost Lake

"What do you think of this Moyra business?" Since they arrived, their four-year-old has been quoting a new friend who seems to know everything.

Leo shrugs, eyes on his book. "Lots of kids have imaginary playmates."

"Yeah, but this one's kind of—"

He puts his book down. Looks at her over his glasses. "What?"

"Well for one thing, where would Leonora get a name like Moyra? There's no Moyra in any of the books we've ever read to her. Believe me, I have those things memorized, and there's no Moyra. And then, this morning she came to me and reached up and grabbed my boobs and said, *Moyra says daddies like these things.*"

He laughs. "She's curious. She's noticing stuff. And it's easier to have this Moyra person voice her thoughts." He play-grabs at Fiona's breasts. "Maybe she saw us fooling around."

"Maybe."

"So what did you tell her?"

"Oh, something vague like, *Mummies and daddies who love each other do like to hold each other and touch.*"

"Was she satisfied with that?"

"For now."

"Enjoy it while it lasts. We'll be into penises and vaginas in no time."

"I wish."

"Oh, *do* you!" He puts his book and glasses on the night table, rolls onto her and buries his face between her breasts. "Daddies like these things," he growls, reaching down between her legs.

Fiona laughs and lets herself have a good time. Tries to put out of her mind the rest of what their daughter told her.

"Daddy likes the other lady's things too. Moyra said! Because he's always looking at them when he thinks nobody will see."

Fiona kept her face still and her voice calm. "Moyra sounds like a very imaginative little girl. Do you know what imaginative means? Im-*ag*-in-a-tive?" She can always divert her daughter with a new word.

Afterwards she told herself to forget about the breast business. Okay, Leonora must have seen her father sneaking a peek at Jennifer's boobs. God knows, she flaunts them enough. But so what? Show me a straight guy who doesn't do stuff like that and I'll show you a eunuch. She couldn't shake off the other thing Moyra apparently told Leonora, though. And she can't share it with Leo, either.

"I know a new word too!"

"Do you? Tell it to Mummy."

"Pub—?" The little girl frowned and tried again. "Pub-ul—"

Fiona smiled and nodded encouragement.

"Ish! Pub-ul-ish!"

"Publish. Wow. That is a very grown-up word. Do you know what it means?"

Leonora nodded, proud. "It's the thing Daddy is never going to do, ever again."

"What?"

"Moyra said! She said, *Your father is never going to publish another word, as long as he lives.*"

Fiona's mouth went dry. Could this be a real person saying these things? An adult? Jennifer, even, with that mean mouth of hers?

"Leonora, is Moyra a grown-up?"

"No."

"Are you sure she's a little girl? Like you?"

The child nodded. Then she said, "But she's real, real old."

They are staying for a week in an old country house on the shores of Lost Lake in the Laurentians. Leo and Fiona Van de Veld and their four-year-old daughter, Leonora, are on the top floor, in the master bedroom and adjoining nursery. Charles and Jennifer Stumpfigge, Leo's former colleague and his wife, have the main floor bedroom.

It is mid-September. On the drive north, Fiona was all but falling out of the passenger window of the car they rented at the airport in Montreal, relishing the cool breeze after a stifling Toronto summer. From the back seat, Leonora kept up a chorus of "Orange! Red! Yellow!" whenever she spotted changing leaves.

They arrived a day ahead of the Stumpfigges. That first afternoon, while she and Leo were unpacking, Fiona kept coming upon Leonora opening closet doors, looking under beds, peeking into cupboards in the kitchen. She was trying to find the Stump Figs, she said. She had heard Leo and Fiona talking about them, had imagined little elf-like creatures and wanted to play with them. She was visibly disappointed when the other couple arrived that evening and turned out to be ordinary people like her parents.

Leo is on sabbatical from Breadalbane College, where he teaches creative writing. He and Charles, who has just retired, are checking out Lost Lake Music Camp as a possible site for a writers' retreat.

Fiona knows Charles a little, and has met Jennifer once, at last year's Breadalbane staff Christmas party. "So how did Chuck end up with Morticia Addams?" she asked Leo that night in bed. "I know for a fact that he doesn't make enough to bag a trophy second wife." Jennifer looked to be at least twenty years younger than Charles, very pale, with makeup verging on Gothic, long straight black hair and breasts that belied her thinness.

"She's his first. He was a confirmed bachelor, then along come Jen. Nobody knows what she's doing with him. But he dotes on her."

"Do you think there's some kind of S&M thing going on?" Fiona could imagine Charles, balding and plump, trussed up in a leather harness. Jennifer wouldn't need a costume.

"That's what I love about you," Leo said. "To the pure in heart, all things are pure."

As a matter of fact, Fiona is trying hard to get along with Jennifer, given that they've been thrown together for a week. In the kitchen of the big house, shortly after the Stumpfigges arrived, she helped Jennifer put away the groceries they had brought and said brightly, "I think you and I both deserve medals for taking our husbands' names."

"Oh really? Why would that be?"

"Well. Stumpfigge and Van de Veld? Not exactly Smith and Jones, right?" She was actually sweating. "Mind you, I was happy enough to stop being Fiona McFee. Everybody used to call me Fifi."

"I was Jennifer Bangs. I spent my life telling people it wasn't a sentence."

Fiona laughed too loud, then realized Jennifer had not meant to be funny. She could only hope Leonora wasn't lurking. If the little girl had overheard their exchange, she would demand a full explanation of "bangs."

It takes Fiona a day or so to decide that Jennifer Stumpfigge is a social black hole. The harder she tries, the more she gives, the more Jennifer will just suck it all in and render it nothing. But Fiona knows she is a giver by nature, so she is resigned to a week of suggesting tea and a slice of banana bread to Jennifer while their men are off hatching plots, only to have Jennifer curl her lip and inform her that she is *attempting* to *detoxify*.

"She's got a long way to go," Leo says in bed when Fiona shares this last detail.

"*Shshsh!*" Into the silence, from the main floor bedroom beneath them, comes the unmistakable sound of Charles. Moaning. Then uttering a little *yip!*

"Holy fuck. What is she *doing* to him?"

"I just hope they don't wake up the Queen of Everything."
Fiona glances at the adjoining nursery door, trying to ignore
the fascination in Leo's tone.

The big main house is flanked by four housekeeping cottages, now closed up for the winter. Nearer the lake there is
a lodge with a meeting room, dining room, and kitchen. A
caretaker drives in once a week to check on things and make
any necessary repairs.

"After the musicians clear out, the place is free every
year from mid-September till the end of October," Leo told
Charles during one of their initial talks. "We could fill those
cottages the first year, no problem. There's enough surrounding land for a campground, too. In time, we could build a
wash house with toilets and showers for folks who can't afford
a cottage, but could stay in a tent. And we could hire our own
cook and staff. It could be another Bread Loaf."

"Well, this all sounds wonderful, Leo," Charles said in
his slightly pedantic way. "But what do we have by way of
money to pay for it?"

"The first year, we'd both have to kick in," Leo admitted.
"But we'd charge anybody else who came, and as the thing
grew, it would pay for itself. Plus, once we were established,
we could apply for grants."

"And what would we be offering these pilgrims in
exchange for their money?"

"Charles. We're talking about writers. What wouldn't
they give for a week in the woods by a lake to get some
writing done? Plus, there'd be courses and workshops."

"Taught by whom?"

"Me! You! To start, anyway." Charles actually taught
economics at Breadalbane, but he was a poet on the side,

and had published a dozen or so poems. Leo's novel, *Olly Olly Oxen Free*, had been up for both the Biggar Prize and the Olympia Featherstone Award For Fiction five years ago, and had helped him secure his teaching job. "And in time, we could recruit more teachers. Make it a rule that anybody who comes on the retreat has to take at least one course. Bundle that into their fees."

"And you're sure the music camp foundation will approve of all this building and all these improvements that you foresee?" The couple who had originally owned the big house had donated it to the foundation in 1973 in memory of their daughter, who once dreamed of becoming a concert pianist.

"Look. Charles. I don't have all the answers right now, okay? All I'm asking you to do is think about it. Come see the place. Bring Jennifer. Have a week by a lake in the Laurentians in the fall. Great way to kick off your retirement."

On the third day, the two men decide to take a break from arguing and envisioning and totting up hypothetical dollar amounts in order to do some writing. Charles asks if anyone would mind terribly if he set himself up at the dining room table. He's sorry, but he needs a straight-backed chair for his lumbar region. That said, he's perfectly willing to go elsewhere if this would cause any—

"Oh, for Christ's sake, Charles! We're paying enough to stay here. You can put your lumbar region anywhere you want." Jennifer retreats to their bedroom, claiming one of her headaches and leaving Charles to gaze, moony-eyed, at the closed door.

"How long before he goes crawling in after her, do you think?" Fiona asks, as she and Leo head for the pond behind the house. Leo has decided to write on the dock. Leonora skips ahead of them.

"That's probably why he writes haiku," Leo says. "Just seventeen syllables, and he's already earned himself a spanking."

"Are you sure you want Leonora with you?" Fiona asks as Leo settles down on the dock with his laptop. "I could take her."

"Nope. You have your walk. Oh, *hey!*" Leonora has just run up to him and tucked a fresh-picked daisy into the neck of his sweatshirt. "Does this mean you're my girlfriend?"

"Moyra said to give it to you," the little girl answers.

Fiona is secretly glad to have some time to herself. On top of everything else, she has become the default cook for the group. She had thought she and Jennifer would share the kitchen duties, but Jennifer seems to have a complicated relationship with food. She claims never to be hungry, to be mystified by others' need for three meals a day, to be lactose-intolerant, gluten-sensitive, and vegetarian-verging-on-vegan. Then she loads her plate with whatever Fiona has put on the table and goes back for seconds. Later she complains of indigestion or headache or both, citing the meat or the gluten or the milk in the enormous meal she has just inhaled.

"Where does she *put* it?" Fiona whispered to Leo on their second night.

"It probably rubs off on Charles." Whom they could once more hear moaning and yipping in the bedroom beneath theirs.

Just before she turns onto the trail leading into the woods, Fiona stops and looks back. Leo is sitting cross-legged on the dock, studying his screen. Leonora is walking the circular path that rings the pond, gathering more wild flowers. As Fiona watches, Leo looks up, checks on their daughter's location, bends his head down to type, then looks back up again. *He won't get much writing done,* she thinks, turning and entering the woods.

She strides along the trail, swinging her arms, enjoying the leaf-crunch underfoot, the smells of autumn coming early. Long, solitary walks are a rare treat now. Of course, once Leonora is more independent ... But if she's honest with herself, Fiona will admit that she can hardly stand to think of her little girl not needing her.

She still can't get over how content she is to stay at home with her daughter. She read all the books during her pregnancy, braced herself for post-partum depression, debilitating fatigue, boredom, and frustration. The whole world was telling her she would live for the day her kid finally started school. Then Leonora was placed in her arms for the first time, and all that went out the window. Talk about not knowing what you've been wanting all your life until it's given to you.

Motherhood filled her with almost superhuman energy. She seemed to thrive on two hours of sleep a night or less. She cherished every stage of Leonora's development, including the terrible twos, and missed it when it was over. Refused to even consider daycare.

That last decision turned Leo into the sole breadwinner. Well. Okay. She supported him for nine years while he was writing his book, didn't she? And his book took off, didn't it? And helped him land his job. Which he likes. Doesn't he?

Dry leaves crackle under her feet. Maybe she should have insisted on taking Leonora with her on this walk. She knows Leo wants—needs—time and solitude to write. He was hoping to have another book in the works at least by now. It must be awful to be surrounded by other people's writing—reading it, teaching it—yet not be able to do any of your own. What if she hadn't been able to conceive? How would she feel every time she saw a pregnant woman or a mother with children in tow? Every time she passed a schoolyard at recess time?

She has hinted that she might go back to work half days, once Leonora's in school. Take some of the pressure off Leo. But she hates the idea. A few nights ago she had a dream that she had a job again. It was ten in the morning, the boss was calling to ask why she wasn't there, and she was still struggling to get dressed and out the door because she had forgotten how.

She'll have to remember how, soon enough, she thinks ruefully, scuffing along the path. And that's just one reason she'll probably burst into tears next year when her little girl lets go of her hand on the first day of kinder—

Something soft. Under her foot. She half-kicks, half-steps on it. A small, brown, furry creature. Not a mouse. A vole? It is obviously badly hurt, on its side, curling into a ball then straightening out. Curling, then straightening.

Oh God. She has hurt this poor little thing. And now she has to kill it. Put it out of its pain. She takes a step nearer. Raises her foot. No. No. She can't do it. The thought makes her sick. Maybe Leo? But if she goes and gets him, Leonora will want to know why and will want to come too, and—

A stone. A big, flat stone. Big enough so she won't have to see. She'll place it gently on top of the little animal, then bring her foot down hard. Yes. She can do that. Except there are no big, flat stones anywhere nearby. She marks the place on the trail where the creature is still writhing, then walks deeper into the woods, searching the ground.

Pebbles. Nothing but pebbles. Biggest one the size of a golf ball. Oh. Here's something. Something shiny and smooth and brown. It takes her a moment to realize it is the toe of a shoe. Above it, a trouser cuff. Above that, a leg.

"Looking for something?"

Fiona jumps back. The man is essentially camouflaged by his brown corduroy pants, tweed vest and jacket and old-fashioned flat cap. "I'm sorry. I didn't see you."

He smiles. A strange, square smile, just a lifting of his upper lip over very yellow teeth. "That's because you weren't looking for me."

"I was looking for a rock. I accidentally hurt a little animal, so now I have to kill it and—"

"Where is it?"

"Just back a few feet on the trail. I—"

"Better take a look," the man says, pushing past her. She follows.

"Ah, here we are." He bends to look at the still-twitching creature, then turns his face back up to Fiona. "So you just left it like this. Hurting all over. Insects getting into it already. Eating it alive."

"No! I didn't just leave it. I told you I was looking for a rock to—"

"Oh, never mind," the man says disgustedly. He stands. "Up to me, then. Do what needs to be done." He raises his foot and brings it sharply down on the vole.

Fiona didn't mean to yelp. It was just so fast. And that *crunch* sound. She swallows. Takes a breath. "Thank you," she says grudgingly. "I couldn't have done that."

"Staying at the music camp, are you?" He is looking at her with a trace of amusement in his eyes. His foot has not moved from the vole.

"Yes. We are. For a week. The four of us." Five, actually. She wants him to know that she's not by herself. But she wants to keep Leonora out of the conversation.

"Yours the little girl, then?"

Reluctantly, she says, "Yes. Our daughter is with us." Maybe he's the caretaker. The one who drives in once a week in the off season. Maybe it is his business to know who's on the property. "She's with my husband right now." She puts emphasis on *husband*.

"Sure of that?"

"I'm sorry?"

"Think I saw her just a minute ago." He jerks his head over his shoulder, keeping his eyes on Fiona and his foot on the vole. "All by herself. Wandering in the wood."

"No," Fiona says firmly. "She's with my husband. At the pond." Sweat is running down her back, despite the cool air.

He shrugs. "If you say so."

"Her father would not allow her out of his sight." Who is she trying to convince?

"And that's a good thing, is it?"

"What's that supposed to—"

"Wee little girl with a big, big man," he whisper-chants, his lip stretching higher over those yellow teeth. "Wee little girl with a big, big man." He's swivelling the ball of his foot back and forth on the crushed vole. "Wee little girl—" Now he's waggling his pelvis.

"You sick—!" Fiona turns and tears back down the path, hearing laughter fading behind her. Straining her eyes for a first glimpse of the pond. Of Leo. Of Leonora. The pond. The pond.

Leo sits cross-legged on the dock, his laptop open in front of him. He waves goodbye to Fiona and Leonora as they walk hand-in-hand along the trail into the woods. The daisy Leonora has just popped into the neck of his sweatshirt is tickling, but he doesn't remove it. She could come running back for another goodbye kiss, and God help him if he's not still wearing it.

He offered to keep their daughter with him, but Fiona insisted on giving him some time alone to write. Now he makes a point of appreciating the sight of his wife's sweet little bum as she walks away from him, head bent to catch what the child is saying to her. He still feels a bit guilty about the dream he had early this morning. He was kneading Jennifer Stumpfigge's breasts, which were blowing up like balloons, getting bigger and tighter by the second.

The cursor is blinking at the top of the blank screen. He types *Lost Lake*, then centres and saves it. Great title. For something. Last year, when he found this place on the internet, he had the strongest hunch that if he could just get to Lost Lake he would write something called *Lost Lake*. It's been five years since he published *Olly Olly Oxen Free*. His breakout book. That just might turn out to be his only book.

He shakes his head. He shouldn't let himself think that way. *Olly* was nine years in the making. So five years is nothing. Except that's what he's been doing. Nothing.

Lost Lake

The cursor is still blinking.

Wrong. He has not been doing nothing. He's been teaching. Supporting his family. Living a life that all kinds of people would envy. Even if he never publishes another word, he'll still survive. Keep on teaching at Breadalbane. The place isn't publish-or-perish. And he's a good teacher. And he likes it. That came as a surprise. He took the job because Fiona was pregnant (another surprise) and he knew he probably wouldn't be offered anything like it again. So yes, he could spend his days reading his students' short stories and novel excerpts. Cultivating a warm, encouraging atmosphere in his classroom.

Except—

Lost Lake

Leo used to despise the kind of man he has become. *Family man.* Something castrated about that phrase, the way it smacks of groceries being loaded into the backs of minivans and Saturdays spent in the children's section of the library. The implied sunniness of it all. The assumption that this was the stuff of maturity. This was what it meant to be a man and put away childish things.

He wants his childish things back.

When *Olly Olly Oxen Free* was still in the news, critics inevitably referred to its *edge* and its *darkness.* He remembers approaching nearer and nearer that edge during the writing, digging deeper and deeper into that darkness. Daring himself, shocking himself with what appeared on the page. The joy of it. The work of it. Chewing through stacks of paper, draining one pen after another, heating up his laptop, exhausting the ink cartridges in his printer. Knowing full well he would never actually get where he was trying to go. But trying and trying anyway. And nothing sunny or mature about it.

It isn't enough just to survive. He has to keep his head above what he imagines as a huge, grey sea of ordinariness. He is in fact terrified of never again seeing his words and his name in print. He had thought the fear would abate when *Olly* was published and got so much attention. Instead, once the excitement died down, he was gripped with a new version of the old fear—of turning out to be a one-book author.

Publishing. His students think it's the Holy Grail. Should he tell them that it's more like a drug? That the more you get, the more you need?

He should be brimming with gratitude for his life, just as it is. For Fiona and Leonora. If he had his priorities straight, he'd be able to put all that publication stuff down and walk away from it. Find all the happiness he needs in being a teacher. A husband. A father.

He was there when Leonora was born. They let him cut the cord. Then, when the nurse had to take her away to wash and weigh her, he followed close behind. His fists were actually clenched. The sight of hands—strange hands, hands not his—lifting and removing his child hiked his testosterone. *Mine! Mine!* A deep, atavistic voice growling from the base of his skull.

Right then, for once in his life, he did have his priorities straight. Everything else shrunk away to nothing. There was only this child. *His* child.

Lost Lake Lost Lake Lost Lake

He closes the file. Shuts down his laptop. For all it's a cool day, the sun is hot on the back of his neck. The surface of the pond is perfectly smooth, a mirror for the sky above and the surrounding ring of bulrushes and wild flowers.

This place is gorgeous. Does he really want to turn it into a writers' retreat? Think of the work involved. And it's such a long shot. He's seen the scepticism in Charles the economist's eyes lately when he's been going on about how the whole venture could pay for itself. Right now, just thinking about it makes him tired. He doesn't want to run a retreat. He doesn't want to run anything. He just wants—

"To be. Yes. Isn't that what you really want? Just to be? Isn't that enough?"

Of course it is. The young woman has put her finger on it. The young woman who is standing at the far edge of the pond, across from the dock. Her voice is practically in his ear.

She smiles and walks around to him. Where did she come from? Even as he wonders, Leo knows somehow that she has been there all along. She is so lovely. Blonde and tanned, about the age of his senior students.

She has stepped onto the dock and is sitting down cross-legged in front of him. He is struck again by her sun-bleached hair, the freckled beauty of her face. He actually yearns toward it. Her vitality. Her youth and potential.

"Keep all that for your little girl," she says, smiling gently at him. She knows him so well. And he knows her too, but in a way he can't place. He senses a huge sadness at the bottom of his knowing and his yearning, and it frightens him.

"Be afraid for *her*." The young woman is suddenly intent and serious.

A wave of sorrow washes over Leo. He feels the threat of tears. "Your poor father," he chokes out.

"Yes. It was awful for him. He found me. He took me in his arms."

Leo puts his hands over his face. No. Never. Never. His life would be over if such a thing ever happened to Leonora, if—

"It won't," the young woman says. "As long as you believe what your little girl is telling you. She's very, very special. They know that. They're drawn to her because of it. But they hate her for it too."

Leo has no idea what she is talking about. But he understands her perfectly. And it fills him with dread.

"You have everything you need. You can do what needs to be done. Just believe her. Believe what she is telling you. Believe her. Believe her. Believe—"

"Where is she!"

Leo jerks awake. Fiona is on the dock in front of him. Panting and sweaty. "Who?"

"*Our daughter!*"

"She's with you."

"No she is not! I left her here with you!"

"No you didn't! You took her with you for a walk in the woods! I saw you both go!"

In the few seconds before they somehow agree to split up and search—Leo the woods, Fiona the grounds and the house—they are mesmerized by the hate in each other's eyes.

Leonora is crying. It is a deep, despairing wail, strangely old, completely at odds with her usual high-pitched little-girl fussing.

"Moyra said! She said I had to stay with the Stump Figs now! Because you don't want me any more!"

Her parents are with her in her bed, up in the nursery. When Fiona came tearing into the house, Charles was still at the dining room table. Jennifer emerged from the bedroom and greeted her with, "Oh, there you are. Can we talk?"

"Have you seen Leonora?"

"Yeah, she's upstairs. But look—"

"She's *upstairs?*"

"Yeah, taking a nap or whatever. But what I wanted to say—"

Fiona ran past her up the stairs into the nursery and found a lump under the covers of the bed. When she coaxed the little girl out from under, the expression of grief on the child's face made her gasp.

She heard Leo downstairs, panting out the same question she had asked, getting the same answer. He sounded hoarse, probably from shouting his daughter's name while running along the trail. He pounded up the stairs, found the two of them, and sagged in the doorway of the nursery, looking close to tears.

Instinctively, he and Fiona lay down on either side of their wailing daughter. It took them several minutes to quiet her, to reassure her that they would never leave her, and to watch her drop finally into a deep, exhausted sleep.

Now they look at each other silently. Ease themselves up off the little girl's bed. Tiptoe hand-in-hand down the stairs.

Jennifer greets them with, "Look, what I was trying to say. I mean, I don't mind looking after your kid for a while if you two want some time alone together. But I'd appreciate being asked, okay?"

"So neither of us asked you to look after Leonora." Leo. Just getting the facts.

"No. She just wandered in here all by herself and said she was supposed to stay with us." At the table, Charles nods.

The parents exchange a look. Then Leo says, "We're sorry. There was some kind of misunderstanding. It won't happen again. Now, could we ask you and Charles to give us a few minutes' privacy?" The cool, firm tone he is taking with Jennifer makes Fiona secretly glad.

"Yeah. Sure. Whatever. Charles! We're going for a walk!" Charles drops his pen, gets up, and stumbles after Jennifer out the door.

"Okay, Moyra. I don't know who you are or where you came from. And I don't care. All I care about is my little girl. You are telling her things that are not true. And you are getting her all upset. And that. Is going. To stop."

Leo is making himself as big as possible—legs spread, shoulders back, chest thrust out. He is speaking—booming—from deep in his diaphragm, sending his voice into every corner of the nursery. Leonora is huddled in her mother's arms on the bed, looking up at her father with huge, dry eyes.

"So you are going to leave my little girl alone. Is that clear? You are not going to talk to her. You are not going to make her sad or scared. Ever again. Because if you do—" He cocks a thumb at his chest. "You're going to have to deal with me."

He falls silent for a moment. Scanning the room. Listening. Then he nods his head as if satisfied, drops to one knee and looks seriously into Leonora's eyes. "Think that did the trick?"

Once the Stumpfigges were out the door, Leo and Fiona sat down across from each other at the dining room table. There was something formal, almost legalistic, in the air between them.

"All right," Fiona began. "What's going on?"

Leo took a deep breath and spoke slowly. "I was convinced she was with you. You were convinced she was with me. And she was convinced neither of us wanted her."

Fiona shook her head. "Could we all have sunstroke? Could there be something in the water?"

"The Stumpfigges are drinking the water too. And they're no weirder than they ever are."

"I read a magazine article a while ago," Fiona said, "about parents who forget that their toddler is strapped into a car seat. And they walk away and leave them in the back of the car in the hot sun and—"

"Shit." Leo runs a hand down over his face.

"The thing is, they're not necessarily neglectful parents that do this. Most of them are as conscientious as we are. But there's been some change in their routine. Say, the one who usually drops the kid at daycare has a dental appointment, so the other one has to do it. And some glitch makes them forget the kid is in the car. Something about the way our brains are wired. So maybe that's what's going on with us. Because we've had a change. We're in a different place. Our routines are different. Right? So maybe—"

They were silent. Then Leo said, "What we have to deal with right away is this Moyra thing. Leonora has to understand that Moyra, whatever she is, is not in charge. We are."

"Think it's time for another monster eviction?"

When she was three, Leonora had a spate of night-mares about a big green monster with long hair and sharp teeth that was living under her bed. Leo listened seriously to her description, then pulled a thick book down from a shelf in his study. He called it the Daddy Manual. "Right," he said, opening it to the middle and running his finger down the page. "Monsters. Green. Hairy. Sharp teeth." He read silently for several seconds, then said, "Okay. I know what to do." He stuck out his index finger for Leonora to hold and the two of them went to her bedroom, where he proceeded to read the riot act to the monster under the bed.

Now he is waiting for Leonora to tell him that Moyra is gone, too.

"Moyra is sad," the little girl says at length. "She got lost and her mummy and daddy could never find her."

The parents look at each other. Fiona hugs her daughter. "You're not lost. You're right here with Mummy and Daddy. And we will never let you get lost." She meets Leo's eyes. "Because from now on we're going to be with you. All the time. The two of us."

Leo nods. He is trying to tell himself he did not see the expression on his four-year-old's face when he asked her if the bad thing had gone away. The child seemed to be strug-gling. Hesitating to answer. When she did, it was with a look of profound pity. For him.

On their last full day together, Fiona suggests a picnic to use up some leftovers. *And clear the air*, she thinks. Leonora has not mentioned Moyra since Leo did his thing up in the nursery. But Fiona can't help wondering if she has merely learned to keep her hidden.

Behind her, Jennifer slouches in the kitchen doorway. "Let me know if there's anything I can do to help," she says with a reluctance so palpable that Fiona almost laughs out loud. *Sure, Jen. You could slice cheese. You could mix lemonade. You could wash apples. You could carry plates and glasses and napkins out to the picnic table. You could get off your skinny butt, open your eyes, use your head, and take and do for a change.*

"Thanks," she says, smiling over her shoulder. "I think I've got it all under control."

It is so warm outside, more like a day in August, that the men carry the picnic table into the shade of a big old oak tree and Leonora demands a swim in the lake.

"Tell you what," Fiona says. "After lunch we'll get you into your shorts and you can go in the water up to your knees. How would that be?" She had thought it would be cooler, so didn't pack her daughter's bathing suit.

"*Well,*" the child says, sounding comically adult. "All *right.* I *guess.*"

Into the adults' laughter, Leo says, "Sometimes I think she was born thirty-five with a martini in her hand."

Up in the nursery, when Fiona is helping Leonora out of her overalls and holding her shorts out for her to step into, the little girl says, "Daddies have things." She taps her fist against her crotch. "Here."

"Yes," Fiona says. "That's right." She and Leo have occasionally let her see them naked, without making a big deal of it. "Honey, please lift your foot so we can—"

"And they put them inside mummies. Here." She pulls down her tiny underpants and points to her pubis.

Right. Here we go, Fiona thinks. *Sooner than we thought.* Calmly, she says, "Yes. Mummies and daddies who love each other sometimes do that. Okay. Let's pull these underpants up. And let's get these shorts on. And now let's go stick our feet in that lake! Okay?"

"And little girls too?"

"Pardon?"

"Do daddies put their things inside little girls?"

Fiona can feel her heart knocking. *Calm down,* she tells herself. *All she wants to know is what goes where. And what the rules are. It's a simple question. An innocent question.* "No," she says, hoping her voice does not sound as sticky as her mouth feels. "That is not for little girls. That is for grown-ups. Just grown-ups."

Leonora gives her a long look. Is it—sly? *Oh please. Not sly. Not cunning.*

"Like the brown stuff that's in Daddy's glass sometimes?"

"Yes! What a smart little girl you are! That's exactly right. It's one of those things that are just for grown-ups. Now let's get you down to that lake."

"Remember that sick fuck of a caretaker I told you about? The guy I met up with in the woods?"

Fiona is showing Leo a drawing Leonora made with her crayons once she got tired of paddling in the lake. She is upstairs now, having her nap. The Stumpfigges are sequestered in their own bedroom, unusually silent. Leo and Fiona have just loaded the dishwasher and are at the table, finishing off the wine from the picnic.

Leo looks at the crayon drawing. "You're not saying—"

"I don't know. Maybe I'm still creeped out by what happened to all of us the other day. Reading stuff into stuff. But look at the hat. And doesn't that look like a vest?"

"Is the man in the picture somebody you know?" Fiona asked, watching the drawing grow under Leonora's hand.

"Kind of."

Kind of was her newest phrase, and she was applying it to everything. *I'm kind of thirsty. I'm kind of tired of that story.*

"Is it Grandpa Van de Veld?"

"No."

"Is it Grandpa McFee?"

"No!"

Okay. Back off, Mummy. All Fiona could do was watch as the crayon in her daughter's fist outlined something she hoped she was not seeing.

"And what's *this?*" Now she's pointing out a second figure to Leo.

"Looks like a little girl to me."

"I asked Leonora if the man was the little girl's daddy, and she said—"

"Kind of," Leo finishes for her, grinning.

"But *look* at her. What is she *doing?*"

"I don't know," Leo says firmly. *Kneeling down in front of the man. That's what it looks like she's doing.* "Look. Let's not read too much into this. Except for that one time, Leonora has not been out of our sight. She's stopped talking about Moyra. She had a great day today. And tomorrow she'll be home."

After a moment, Fiona nods. They finish their wine, not talking about the crayon drawing, but unable to keep their eyes away from it for long.

Charles emerges from the Stumpfigge's bedroom, all flushed and with his hair standing up in spikes.

"Charles," Leo asks. "Have you had any dealings with this caretaker who's supposed to show up once a week?"

"Oh yes. She was by to check on us the other day when you two were out and about."

"*She?*"

"Yes. Very nice young woman. Math major at McGill. Working here is her summer job, and she's just wrapping up. We had a lovely talk about polynomials."

"Did she mention anything about anybody else staying in the vicinity?"

"Actually, she said we were her only charges. The summer people are all gone. Once we leave, she's going to batten down the hatches for winter."

"Mummy!" Leonora, calling down from the nursery.

"Her Majesty awakens," Fiona says, pushing her chair back and heading upstairs.

Once the two men are alone, Leo says, "This young woman. Was she by any chance blonde? With freckles?" He has been strangely disinclined to tell his wife about the dream he had on the dock.

"No, actually. She looked to be Japanese. Why?"

The Stumpfigges pack and leave for Montreal shortly after dinner. They're going to touch down in Toronto, then catch the red-eye west to visit Jennifer's family in Alberta. "Say hello to Lurch and Thing and Cousin It for us," Fiona calls as she and Leo wave to the departing car.

They put Leonora to bed early, then turn in themselves not long after. They're going to pack in the morning in time to get to Montreal and take the noon flight home. It is past midnight when Leonora's wails wake both of them.

"I'm sorry! I'm sorry!"

"Oh, honey, that's okay. Everybody does that sometimes. Were you scared? Did you have a bad dream?" Fiona gathers the little girl up and away from her sodden sheets. Leo is standing behind her in the nursery doorway. "We'll get these wet pyjamas off you and put you in one of Daddy's big old T-shirts. Won't that be funny? You in one of Daddy's big old—"

"They told me I have to go out to them! I have to go out in the woods and be with them!"

"Who?" Leo. Fiona turns and shakes her head at him. He ignores her. "Who told you that?"

"It was just a dream," Fiona says, holding her daughter tight and glaring at Leo. "You're not going anywhere. You'll sleep with Mummy and Daddy tonight, all warm and safe."

"No! They'll come inside me! If I don't go where they are, they'll come inside me! And they'll stay inside me! For ever and ever and ever and ever and—" The child clutches her groin and twists in her mother's arms, her voice rising in a wordless scream.

Leo has no idea what he's doing. Or where he's going. Or why. Fiona, to judge from the look she threw at him over their shrieking daughter's head when he turned and left the nursery, thinks he's copping out. Making himself scarce just when things get tough. And maybe she's right.

He's thrown on some jeans and a sweatshirt. Thrust his bare feet into his running shoes. Now he's walking the path into the woods. Armed with a flashlight he found in a drawer in the kitchen and—what? A dream?

Believe her. Believe her. Believe her.

It's pitch black. He shines the light in front of his feet. Sees a dark mass. Bends down to look. The mangled remains of a small animal.

To the right, the land slopes sharply down to the lake. Fiona would have gone to the left, looking for a flat stone.

He steps carefully through the undergrowth. Not too far in, he stops. Stands perfectly still. Listening. Feeling the cool night wind on his face.

Leo is gone long enough for some of Fiona's anger to change to worry. Then, when she hears the door opening and his step on the stair, she hardens up again. Turns carefully in bed so as not to wake Leonora. Keeps her back to her husband when he enters the bedroom. Says nothing.

It had taken half an hour of rocking and crooning, a warm bath and a children's aspirin crushed in orange juice just to get Leonora settled down. Then it was ages before she fell asleep. And all that time Fiona was as mad as hell, thinking she might as well be a single mother. The worst thing about it was how close she came to taking it out on Leonora, when the kid *just would not shut up*. How close she was to losing it. For the first time in four years.

Leo is taking his clothes off. Now he's sitting carefully on the bed so as not to wake Leonora. "I'm sorry," he says. Fiona keeps her back turned. Says nothing. "I wimped out. I left you here to deal with her because I couldn't take it. You know I can't stand it when she's really upset the way she was. But I'm sorry." A pause. Then, "Do you want me to sleep in the other room?"

They've never done that—slept apart after a fight. His suggestion strikes her as absurd, like something out of a situation comedy. "Oh, for God's sake," she mutters. "Just get into bed." She gives it a few more minutes before turning and putting her arm around him.

"Leo. You're shaking."

"Yeah. Well. Cold out there."

The next morning shows signs of turning into one of those perfect days that tend to greet the end of a holiday. Leonora is full of beans, running around the breakfast table reciting the names of all the toys and dolls and stuffed animals that she can't wait to see again. She appears to have completely forgotten about her hysteria in the night.

"Are you okay?" Fiona asks Leo. He has barely touched his cereal.

"Yeah. Just a bit of a headache."

"Tell you what. I can finish the packing. Why don't you take a walk or whatever you want to do?"

He nods. Gets up. "Think I'll go down by the lake."

"Take your laptop with you?"

"Yeah." Then, "No."

"I'll pack it then?"

After a moment, he nods.

The surface of the lake is calm, reflecting the spreading fire of the colouring leaves. On the far shore is a tall stone outcropping. Sheared off, he imagines, by a glacier that melted eons ago.

Lost Lake.

Leo perches on a rock at the edge of the small, pebbly beach where his daughter paddled in the water yesterday. Was it just yesterday? He feels as if he's aged years.

Last night in the woods, as he stood waiting and listening, he began to feel like a kid taking a dare. *Turn the flashlight off,* he dared himself. And so he did. He'd never been in darkness like it. He might as well have been blind. Gradually, as his eyes adjusted, the moonlight helped him pick out varying densities of shadow. A tree here. A break in the foliage there.

take off your clothes

Could the dare be coming from outside himself? Easy to imagine anything in the dark. But it still felt a little like playing a game. So yeah. He would play along. At this point, he'd do anything. What did he have to lose?

He stripped naked. Put his clothes in a pile at his feet, the flashlight on top. Stood shivering, trying to send out feelers from every inch of his body.

Nothing. So what now? Do a dance and see if it rains? One more try. Then he'd put his clothes on, go back and face the music with Fiona.

"All right. Who the hell are you? And what do you want?"

His voice was shocking in the silence. He listened. Hard. Nothing. He was just bending to reach for his clothes when—

Slowly, he straightened up. There was a thickening of the darkness in front of him. A figure? Two. One big, one small.

He swallowed. Whispered, "Who are you?"

you know

"What do you want?"

what you want

"All right, look. Leave my daughter alone. Get out of her head. You can't have her." He was shaking. He could barely get the words out.

The figures separated. Did he feel a touch—small fingers—on the back of his right hand? Hear a ruffle of wind like a breathy giggle? Then a touch on his left hand? It was a game Leonora sometimes played, touching his hand, making him turn, then slipping round behind his back to touch his other hand and make him turn the other way.

He snatched his hands up to his chest. "Please," he begged. "Stop." And she did. But now she was right behind him, reaching between his legs, grabbing his balls in a small cold fist. Then in front, gripping his cock. And now—

"No. No. Don't!"

Cold breath on him. Small cold lips ringing him. A tongue. Lapping. Fluttering.

"No. Stop. Don't. Yes. Don't. Stop. Yes. Yes!"

He bent double. Groaned. Heard laughter on the wind.

"What do you want?" he groaned again, still bent.

you know

"Look, do anything to me. Just leave my daughter out of it. Don't let it involve her. Take anything I've got. My sight. My sanity. Put me in a wheelchair."

more

"What! What!"

you know

And he did. He did know.

The wind is starting to rise. The surface of the lake isn't perfect any more. He should be helping Fiona pack. In a minute he'll get up. Go start loading the car for home.

His hands feel twitchy. Maybe he should have brought his laptop with him. Gotten it over with. Booting up. Opening the *Lost Lake* file. Then—

What? Will he simply delete it? Or will he keep it, like the unopened bottle of booze a dry drunk keeps in a desk drawer? Is that what it will be like? Always wanting, always denying himself, every minute of every day? Or will it be more like the phantom pain of an amputated limb?

Steps behind him.

Breath in his ear.

Small hands over his eyes.

"Guess who?"

Dog, Boy and St. John River, 1958.

CROOKED LITTLE HOUSE

"HI. MR. SPARKS? I'M AHMED. From the vet's?"

"Oh." Len wasn't expecting the new guy. "Good morning." Hardly seems old enough to be a veterinarian. Hair in one of those man-buns, if that's what they're called, that make everybody look like a samurai. "Please come in."

Ahmed steps into the front hall and puts down what he's carrying—a small black case with a handle, and something that looks like one of those lifters for fireplace logs.

In the living room, Sister is awake in her bed. She did raise her head when the knock came and made the soft *Whuff!* sound that is as close as she can come these days to a bark. But then she just lowered her head and closed her eyes. Time was when she would have been up and crowding the backs of Len's legs, eager to see who was coming to her house.

Len leans on his cane, bends, and puts his hand on her head. "This is a friend, Sister. Friend." The old beagle peers dimly at the visitor, stretching her neck and flaring her nostrils for a whiff.

"Hello, Sister." Ahmed crouches, his knees cracking. "May I pat her?"

189

Len nods, not trusting his voice. An hour ago, he changed into a suit and tie. It seemed fitting, and it was his only deviation from routine. He wanted this morning to be exactly the same as any other, from Sister's standpoint. So he fed her the little bit she was likely to get down. Helped her onto the newspapers he's had to put by the door. Wished he could have taken her for one last walk through the waterfowl park, but these days it's all she can do to stand. Gave her a good brushing. That was tough. For him. Sister loved it.

"Okay if I sit down?"

"Yes. Of course. Forgetting my manners." Len gestures to the couch, and Ahmed sits. "Would you like some coffee? Tea? A cold drink?"

"No, I'm fine, thanks. But maybe you'd like to fix something for yourself?"

Len shakes his head, easing down into his chair.

"Okay, then." Ahmed leans forward. "Mr. Sparks, I want to do whatever's right for you and Sister. I've done this a few times before, and some people like things to happen as quickly as possible. Others want to talk about their pets. Maybe look at some photographs ...?"

"I think we'll go for the quick option."

"Okay. And afterwards, again, it's up to you. I can leave Sister with you for a while and come back for her later, or—"

"Again, quick. Please."

"Okay. I'll just get my bag."

*

"Mom, I could make my own breakfast. You don't have to wait for me to get up. And this is—"

"Oh, go on. High point of my day, watching my boy eat. Then heading off to work."

All Curtis wants is coffee, but that doesn't seem to be on order. Maybe he can drop into Starbucks. If he has enough pocket change left for a small regular. He picks up his fork. Scrambled eggs on toast. Never fried.

"Maybe it's just as well you slept in a bit …" His mother's voice is tentative, her old eyes big.

Oh, shit.

"… There's a special service tonight. Pastor Peter …"

"Mom, I might have to work late. The other pages are booking off because it's Thanksgiving this weekend. So Sondra might need me." *Right. Like the earth will stop turning if two carts of library books don't get shelved on a Friday night.*

"Oh. Well." He can see his mother struggling between pride that he has a job and disappointment that she won't be able to show him off again at Kingdom Come Pentecostal.

He went once to one of those special evening services. They were almost late, so Curtis ended up escorting his mother down the aisle to a pew near the front where there were still some empty spots. They must have looked like some oddball bridal couple, her white head barely level with his shoulder, her ancient hand light as an insect on his arm. And the organ-saxophone-drum combo booming and hooting and banging away. Pastor Peter was already front and centre, his lantern-jawed grin catching the light.

"*Wel*-come to our *ser*-vice of *heal*-ing and for-*give*-ness!" Do they learn that weird way of talking in minister school, Curtis wondered, slumping in the pew. "We have a very special guest with us this evening." *What?* A drop of sweat tickled down Curtis's spine. "But I'll let his best friend in the whole world, our own Doris Maye, introduce him."

Fuck. No. Pastor Peter had turned the glare of his smile onto his mother, who was struggling to her feet.

"My prodigal son who was lost to me is now found," she croaked into the sudden hush. And then she told them. Told a room full of religious nuts the whole fucking story.

Pastor Peter led the applause. His mother poked him till he stood up and turned around. All six feet of him. With his thinning hair and greying beard. At least they couldn't see what he was thinking. How easy it would be to kill his mother. That night. Pillow over the face. Not much pressure. Just long enough for the jerking to stop.

"Thanks, Mom," he says now, wiping his mouth. "That was great."

"But you've hardly finished—"

"Gotta go." It's ten-thirty. Though he doesn't actually start work till one, he's told her he has to be there by eleven. Some morning she might want to come with him, and the jig will be up. But till then, he has two hours, five mornings a week, outside by himself. Long as he doesn't leave town, he can go anyplace he wants. Look in store windows. Sit on a park bench. Breathe the air.

"Don't forget your lunch. It's in the fridge."

It always is. And he never forgets it, because if he does, he'll go hungry. Not like he can just skip out to a restaurant on what he makes shelving books in a public library. A packed, brown-bag lunch. Same as when he was in high school. And in a couple of hours, he'll be doing a job he could have done when he was in high school. Not that he's complaining. He never complains. Just keeps his head down. Does his time.

*

The minute Mary tells Dave, she knows she's made a mistake. She can see it in his eyes. He is weighing the news. The implications for his marriage. His career. And the leverage he has just gained.

"Well, Miss Somers," he begins.

He could call her Mary. His office door is barely cracked. She wanted it closed. It's recess, after all, and there are no kids in the hall. No teachers, either. They're all out supervising the playground or catching a bathroom break. So the two of them are essentially alone. But it seems that the rules are once more the rules.

"I appreciate your coming to me with this," he starts in. "And I understand your concern for your students. My hunch, however, is that, as the officer made clear to you, you are in no actual danger. And, school safety notwithstanding, if we were to overreact—say, by putting you on paid leave and bringing in a supply teacher—it would do more harm than good. Plus, there's the fact that these people—the ones who issue these kinds of threats—are hoping for just such an overreaction."

He folds his hands on his desk and gives her one of his the-Principal-is-your-pal smiles. His together-we-can-deal-with-this smile. Except they're not together. Not any more. If they ever were. And she did hear his own implied threat. *Paid leave. Supply teacher.* This early in the year, when it's so important to bond with your class. Afterwards, when she came back—*if* she came back—the kids wouldn't even know her.

So she's blown it. Completely. But what was she expecting? That when he heard her news his eyes would soften with concern? That he would take her in his arms? Promise to be her big, strong protector? Stupid. Stupid. She has in fact just handed him the weapon he needs. If she goes to the Board and makes trouble for him, he can deny her accusations, impute them to stress brought on by this terrorist target list nonsense, and put her on leave. Medical. For her own good.

"Dave—"

He clears his throat. Glances at the cracked-open door.

"Mr. Edgehill—" The last time she called him that, they were in bed. She said it teasingly enough. But his expression changed, and she felt him starting to withdraw from her, their skin sticky in the late summer heat.

They had met on the street one morning last July outside the town hall near Charlotte and Main. School had let out for the summer not two weeks before. She was surprised when he seemed to want more than just a nod and a few pleasantries. Pleased when he suggested coffee, so they could have a real talk for a change. Then not surprised at all a few hours later when she was in the backyard working in the garden and heard the gate open. There he was. Husband. Soon to be a father. Walking toward her with his arms out.

Two months. Less than that.

On the Labour Day weekend, when she was out shopping for school supplies, she once again encountered him on Main Street. This time, he was arm-in-arm with his pregnant wife. *Mary! How's the summer been treating you? Cynthia, you remember Mary Somers, our kindergarten teacher?* Small talk. Actual small talk. She thinks she may even have congratulated Mrs. Edgehill. *See you in school, Mary!* And the two walked away, once more arm-in-arm. Leaving her to try, with her shredded mind, to remember where she had been going in the first place.

"Yes, Miss Somers? Is there anything else?"

The bell. Recess is over. She has to go and relieve the teacher who's watching her kids.

"No."

He nods. His look makes it clear that there will indeed be nothing else.

Out on the playground, she calls, "Room one! Come inside now, please!" At kindergarten age, they still come when called. Crowd around her legs as she leads them back to their classroom, some grasping her hands, some the fabric of her pants or the edges of her smock. Filling her nostrils with that morning childhood smell of soap and cereal.

She is thirty-three. She told him she was on the pill.

*

"I'm sorry. What do I owe you?" Len pulls his billfold out of his lapel pocket. Can't see. And his damned hands are shaking. He blots his eyes quickly on his cuff.

Ahmed puts his hand on Len's wrist. "Tell you what. I'll bring you a bill on Tuesday when I deliver Sister's ashes. Sorry it can't be sooner, but it's the long weekend."

"Fine. Fine. We'll do it that way." Keep it brisk. Close the billfold and put it back—Oh, hell.

"Hey, no worries." Ahmed bends, picks the wallet up off the rug and hands it to Len. "I'm going to take her now, as we agreed. Some people like to be there for that. Others prefer not to be present."

Oh, Jesus Christ, will this never end? "Just take her." Len turns and stumps away into the kitchen.

He sits looking out the kitchen window for a long time. Wonders if he will regret not witnessing Sister's final exit from the house. Decides he doesn't have to make an issue of it if he doesn't want to. Just a simple, necessary procedure, after all.

"No big deal, right, Girl?" Before he can stop himself, he drops his hand for Sister to nuzzle.

*

Curtis actually likes shelving books. First putting them in order on the cart. Then wheeling up and down the stacks, finding each volume's precise place on the shelf. Sliding it in between its fellows. Checking three books to the left, three to the right. Shifting the spine in or out to be flush with the metal edge. He likes straightening, too. It's purely physical. You could be from Mars, have no idea what the letters and numbers at the bases of the books' spines mean, and still be a good straightener. When he's finished a bay, he always takes a step back and eyeballs it, top to bottom. Pushes or pulls anything that's even a quarter of an inch off.

Should maybe have gone into the army ...

Quit it. Put a stop to the maybes and the what-ifs and the if-onlys right now. Just shelve books. Do your job. Like you did inside. Like you told the new guys to do.

That's the only thing he misses. He was sort of a counsellor in the last five years or so. *Keep your head down,* he would tell the new guys. *Volunteer for some kind of job and do it the best you can. Respect the authorities. Whatever shit you're given to eat, just eat it. The time will pass.* It was the same advice he got, his first night, from Larry. When he was new, before he'd had a chance to bulk up, Larry protected him. For a price.

"Excuse me?"

Curtis looks down. One of the regulars.

"Could you tell me who wrote *Pudd'n'-Head Wilson*?"

Mark Twain. He's so close to saying it. He had thirty-five years to do not much more than read.

"Sorry. Could you ask Ms. St. Clair? She's the librarian."

Once, only once, he did answer a patron's question about a book. Sondra St. Clair had a little chat with him in her office afterwards, about what his duties as a library page did and did not include. And all the time, her eyes were stroking his pecs through his thrift shop T-shirt. Lingering on his tatts that the sleeves didn't quite cover. Reminding him of Larry.

He can hear her now over at the circulation desk. *"Pudd'n'-Head Wilson?* That's a new one."

No it's not. It's old. And it's by Mark Twain.

"I'm going to have to look the author up."

Mark Twain. Mark Twain. Mark fucking—

He grips the edges of his book cart. Thirty-five years. He never lost his temper. Not once. Now, every single day, he's afraid he's going to blow.

*

After school, Mary stashes her stuff at home, grabs her keys, and heads next door. She crosses her arms against the early October breeze. Should have kept her coat on.

She climbs the porch steps and taps on the door. Waits. Wishes again that Len would agree to leave his side door open so she could just poke her head in and call hello. Be able to get inside if she didn't hear anything. But no. Len likes to maintain that little bit of distance. It must have been hard enough for him, last year, when he asked her to touch base with him once a day. *It's for Sister's sake. She's the one I'm worried about. In case I have a fall or something. Can't get up. Who would look after her? Not as if she can pick up the phone and dial 911.*

Mary is just starting to wonder if she should knock again when the door cracks open. Len looks terrible—shrunken and pale. Eyes red.

"Hi, Len. Just me, as usual. You and Sister okay?"

"Oh. Yes. Mary." He sounds as if he's just remembering something long forgotten. "Of course it's you. So it must be four-thirty."

"Len, how are you doing? You look a little—"

"Fine! I—we're fine. Both of us."

"Okay. That's good." Usually, he invites her in. Usually, she declines. But it's part of the ritual. Not today, it seems. "Hey, don't forget about Sunday." All she gets is a blank stare. "Thanksgiving dinner? I'm cooking us up a turkey." God. He really is out of it.

"Oh! Yes. Of course. Thank you."

"Just drop over around five."

The old man nods, then all but closes the door in her face. No. Not like him at all.

As she walks back to her house, she decides not to tell him about her name showing up on that list. He's too frail these days for her to dump her problems on. There was a time when she would have sat on his couch, Sister's head in her lap, and spilled the whole thing. Taken comfort in the posture he would have adopted for listening—elbows on his knees, good ear cocked in her direction, eyes on the rug. And then it would have been her turn to listen as he paraphrased what she had said, minus the emotion. *All right. As I understand it, this Mountie contacted you because it's procedure. Duty to inform, as he said. And the fact that your name showed up on this—United Cyber Caliphate? That what it's called? This list? It doesn't mean you're in any actual danger. If you were, the feds would be doing more than just telling people about it. So it's nothing to do with you personally. And if it was me, I'd put it out of my mind. Get on with my life. Hell. You could step off the curb and get hit by a bus—God forbid—tomorrow. So what are you going to do about that? Hide under the bed? Never go outside?*

And he would be right, of course. But she's not sure that she would be convinced. That she wouldn't still feel as if there were a bullseye on her back. Or as if she carried some infectious disease. Typhoid Mary. Especially when she was around the kids.

Once home, Mary heats up some chili. Pulls some pita out of the freezer and puts it in the microwave. Len really is slowing down, from the looks of it. Every morning for years, when she did her morning walk before work through the waterfowl park, she'd find him and Sister already there, taking a break on one of the boardwalk benches. But the old dog never even leaves the backyard now.

As she carries her plate and bowl to the dining room table she glances at the wall calendar. It's the seventh. She's been too distracted all day to think about that. Now she can't ignore the odd feeling it always gives her in the pit of her stomach. Not nausea. That's for the mornings. No, this is more tingly. Anticipation. Or dread. She's never done hard drugs, never been hooked on anything. Maybe this is how it feels. Hating and wanting at the same time.

She always calls on the seventh. Never on the first or the middle or the end of the month. Nothing that would be too easy to notice. And she always picks a different time of day.

Last month, it was early, before she left for work. So this time it should be—

She eats quickly. Rinses her plates and stacks them in the dishwasher. Takes a few deep breaths to calm herself before picking up her phone and thumbing the Toronto number.

"*Hello?*"

He's always home. No matter when she calls.

"*Hello?*"

How many times has it been now? Hasn't he started to notice a pattern?

"*Who is calling, please?*"

She breathes through her nose with her mouth slightly open. The most silent breath you can take. Hears a sigh. Then a click. Then the dial tone.

Her heart is pounding. One of these times he's going to call back. She's been counting on him hanging on to that antique red dial phone he plugs into the wall as a conversation piece. He uses his cell for anything real. But the old phone can still take calls. So that's the number she uses. If he ever decides to get a new landline, something with call display—

She doesn't know what she would do if he ever said, *Mary? Honey? Is that you?* Would she just hang up? Or would she say, *Hi, Dad. I've been targeted by terrorists. And I'm pretty sure I'm pregnant. What's new with you?*

*

He's put on his heaviest coat. Boots too. More than he needs for the night's chill. But the weight will help—

He descends his porch steps carefully, hanging on to the rail, leading with his cane. Would have been easier to come out the side door. But it seemed more fitting to use the front. And he still has on his suit and tie.

As he taps past Mary's house he sees lights on in the living room—one of them blue and flickering. She must be watching TV. Why doesn't somebody just marry her? Lovely girl. Seems lonely. He left a letter addressed to her on the kitchen table. Left both the front and side doors unlocked.

There are lights on the boardwalk, but it's still pretty dim. Deserted, too. He's never been here this late. The water on either side is pitch black. Don't think about it.

He leans on his cane. Lands heavily on one knee. Eases the other down. Sets his cane off to the side and gets on all fours. Lies down on his stomach. Rolls carefully onto his back. Is he close enough? He reaches out to the right. Feels the rough edge of the board.

The cold might do it. If not, the coat and boots will fill and pull him down.

Don't think. Just roll. On the count of three.

One. Two—

*

The second Mary sits up in bed, a wave of nausea drives her back down under the covers. It's Saturday. Thank God she doesn't have to work. But there is so much she does have to do. Should have done by now. Gotten to a pharmacy. Peed on a stick. Learned what she already knows. Made a decision.

She buries her face in her pillow, willing her stomach to settle down. She hasn't actually vomited yet. Once that starts, if it starts, if she allows it to start, how will she handle a class? She can't keep running out on a bunch of four- and five-year-olds to throw up. And what about Dave? Will she have to lawyer up? Get some kind of support from him? Or could he duck out of it because she lied to him about being on the pill? Maybe even turn around and sue her?

It's all such a mess. And her house is a mess. And she needs groceries. And she wants her mother.

The last time she saw her, her mother gave her a cold once-over and said, "You look just like my daughter."

"I am your daughter."

"Oh no. My daughter's dead."

"Mom—"

"Don't you call me that. My name is Caroline. And my daughter is dead. That's why I'm here. They put you in here when your children have died."

Carefully, Mary sits up. The nausea is gone. For now. She goes into the bathroom and urinates, thinking again about what she has to pick up from the pharmacy. Will she be able to find it on the shelves without having to ask? And will the cashier please, please not be the teenaged kid of somebody she knows? *Guess what I rang up for Mary Somers today, Mom.*

In the kitchen she puts the kettle on for herbal tea. She can usually get that down, with dry toast. Then, if she's up to it, she'll clean the house. That always cheers her up afterwards, to have everything neat, smelling fresh. She takes after her father that way.

Her father. How long ago did she stop talking to him? Long enough that she has to work a bit to remember why.

She couldn't forgive him for giving up. Putting her mother in an institution—a place full of people who slumped and drooled. She hated the way he had resigned himself. Could not accept his acceptance.

The kettle starts to whistle. She pours hot water over her chamomile tea bag, thinking about that cockamamie scheme she found on the internet. She must have been in a real state. How could she have let herself be taken in by it? Some so-called American doctor who claimed he could cure dementia, no matter how advanced. For a price, of course.

What finally broke it for her was her father's utter calm. What he said when she was pushing him to go for that so-called miracle cure. And the way he said it. "Mary. You have an education. Consider the source." *Use your head*, in other words.

She carries her tea into the living room and puts it on the coffee table. Pulls her bathrobe closed. Opens the front door to retrieve the paper.

There is a man on her porch. His fist is raised.

*

"Hey, buddy. You don't want to do that."

Curtis had run and managed to catch the old guy in a bear hug just as he was about to roll off the edge.

"I did, actually," Len said into his shoulder.

"Yeah, well, it's not going to happen."

They lay together like lovers on the boardwalk until Len was still.

"Okay. If I let you go, do you promise to—" He almost said *behave*. But the guy could be his father. After a pause, he felt Len nod. Loosened his grip. "Come on, then. I'll help you up. Take your time. That's right. I've got you. Get a leg under. Now the other one. Good. This your stick? Where do you live? I'll see you home."

"I'm sorry," Len said, once he was on his feet. "I don't know what came over me. And I'm so ashamed of myself."

Same thing Curtis said at his inquest all those years ago. Meant it, too. Not that it made any difference. "Let's just get you home," he said now. "Cold out here."

But the old man braced himself with his cane. Held his hand out. "I'm Len Sparks."

Well, howdy do. Come here often? "Curtis Maye." They shook.

"I just want you to know one thing, Mr. Maye."

"What's that?"

"I'm not—irrational. It's just. I had my dog put down today. Sounds like a pretty poor excuse now. But at the time …"

Curtis shrugged. "Doesn't take much, sometimes."

"You from these parts, Mr. Maye?"

So now we're going to have a conversation. As if nothing has just happened. Okay. "I grew up in Moncton. My folks moved to Sackville when I was going to Carleton." Part of the script he worked up while he was waiting to be released. Normal-sounding small talk. "After I graduated I worked in Ottawa for a while. Then Kingston. Moved here six months ago. I live with my mother over on Salem. She's—" *A big part of my parole ticket.* "She's at an age when she can use my help."

"Well, she's lucky to have a son like you."

I wish you'd never been born. Last thing his father ever said to him. "Hey, you're starting to shake. Can we get you home?"

"I'm on Bridge Street. Not far."

When they got to his house, Curtis lent his arm up the porch steps. Insisted on seeing the old man safely inside. "I need to change," Len said, keeping his coat on. "I had—a bit of an accident."

"I don't wonder. You do what you need to do. I'll just hang around until I'm sure you're okay. Then I'll split."

"Please don't call anyone. Please."

"I won't."

He glanced at his watch while the old man mounted the stairs, one step at a time. He'd told his mother he was working late. The library closed at nine. She would expect him home soon after that. If she got back from her church service and he wasn't there, she might do some damned fool thing like call his parole officer. *I was just so worried, dear.*

While Len was upstairs, Curtis looked around a bit. There was a sealed envelope propped against a napkin holder on the kitchen table. PLEASE DELIVER TO MARY SOMERS. Then a Bridge Street address. Nearby. Next door, even? He'd check. Pay a visit tomorrow morning. Let this Mary Somers know she should maybe keep an eye on her neighbour.

Len was coming back downstairs. He had changed into pyjamas and a bathrobe and slippers. It made him look oddly boyish.

"Mr. Maye, I owe you an apology. I ruined your evening walk. Actually, I owe you more than that." He reached into the pocket of his robe. Pulled out a wad of bills.

"No," Curtis said. "I don't want anything." But he couldn't take his eyes off the money.

"Please. I insist. When you get to be my age you don't have as much use for this stuff."

By the time he was home, Curtis had almost stopped feeling like a shit for taking the old man's cash.

*

"So you thought I was some kind of terrorist." *Been called worse.*

Curtis is perched now on Mary Somers's couch, sipping coffee from a mug with a cartoon of a cat on it. He'd like to lean back, but there are about a dozen little pillows behind him that seem to have been arranged just so. His mother's living room is like that. Tiny useless tables everywhere. Doilies. Bits of china and glass all over everything. If he breathes, he knocks something over.

Mary is curled up in the one chair that looks comfortable, sipping tea. Once they'd established who each other was, and what he was doing there, she offered him some. He caught a whiff of it and said no thanks, so she said, "You more a coffee man?" He snuck a look at the back of her as she headed to the kitchen. Bit of flesh on her bones, to judge from the hug of the bathrobe. Long, tangled hair the colour of pine.

"Sorry I screamed," she says now, moving around to get comfortable. Her robe falls a little open, showing him a nice bit of curve. He drops his eyes to his mug. "For long stretches I forget all about being on that stupid list. Then something happens—like opening the door and there you are—and I think I'm going to be murdered."

Curtis drinks his coffee.

"I'm so glad you were there on the boardwalk last night right when Len … I could tell something was wrong yesterday when I checked in on him. But I never thought he'd—"

"Yeah, well. I'm pretty sure it was a one-off. He'll be okay. He was just feeling low. Upset about his dog."

"What about his dog?"

"Had it put down yesterday."

"Oh no! Sister? He had Sister put to sleep? I loved that old dog!"

"Sorry. Guess I could have broken the news a bit more—"

"It's okay," Mary says, dabbing her eyes with a Kleenex. How do women do that, he wonders, watching her. Pull a Kleenex out of thin air? "You couldn't possibly have known. But damn it. Poor old Len. Sister was all he had."

"Oh, I don't know. I'd say he has a pretty good neighbour."

She doesn't respond. She's gone all still, and is looking at him strangely. "*That's* where I've seen you!"

His armpits go cold. When he was released, his name and picture made it into some of the papers.

"You work at the library, don't you?"

"Yes. Yes, I do." His heart begins to slow.

"Right. I teach school. I'm in there a lot." She continues to study him. Maybe wondering why a man his age is doing a teenager's job.

"It's just a stopgap for me," he says. "I'm new in town. Hoping to set up a business." Another part of the passing-as-ordinary script he's worked up.

"Oh yeah? What kind of a business?"

"Carpentry, mostly." They taught him woodworking inside. "Maybe some electrical, too. Repairs. Installations. Handyman kind of thing. But mostly, I'd work with wood."

Right. Where's he going to get the capital to start a business? Even buy tools? Any banks out there loan money to ex-cons? Still, for all it's bullshit, it's nice to sit and talk like a normal human being. Nice to have somebody listening to him who thinks he's a normal human being.

"I should show you my back porch," Mary says now. "It's a disaster. I'd love a real deck."

"Glad to take a look at it. Some time." He checks his watch. "But I'll have to head over to the library. Anyway, thanks for the coffee."

"Well, thank *you* for coming and telling me about Len. I should hustle too. I've got some shopping and cleaning and cooking to do."

It's the cue for both of them to get up. But for a second or two they just sit and look at each other.

*

Len is wrestling Sister's bed into a garbage bag. He thought about donating it to the SPCA, then decided it was too old and worn. Her food and water bowls, her toys, her collar and leash went straight into the trash. Easier that way. And it keeps him from thinking about the damned fool he made of himself last night.

He slept like a baby, then woke up feeling sheepish and relieved, the way he used to after a deserved bawling-out by his father. Strange to think that he could have been dead now. Floating. His body yet to be found. Strange, too, to be the only living thing in the house. That'll take some getting used to.

The thing about Sister was, she was *there*. For the last thirteen years. And he has the photographs to prove it. Him and Joan up at the lake, sitting at the picnic table outside the cottage they always rented. Sister down front, dog-grinning into the camera. Christmas morning. Joan sitting at the foot of the decorated tree in her red velvet robe, Sister's head in her lap.

But in the years since Joan died, it's been going back farther than that. Farther than can be caught on camera. Sister now inhabits his boyhood memories. She's there with him, those mornings he was—what? Fourteen? Heading down to the river. Toting the air rifle—couldn't do much more with it than scare crows—that his father gave him over his mother's protests. His mother who thanked God every day for the very thing he pretended was itching him crazy—that by the time he was old enough to sign up, the war would likely be over.

He would never have admitted it, but he was just as glad to be out of harm's way. Still, every Saturday morning he took his rifle down to the banks of the St. John. Crouched behind a bush to watch and wait, half-hoping, half-fearing to see the swastika-decaled turret of a submarine breaking the surface.

And now, when he thinks of those mornings, Sister is by his side. Taking her cue from him. Watching the water.

He drags the garbage bag out the side door and down to the curb. And here comes Mary. Was she watching for him? Soon as he sees her face, he can tell that she knows what he went and did last night. Tried to do. Doesn't matter how she found out. This town, secrets blow around on the wind. Her eyes are fierce as she marches toward him, reminding him of his mother. Yes, she knows, all right. And all at once he knows something about her, too.

He couldn't put his finger on what it is that makes him so sure. But he's always been able to tell. His father was a country doctor. Maybe he picked the knack up from him.

When he was teaching, once a year or so a high-school girl would get into trouble, as they used to say back then. There'd be a special staff meeting about it, everything very hush-hush. He'd have to bite his lip. Because he already knew. Was it the way they walked? Or a kind of glow about them that came through, for all the worry and shame?

Oh, Mary, he thinks. Standing his ground. Bracing for a bawling-out.

*

Mary pulls a bag of torn-up bread out of the freezer and leaves it on the counter to thaw. Whenever she has a stale end of a loaf, she rips it into small pieces and drops them in the freezer bag. Then, when she needs bread for stuffing, it's there. Just one of the tricks her mother taught her.

Her mother. Does she even know it's Thanksgiving? Will they give her any kind of a decent dinner in that place in Hamilton? What if she drove to Moncton, right now, and took the next flight west? Showed up in her mother's room. What if her father just happened to be there?

Pick up the turkey, Mary. Get potatoes, squash, carrots. Pick up the pie. What else?

Pharmacy.

No. Do that on Tuesday. Don't think about it till then.

She gathers her shopping bag, purse, hat, and gloves. Pulls on her coat. Was that a little reckless, sitting talking to a strange man in just her nightie and robe? Asking him in in the first place? But once she got over the shock of seeing him there on her porch, he seemed—

Not just familiar. Comfortable. As if she'd known him for ages. It felt right, having him there. She could almost have asked him to hang around and help her while she shopped and cooked and cleaned.

Len suggesting she invite him for Thanksgiving dinner was a surprise. But then when she thought about it, it gave her that same comfortable *of course* feeling.

She hopes he'll come. It would be nice—the three of them sitting around her table. The lines of a song she teaches her kids each year runs through her mind: *They all lived together in a crooked little house.*

*

Fuck. Fuck. Fuck. Some days. And this one's a dilly.

Started with wanting to kill his mother. Again. So he did that good-Samaritan thing, dropping in on Mary Somers to tell her about Len. Hoping to cheer himself up.

He was expecting a woman around Len's age. Instead, what he saw was—Ripe. Yes. A ripeness about her. Those sleepy eyes and tangled hair. That waft of bedclothes rising from her whenever she moved.

Don't even think about it. Look at you. Ex-con. Did your twenty-five, then ten more getting parole. In your sixties now. Earning chump change at a nothing job. Living with your mother.

"So, Mom," he said that morning at breakfast. "You want me to help you get groceries or anything once I'm through work today?" She had been oddly silent about Thanksgiving dinner. Didn't even have a pumpkin pie baked. When he was a kid, the pies were the first thing she did. He was looking forward to a decent feed on Sunday. His mother didn't have much of an appetite, and she sometimes forgot that he did.

"No, that's all right, dear. We won't be needing any-thing." There was a bit of mischief behind her eyes. *I know something you don't know.*

"What do you mean? It's Thanksgiving."

"Yes. It is. And last night at the special service Pastor Peter issued the most wonderful challenge to us all."

He didn't like the way this was going. They'd been United Church when he was growing up. Then, once he was inside and his father was dead, his mother went a little strange. Switched denominations. Started including phrases like *the reign of Christ* in her letters. Confessing that she envied the ones in her new congregation who could *speak in tongues* and *faint in the spirit*. That one time he went with her to Kingdom Come Pentecostal, a woman next to him kept slamming her hips into the back of the pew in front of her, gasping out "Jesus! Jesus! Jesus!" He didn't know where to look.

"We are going to *fast*," his mother was saying. "As a com-munity. We will gather together on Sunday at Kingdom Come for a day of fasting and prayer, then donate what we would have spent on food to our African mission."

"You're fasting? On Thanksgiving?"

"You can join in, Curtis! We would love to welcome you to our fold!"

"Like hell." He was starting to heat up. He'd better watch it. But shit. His pay cheque went straight into her bank account. She handed him twenty-five bucks every Monday morning. Twenty-five bucks for the week. When she remembered. "Some of that money you're sending to Africa is mine, you know. And will you get a receipt? Some kind of proof that you're not just lining Pastor Peter's pocket?"

Oh, look at her. She was getting that pinched little look. He had *disappointed* her. Again. And so it started up—that murmuring little whimper that ate under his skin.

"All those years … I took the train … all alone … to that place where they searched my bag … and your father would never come …"

His only visitor. Year after year. They watched each other get old through plexiglass.

"… to have to see my own son …"

He wiped his mouth. Threw down his napkin. Got up and left the house.

Sondra's got him shelf-reading today. His least favourite job. It's picky. He has to check every Dewey decimal notation on every single spine—the skinny ones have it stamped on sideways, so he has to bend and twist—and catch any rogues and put them where they belong.

Sondra hired him through the Second Chance Program. He was lucky, and he knows it. He could have ended up bagging groceries or cleaning toilets. "That's *Sin*-Clair," she said to him his first day when he stuck out a sweaty hand and mispronounced her name. "I'm no saint."

No, she isn't. And she's really laying it on today. She always lets herself dress down on Saturdays. This week's jeans are skintight. And that low-cut flowered blouse. Plus her perfume, that manages to creep into every corner of the place.

She's curious. Written all over her. Some days like this one, when he could cheerfully blow everything out of the water, he imagines going into her office and saying, *Okay, Sondra. Since you want to know. Inside, everything that doesn't smell like damp concrete smells like shit. And you hear every cell door slam, every whimper, every scream, because there's not a scrap of rug or curtain to soak up the noise. And yes, the guys lucky enough to have a woman on the outside do get conjugal visits. In the fuck truck, as it's called. And yes, it hurts like hell to get it up the ass. Anything else you want to know?*

Just read the shelves, Curtis. Wouldn't be so bad if people would leave books on the tables for him to pick up. But oh, no, they want to help. So they put the fucking things back on the shelves, only in the wrong—

"Curtis?"

He looks down. Does a double take.

"Sorry to interrupt you at work."

"No! No, that's fine. That's no problem." She's wearing a fuzzy little blue hat. Out of the corner of his eye, he can see Sondra at her desk. Watching the two of them.

"Um, look, this is really a long shot. Like, you probably have plans. But I'm having Len over tomorrow for turkey with all the trimmings, and we'd both really like it if you could join us. I think Len's kind of embarrassed. He'd like you to see him under different circumstances." Curtis is still stuck on *trimmings.* Stuffing. Mashed potatoes. Gravy. Enough to make him believe in God.

"Anyway, if there's any chance at all that you're free—"

"Yeah! I am. And that's. That would be. Thank you. Yeah. I could come."

"Great. So. See you around five?"

"Five. Okay. Anything I can bring?" That's what you say, isn't it, when you're asked over for dinner? *Anything I can bring.* Just like a normal person.

"How about a bottle of wine?"

"A bottle of wine."

"Yeah. I'm not much of a drinker, so I'm not really sure … Red, maybe? With turkey?"

"Red."

"Unless. Like, if you prefer white—"

"No! Red. Red's just fine."

"Okay. See you tomorrow at five."

And the blue fuzzy hat is bobbing away from him out the library door. And he can feel Sondra St. Clair's eyes on him.

He turns back to the shelf. Pretends to be reading Dewey decimal notations.

Bottle of wine. Red.

May not consume alcohol. One of the conditions. Consume. Nothing about buying a bottle to bring as a gift, though. He could do that. He'll just have to put his hand over his glass when Mary tilts it his way. *Thanks, but I don't drink.* Another line in the script.

He has Len's cash in his pocket. And right across Main Street, smack in between this library where he works and the Town Hall / RCMP building where he has to check in every week, is the cutest, sweetest little wine store you're ever going to see.

Not that he's ever been in it. Or ever even looked in the window. Or so much as let himself walk the side of the street that it's on.

*

Grace Morgan Pettingill ... twenty-one ... only child of the Reverend Dr. Ramsay Pettingill, Dean of Christ Church Cathedral in Ottawa, and his wife Clarissa ... musical prodigy ... accepted at Juilliard ...

Len wishes he hadn't booted up. Hadn't keyed *Curtis Maye* into the search field. He shuts down his laptop. Takes his cane and goes carefully down the basement steps. He doesn't often visit the basement any more. No need, since he had the washer and dryer installed in the pantry off the kitchen. But he's been thinking about his old potting table. And there it is. A bit cobwebby. Clay pots still lined up on the shelf. Fork and trowel hanging on the wall. Gloves folded. And yes, the grow light still clicks on.

... died of injuries sustained during an attack by ex-boyfriend Curtis Maye ...

It's been years since he planted or potted anything. Maybe come spring he could have some soil delivered from the gardening centre. Give him something to do. *Right, Sister?* he almost says, then catches himself.

... previous drunk-and-disorderly convictions ...

The plants were always his thing, as far as Joan was concerned. Oh, she liked seeing them in the back garden and in the sunroom. But she had no patience for the work, for witnessing the slow growth. So it was up to Len to putter and pot. One year he grew a whole bank of coleus from seedlings in discarded egg cartons. Spooned water each day carefully over each tiny sprout.

Panicked and fled the scene ... Kingston Penitentiary ... no chance of parole for twenty-five years ...

One spring, when he was watering the houseplants in the sunroom, he discovered a weed poking up near the rim of one of the pots. Just two leaves on a single stem, like a tiny green propeller. Dandelion, most likely, from a seed that blew in through an open door, or rode in on Sister's coat. If he didn't pinch it out by the root right away, it would spread to all the other plants.

He eased it out with an old spoon and gave it his smallest pot, not much bigger than a thimble. He set it on the high basement window ledge. Then, telling himself that it was foolishness, he tended it the way he did all the other seedlings.

It grew. One morning a many-petalled yellow head was leaning into a shaft of sun coming through the dirty basement window. Now it was harder to do what he should have done in the first place. The thing could burst into seed any day, and even the faint breeze of his passing would break the tiny parachutes away from the mother plant and send them flying.

He dropped the dandelion, pot and all, into a garbage bag and tied a knot in the neck. "Sorry," he heard himself mutter. When he turned to carry the bag outside and tuck it into the can at the curb, he found Sister looking at him with those big, questioning beagle eyes.

*

full-bodied … provocative, light and mischievous … deep, dark, delicious … stirs the senses … intense … succulent …

Christ. He's trying to pick out a bottle, not get laid. And just about everything has a screw top now. Last time he bought wine, screw tops were for rubbies.

He's sweating. Feels as if there's a spotlight on him. He's convinced that if he turns around he'll see Sondra. Or worse, his little prick of a parole officer. Jesus. If he's going to buy booze, why does it have to be on Thanksgiving weekend, when half the town is in here doing the same thing?

He gets through the checkout. Slips the bottle into the inside pocket of his coat. Steps out into the sun. Crosses Main. Turns left onto Charlotte. Heads for Salem and home. The whole time, he can feel the bottle bumping against his hip. Once inside the house, where his mother is still making a show of not speaking to him, he manages to smuggle the thing upstairs to his room. Stashes it inside a boot in his closet.

Five o'clock, Mary said. Twenty-three hours from now.

*

She can't believe what she just did. She's never called twice in a month, much less twice in a weekend. And it was so close.

He picked up on the second ring. Did his usual two *Hellos*. Made a pettish little sound with his mouth, as if he were just about to slam down the receiver.

And that's when she drew her breath in. Loud. Even to her it sounded like the kind of breath you draw right before a sob.

Stupid. Stupid. It's such a personal thing, breath. Once you've lived with someone, once you really know them, you can recognize the way they sneeze or cough. Or breathe.

He must have heard it. Because he didn't hang up. Just waited. Absolutely silent. Listening.

She held her breath as long as she could, then ended the call. First time she's ever been the first to disconnect.

*

Why couldn't the damned thing at least have a cork in it? He'd bet money that his mother does not possess a corkscrew. All that's keeping the cap on is that perforated tin ring. How easy would it be to close his hand around the neck of the bottle? Give it the slightest little twist? Hear the crack?

Tonight the what-ifs won't leave him alone. Having a bottle stashed behind a flimsy closet door just a few feet from his bed doesn't help.

What if he hadn't taken the job in Campus Admin after he graduated? Or just hadn't been on counter duty the day when she walked in? She needed to have her transcripts forwarded to that music school in New York. Grace Morgan Pettingill. What a name. "*Morgan*," she corrected him, rolling her eyes when he called her Grace.

What if he had just helped her fill out the forms then let her go back out the door? Put those freckles and that incredibly assured manner of hers out of his mind instead of dreaming up all kinds of unnecessary questions and procedures—anything to keep her at the counter?

What if he hadn't bumped into her on campus a week later on his lunch break—okay, he had been deliberately hanging around the arts complex—and asked her to go for a coffee? What if she hadn't said yes?

Fast forward. What if he hadn't already had the two of them married with kids, in his mind, when he asked her? Would he have handled it better, when she inched away from him in bed and repeated that she was serious about Juilliard? That she intended to live the life of a concert pianist—travelling and performing? Besides, as she'd said before, that wasn't the only issue. There was also—

But he didn't want to hear about his drinking. He was fucking sick and tired of her going on about his drinking.

Fast forward. His last day as a free man. What if he had given up after he called her a hifalutin elitist bitch and threw her out of his place? Hadn't spent the next week going over their last conversation in his mind, convincing himself that he should try again, with different words. Better words.

What if he hadn't stopped in for just one drink after work? Just one, to take the edge off. Mellow him down a little before he approached her and had the conversation that he was so sure was going to change her mind. What if he'd known better than to head back to campus, after the fifth or sixth or whatever it was, and wait outside the library where he knew she was studying. Try to talk to her when she came out.

What if he'd just let her go after she told him he was drunk and to leave her alone? Instead of following her into that laneway she took as a shortcut. Grabbing her by the shoulders. Spinning her around. Trying to shake some sense into her.

He could what-if his way back to the first drink he ever took. It all leads up to the same thing. One minute, he was one kind of person. The next, he was another. Forever and ever, amen.

What's he going to talk about at the dinner table tomorrow? What charming anecdotes does he have to share? When exactly will that *look* appear on Mary Somers's face? How soon before she takes that step back that everybody takes, once they figure out where he's been for over half his life?

There's no point in trying to tell people that as soon as Morgan Pettingill started to yell, he panicked. Tried to cover her mouth, but she bit his hand. So he tried to choke off the noise she was making. Just a little pressure. Not too much. No point in trying to tell people that from the second he felt her windpipe collapse under his thumbs, he was inside. Nobody had to lock him up. He'd already put himself away.

*

Mary has just put foil over the platter of carved turkey and is sliding it back into the oven to stay warm. At five forty-five, when the candles on the table had burnt down to half their length, Curtis still hadn't shown. That's when Len said, "I think I know what's happened. Just give me a few minutes."

She's just about to blow the candles out when she thinks, *Oh, for God's sake.* All day, she's been rehearsing the words in her mind. *"Dad? It's Mary. How are you?"* What could be so bloody hard about that?

She's reaching for her phone when it rings.

*

Len finds Curtis on the boardwalk, not far from the spot where they met the other night. He's sitting hunched on a bench, rolling the bottle of wine back and forth between his palms. When he looks up, Len says, "Aren't you a little late for dinner?"

"I'm late for everything."

Len points at the bottle. "If you'd opened that, I wouldn't be saying what I'm about to say. Mary tells me you want to start a business. I'm prepared to advance you the capital. On two conditions. First, that before you sit down at her table you tell her where you've been for the past thirty-five years and why. Even if she shows you the door once she's heard your story, my offer still stands. Provided—and this is the second condition—you stay sober."

*

She's given him one of the drumsticks. It's huge. The skin is dark gold. Crispy. The mound of mashed potatoes has a perfect round lake of gravy in the middle. The stuffing has nuts in it. He's never had stuffing with nuts. Carrots and squash off to the side, shiny with butter and sprinkled with bits of green.

The bottle is sitting on a coaster in the middle of the table. He reaches for it. Twists it open. He'll have to listen to that delicious glugging sound of the first pour. Watch the red swirling up against the sides of Len's and Mary's glasses. Breathe in the smell of it, sweet and dark.

"Len? Can I pour you some of this?"

"Thanks, but alcohol does not play nicely with my heart pills."

Mary shakes her head too. "I shouldn't be drinking right now either."

"Well. I guess it's all mine, then." Curtis pushes his chair back. Carries the bottle into the kitchen. Pours the contents down the sink.

*

It's chilly on the boardwalk this morning. First frost. Len is holding a small box made of sturdy cardboard on his lap. Ahmed delivered it that morning, along with the vet's bill. He looks at his watch. Better get on with it. He's got an appointment in less than an hour with his accountant.

He levers himself up with his cane. Carries the box to the handrail. Pries it open and upends it over the water. "Okay, Girl. Go get that muskrat that always drove you nuts."

He waits for the cloud of ash on the surface to darken and sink. Drops the box onto the boardwalk and flattens it with his foot. Braces with his cane, lowers himself down and picks it up. *Have to keep an eye out for a recycle bin,* is what he's thinking as he sets off toward town.

Three Girls on a Wharf, 1953.

FLESH

THE YOUNGER WOMEN—NOT MANY OF those—are the modest ones, undressing awkwardly under towels they've tucked round themselves. Women more Harriet's age get matter-of-factly naked and take their time squeezing into their bathing suits, not seeming to care how they jiggle or bulge. *Have we all just given up?* Harriet thinks, hanging her suit on a hook in one of the shower stalls and rinsing down. *Or is this wisdom?*

What she'd really like to do is set up her easel in a corner of the change room. She's never seen so much mature naked flesh together in one spot. She would enjoy capturing the soft weight of buttock and breast with chalk on rough paper.

Boobs and nipples and bums, oh my! Boobs and nipples and bums, she chants in her head as she pulls her bathing suit on over her wet skin and follows the others out to the pool. She's always liked to look at naked bodies, the fleshier the better. She loved life class when she was a student, especially when the model was a large woman with lots of swellings and folds.

"Do you think that makes me a little bit lesbian?" she asked Halvor during their honeymoon in Vancouver. That afternoon they had visited Wreck Beach, and Harriet had surprised herself with how readily she stripped in front of dozens of naked strangers. Halvor, being Danish, was an old hand.

"Believe me," he said, "you are not lesbian." They were back in their hotel room, naked together in bed. She had just told him about preferring the heavier models in life class. "We all like it. Woman flesh. Because we were all once babies." He kneaded one of her breasts and planted his mouth on the other.

This is Harriet's first time at Aqua Fit. Her doctor has told her to take off fifteen pounds, so she's trying to get more exercise. She stands waiting near the edge of the pool with the rest of the class. They all chatter familiarly with each other, having obviously done this for ages. One or two give kind, welcoming smiles to Harriet, who smiles back but does not join in.

My daughter, my husband, my son, my niece, my dog. The my-my litany. She could do it, too—*my husband, Halvor, who drowned at the cottage while I was arguing with the radio; my son Ranald the gay architect whom I can hardly stand; my son-in-law Patrick whom I wish was my son.* What is it in aid of, this constant, other-directed talk? She's always wondered if it isn't in fact some kind of bluff. For all their giving and sharing, there's something essentially secretive about women. Tucked up inside. Not like men, hanging and swinging for all the world to see. Whenever she's been in a group of women going my-my this and my-my that, the phrase *sitting on our secrets* has gone through her mind. She imagines being able to enter and travel her own vagina. What would she find in there? Cave paintings? Glittering cities? An entire alternate universe? Maybe that's what men are trying to do with their relentless push push push. Explore. Discover. Claim.

She would love to talk about this with Halvor. The two of them were cheated out of their old age together. Now it's just her and Ranald, with whom she is going to have lunch as soon as this class is over. That's another secret women keep. She can't be the only mother who feels relief when a visit with her adult kid shows signs of coming to an end.

Their teacher has arrived—a young black woman in spandex that shows off her muscled perfection. She gets them going even before they've finished stepping down into the water and spreading out. Running on the spot. ("Get those knees up!") Cross-country skiing. ("No bent elbows!") Leapfrog. ("I see bums sticking out! Straighten those torsos!") Jumping jacks. ("To the left! To the right!") One-leg figure eights. ("Clockwise! Counter-clockwise! Other leg!") Cross-country skiing again. ("Shoulders under the water! For every pair of shoulders I see, I will add five seconds to this exercise!")

"Oh, shut up, little girl," Harriet grunts under her breath. "When you're my age you'll—"

"I hear talking! If you are talking you are not working hard enough!"

She says it all with a grin, and Harriet knows she's just kidding. But an old resentment wells up, born of long-ago high-school phys-ed classes. *Physical education.* Who thought that one up? Might as well have been *corporal punishment.* Twice a week for two hours. God. And there was—there *is*—something sadistic about one professionally fit individual forcing a class of the feeble, the fat, and the maladroit to huff and heave, aching for the whole thing to be over.

Then, all at once, it is over. Harriet admits grudgingly to feeling marvellous. Loose-jointed and floaty. She could happily go home and sleep. But she has to have lunch with her son.

"Something is leaking in the bottom of your bag." This is how Ranald greets her in the Rendezvous, where he's reserved a table near the back.

"Nice to see you too," Harriet says, kissing his remarkably smooth cheek. How many times a day does he shave? And why are they sitting in the dark? He usually insists on a window table. "That's my wet bathing suit leaking. And if you smell chlorine, it's me."

She wants the club sandwich, but orders the large Caesar salad. Hopes it comes with bread. Ranald orders the soup-and-sandwich combo. They decline drinks. He's returning to work, and she wants to paint this afternoon. Wine at lunch makes her logy.

She's glad to have Aqua Fit to talk about. Whenever she's going to meet with Ranald, she tries to line up some topics— hooks to hang the conversation on. *Oh, Halvor*, she thinks at times like this. *You could have made this so much easier.* As she prattles on about the fitness class, she wonders in the back of her mind if Ranald is thinking the same thing. What if his father had lived? Would the two of them get along better if they had Halvor as a buffer between them? Maybe. But then, would Ranald have sought out and married Patrick, who is sunny and sweet, like the grade threes he teaches?

"I have some news."

"Oh? What?" She was just going to tell him about the pool noodles, which was the only part of the class she enjoyed, but it can wait. Is he up for some architecture award?

"I have a small lump under my left nipple. It seems to be growing. It's going to be needle biopsied next week."

She stares at him.

Into the silence, Ranald says, a bit defensively, "It is not unheard-of for a man to have breast cancer."

"Yes. I know. But—"

The waiter arrives with their food. Ranald starts right in on his soup, so Harriet picks up her fork and stabs some romaine. "When did you find out?" She is furious, but keeps her voice neutral. She knows that if there's even a hint of *why didn't you tell me right away*, he will ice over the way he does.

"Two months ago. My doctor noticed a slight dimpling during my last checkup and sent me for an ultrasound. I had a second ultrasound last week. That's how they can tell it's growing. The needle biopsy will determine whether or not it's malignant. If it is, I'll do chemo. It's faster than radiation. And now I would like to talk about other things." He gives her a look, picks his spoon back up, and carries on drinking his soup.

She knows there is no point in trying to push for more. Or in reminding him that the growth might very well be benign, that cancer isn't the only thing that manifests as a lump, that the worst-case scenario isn't the only one or even the most likely one. She can just imagine what Halvor would say to that. *He is an architect, Harriet. He is trained to imagine every contingency. Second-guess any possible disaster.*

"How's Patrick taking it?" Surely she can ask Ranald about his husband. And to her relief, she gets a wry smile from him.

"Patrick is Patrick."

She smiles back. Patrick is the heart, the emotional worker in the marriage. It would have been his job to go into shock, then do the crying and the worrying for the two of them. Her son-in-law is easy to love. When they met, he practically sprang at her like a puppy, wanting to know her, wanting to adore and be adored by her.

Patrick probably put Ranald up to this lunch. Would have insisted, with threats of telling her himself, on his at least giving her the facts. And facts are what she is going to have to be satisfied with. Ranald is Ranald. Cold and severe, like his buildings. Yes, his buildings serve a purpose. But they do it grudgingly, as if they regard function, and the people who make it necessary, as secondary to form.

Harriet eats her salad, for which she is actually hungry. It did not come with bread. *You gets no bread with one meatball.* That old song from the Depression. Would the lump look a bit like a meatball? A meatball that's growing. Right now. Inside her son. She puts her fork down and tries to distract herself by listening in on the conversation of two men at the next table. They're talking about going to the aquarium. Didn't Patrick say something about taking his grade three class there? God, the thought of taking a bunch of kids on a field trip. The memory of that one summer when she was a camp counsellor still wears her out. But Patrick seems to thrive on all the neediness and chaos.

Ranald has finished his soup and started in on his sandwich. He still eats the way he did when he was a little boy—completely devouring one item on his plate before proceeding to the next. Sitting across from her son, watching him take food, nourish himself, she feels a yearning for his body—its life, its health, its continuance—that she hardly ever felt when he was a baby. The way some mothers talked about loving to breathe in their baby's smell, about wanting to nip gently at the tiny buttocks with their teeth, about breastfeeding being a sexual turn-on, frankly mystified her.

She was alarmed by Ranald's dense heaviness in her arms, even when he was newborn. Too often, he smelled like shit or spat-up milk. And he was a gobbling little vampire to feed. Her nipples cracked till they bled.

Now she does want to touch him. She would like to strip and feel his naked skin on hers all the way down. She wants to cover and warm him. Absorb any shock or hurt. Keep him whole.

All she can say is, "How's the sandwich?"

"Want me to come and stay for a while?" Jill. Phoning from Hamilton, in response to Harriet's email about Ranald.

"Yes. Come. And bring your bathing suit. We'll be doing Aqua Fit."

They have been friends for over fifty years. The last time Jill came to stay for a while was a few weeks after Halvor drowned. Harriet doesn't like to remember that visit. She knows it's too much to hope that Jill has forgotten about finding her in Halvor's closet late one night.

Jill had gotten up to go to the bathroom, had peeked into the master bedroom to check on Harriet and had seen the bed empty. The sliding door onto the balcony was open. They were fourteen flights up. Just as her mind was forming a *No!* she heard sounds coming from the closet. Harriet had wedged herself in between Halvor's suit jackets and pulled the door shut. She had picked up one of his shoes and fitted it over her nose and mouth like a mask. Breathing in. Wailing out.

The memory of Jill's skinny arms wrapped around her plumpness still embarrasses Harriet. True, she's seen Jill through heartbreak too, more than once. Jill never married, and has a talent for falling in love with men who are emotionally inaccessible. Her last affair was just a few years ago, with someone named Eliot. Harriet had to watch the same old girlish joy in Jill's eyes become the same old misery. Had to listen as she read aloud the letter she was sending to Eliot—a letter he never answered. Surely by now she's stopped checking the mail twice a day?

Sometimes Harriet wishes she could wave a wand and do away with sex and romantic love and parenthood. All the fleshly ties that hurt so much when they're even tugged. Friendship, though, she would keep. Purely chosen attachments. Breakable, yes. But a cleaner break.

For Jill's visit, she clears out Ranald's old room, where she has been storing canvases. She tries to make it tidy. Attractive. Jill was always such a neat little thing, every hair of her dark bob in place, even at camp.

They met in the summer of 1970, when they were both counsellors at Onteora Arts Camp in the Caledon Hills. Summer jobs for students were scarce that year, otherwise they would never have applied. But then they would never have met each other. Or Morgan.

Harriet and Morgan and Jill, oh my! Harriet and Morgan and Jill!

At the beginning of the summer, during the counsellors' orientation, the camp director kept emphasizing that a focus on the arts should not interfere with the process of turning out a well-rounded camper. "I resent that," Harriet muttered after the third iteration of *well-rounded*. A slight, dark-haired girl sitting beside her, who turned out to be Jill, gave her a grin.

The camp director went on to health, safety, and morale. They might have to deal with homesickness and nightmares, especially with the younger campers. Anything a counsellor can do or say to calm the little ones' fears and reassure them that nothing will harm them—"

"Lions and tigers and bears, oh my! Lions and tigers and bears!" That line from *The Wizard of Oz*. Chanted wickedly, just under the breath, by someone behind them. Harriet and Jill both turned. Saw a tall, blonde, freckled girl meeting their gaze. As if she had been waiting for them to notice her.

Morgan.

All three of them were students—Jill at McMaster in Hamilton, Morgan at Carleton in Ottawa and Harriet at the Ontario College of Art in Toronto. Harriet was to be the so-called crafts specialist at Onteora. Jill, who wrote for her campus newspaper, would do something involving stories and drama. Morgan, who had started piano at three, would be in charge of music. None of them had ever been to summer camp as kids. All of them were bored by children, had a horror of sports and had hoped and prayed not to be hired.

Harriet and Morgan and Jill, oh my! Harriet and Morgan and Jill!

"What we evidently need to do," Morgan intoned, imitating her Anglican priest father, "is come to grips with the *crucial*, one might even say the *dire*, importance ..." Here she sucked on a cigarette, then passed it to Harriet and Jill, who each took a puff and wished they hadn't, "... of getting the *ball* in the *hole*."

They were in their hiding place behind the supplies cabin. They had just been summoned to the camp director's office to be reminded that Onteora's paying parents had paid for a well-rounded experience for their children. And it had been noticed by more than the camp director that the support and enthusiasm demonstrated by all three of them for the athletic side of things had been somewhat less than—

Harriet and Jill responded as one, "The *ball* in the *hole*." Trying not to cough.

"Even if the reason eludes us."

"*Especially* if the reason eludes us."

"Do you ever think about Morgan?" Harriet asks Jill on the third night of her visit. They are draining a bottle of pinot grigio and picking the last fluffy bits out of a bowl of popcorn, having just watched their favourite DVD, *Stand By Me*. They haven't talked much about Ranald. They did try. But once Harriet had come out with the words *malignant* and *chemo*, there didn't seem to be much else to say. Or much point in saying it. What she knows is what Patrick tells her when he phones. Ranald is losing weight and losing hair. No, a visit from his mother at this time would not be a good thing. This is Ranald, after all.

Harriet suspects that she and Jill may even have used Ranald's cancer as an excuse to get together. *Ranald's cancer*. She hates that. The way you come to possess something that you would never have chosen. A year after Halvor died, someone asked her how far she was into *her widowhood*. She wanted to tell them that it wasn't hers, that she didn't ask for it, didn't want it, and that they could take it and shove it up their ass.

"I do think about Morgan. Sometimes," Jill says now in answer to her question. "But I still can't write about her." Jill has published seven books. Harriet goes to her launches and readings as often as she comes to Harriet's gallery shows. "Could you paint her?"

"I've sometimes tried to paint the pond from memory." Then, "Do you ever wonder what we all would have been like? If Morgan ...?"

"Yeah. I do. But I can't imagine it."

Harriet can. She is convinced that neither she nor Jill would have accomplished anything much. Instead, they would have followed Morgan's career in the papers. Shown up for her concerts whenever she touched down in Toronto. Made awkward small talk with each other during the intermissions.

Morgan's family had a summer house on the edge of Lost Lake in the Laurentians. When camp ended that year, she invited Harriet and Jill up for the Labour Day weekend. It was the start of a tradition, the three of them coming together just prior to going back to their respective schools in the fall.

They each had their own room in the two-storey fieldstone house. When Harriet first saw hers, she wanted to paint it. The pine four-poster with the faded antique quilt. The braided rag rug. The rush-bottomed rocker. The table under the window with the mayonnaise jar—label still on—full of wild flowers. *I could live here.*

Downstairs, everything was just shabby and peculiar enough to hint at the kind of wealth that can afford to let its shabby, peculiar side show. There were dried bats in sealed mason jars on the mantle. ("Mummy is a frustrated naturalist.") There was a glassed-in bookshelf filled with collector's editions of *Le Morte d'Artur, Idylls of the King* and *The Once and Future King.* ("In another life Daddy was an Arthurian scholar. I was in danger of being named Guinevere, but Mummy for once put her foot down.") Morgan spoke of her parents indulgently, as if they were characters in a favourite childhood book. When asked where they were that first weekend, she replied, as if stating the obvious, "Switzerland."

She did not seem to know how extraordinary she was in the eyes of Harriet and Jill. That first time up at the summer house, she taught them how to make a cheese fondue. As she lifted handfuls of grated Emmental off the marble cutting board and stirred the melting mixture with a wooden spoon, she apologized for using Canadian cheese, but assured them that the recipe was authentically Swiss. Harriet's and Jill's eyes met. Prior to that weekend, neither of them had ever even heard of cheese fondue.

Morgan described her own future in a way that would have been preposterous coming from anyone else. After getting her BA from Carleton, she told them confidently, she would attend Juilliard in New York, where she would either be discovered or win a global competition. Either way, she would step onto the world stage as a concert pianist. Furthermore, she expected the same level of achievement from the two of them. "What do you mean, *if* you publish? What do you mean, *if* you get shown in a gallery? *When! When!*"

What had she been doing at Onteora Arts Camp? Surely not, like Harriet and Jill, earning her next year's tuition. Harriet did ask her, one morning when she found her watering plants on the deck of the summer house. Jill was still asleep upstairs. Harriet had come down to the kitchen to get coffee and had heard Morgan half-humming, half-singing one of the hymns that, along with old Beatles and Beach Boys tunes, formed her personal hit parade. *And did those feet in ancient times ... And was the holy Lamb of God ... among those dark Satanic Mills ...*

"It was Daddy's idea," she said with a sigh and an eye-roll when Harriet asked her about Onteora. "He insisted that I take at least one opportunity to render a service. So I did. And all I can say is, thank God that's over."

It was right then that Harriet knew she was in love with Morgan. As strange as that was, it made sense. It explained why, toward the end of each summer, she would watch for the mail, hoping for a letter from Ottawa addressed in Morgan's hand. If no letter was there, she would feel the need to hide her disappointment from her parents. When it finally did arrive, inviting her once again up to the summer house for the long weekend, her joy and relief would be so sharp it hurt. And from the moment she and Jill drove up the lane to the house and caught sight of Morgan grinning at them from the deck, she would start to dread the visit's end.

Did Morgan know how she felt? Harriet both did and did not want her to. Nor could she imagine telling her. What could she say? She could barely describe her feelings to herself. It wasn't as if she wanted to *make love* to Morgan. A young nineteen, she was still slightly vague in her mind about how she would do that with a man, let alone a woman. It was more that she wanted to follow Morgan through life. Worship her. Be known by her. Seen by her. Yes. Be the one. The apple of Morgan's eye.

"You are the boss of your pool noodle!" The Aqua Fit instructor.

"Like hell I am." Jill's has just reared up through the water and bopped her under the chin. "Tell me again why we're doing this?"

"Hey, this is the fun part," Harriet says, bobbing past with the end of her own noodle sticking up from between her legs. "This is as close to sex as I've gotten in years."

"I hear talking!"

Harriet has enjoyed letting Jill in on every aspect of her life. Her long mornings of drinking coffee and reading the paper. Her afternoons kept strictly for painting in her studio, which Jill has respected by staying in her—Ranald's—room and working on the manuscript she brought with her.

More than once, Harriet has toyed with the idea of asking Jill to live with her. There's room. They're both alone now. And Jill has finally retired, after selling that frame shop in Hamilton.

But each time Harriet has felt ready to raise the possibility, something has stopped her. She senses the impulse is disingenuous. That it is not really about her and Jill, here and now. That it is really about her and Jill and Morgan. There. Then.

There was a pond behind the summer house. It was almost perfectly round, ringed with bulrushes, spring-fed and very cold. After lunch the three of them would get into their bathing suits and go in. Not for long. The point was to get out, lie on the dock and dry off in the hot sun.

Whenever Harriet thinks of those weekends now, it is the pond and that sun-warmed dock that come first to mind. She can hardly believe how little time the three of them had together.

One weekend—the last, as it turned out—they were all drowsing on the dock. The pond was smooth and cold beneath them. If waves had slapped up between the boards they would have iced their stomachs in stripes. Their few words hung like smoke in the still air. Jill murmured that her back was burning. Harriet said another cucumber sandwich would be nice.

Morgan got up quietly and stood on the warm dock. Harriet looked at her feet and thought, *You can't be going in again. Not into that cold water, after being so hot.* The feet stood still for a long time on the weather-silvered boards, as if making up their mind. Then they walked swiftly, softly off the dock onto land.

Jill was asleep, snoring in little sighs like a cat. Harriet pretended she was too, while watching Morgan through her lashes. Morgan circled the pond. Stopped on the far side, opposite the dock. *We only see you in the summer,* Harriet thought. *When your hair's almost white from the sun and your face is all freckles and your shoulders and thighs are such a smooth brown.*

As she stood there, Morgan raised one hand. Spoke. Harriet could see her mouth moving, but could not make out what she was saying.

Jill leaves after a week. They both know that being together is not so much about keeping Harriet company as keeping her from dealing with Ranald. In the cab on the way to Union Station, Harriet keeps wanting to say, *Morgan would be proud of us,* but is too afraid she might cry. On the platform beside the idling Hamilton bus, she and Jill hold each other close for a moment.

"We got old."

"No we didn't."

Later that day, when Harriet is stripping the sofa bed prior to moving her canvases back into what used to be Ranald's room, it occurs to her that her life is all wrong. Halvor was more a mother to Ranald than she ever was. Would be more of a help now. And if anyone was going to get breast cancer, surely it should have been her.

She thinks the wrongness may have started with what happened to Morgan, just months before she would have been packing for Juilliard. The absurdity of it. She and Jill should have been old at that funeral. Losing friends is what happens to old people.

Once she has bundled the sheets into the laundry hamper and collapsed the sofa bed, she stands for a minute looking around, thinking how nice the room is, all cleared and tidied. But then she sighs and starts carrying canvases two by two from her studio, where they have leaned against the wall during Jill's visit.

Morgan. Morgan's funeral. She searches her memory. No. Still nothing. She knows she was there. She just can't remember it. Can't even remember if *Jerusalem,* the hymn Morgan was singing while she watered the plants, was part of the service.

Remembering, Harriet has decided, is not like reading a book cover to cover or watching a film from lights down to credits. It's more like viewing a collage that keeps changing and rearranging its parts. A pale, tiny piece in the corner might suddenly shift to the centre and start to glow. A brand new colour will seep through from the back, where it always was, unseen till now. A defining shape will all at once be gone, leaving you wondering if it was ever there in the first place.

She can't remember getting the news of Morgan's death. She can't remember going on the train with Jill to Ottawa. Attending the funeral. (Open casket, according to Jill. Filled with spring flowers clustered close under Morgan's chin, as if she were hugging them to her.)

Her memory of the whole episode kicks in the morning after. She and Jill were eating an enormous breakfast in a B&B near the Byward Market. Spearing a piece of sausage, Harriet looked at Jill and said, "We never heard Morgan play!"

Even now, it's absurd. A piece of the collage that should have been discarded because it isn't right. Couldn't possibly fit. Morgan was studying late in the Carleton campus library. Her father was going to drive her home, and was waiting in the parking lot. When she was more than half an hour late, he got out of the car and went looking for her. He found her in the lane between the library and the arts complex. Her books were scattered, just out of reach of her outstretched hands. One was face up, pages turning slowly in the evening spring breeze.

Oh, stop it, Harriet hisses at herself as she stacks canvases in Ranald's old room. *You don't know any of those last details. Quit romanticizing.* But the facts are just too banal. Morgan had been seeing a man who worked on campus. They had quarrelled about her plans to attend Juilliard. The night of her death, he got drunk. Waited for her outside the library. Followed her into the lane. Claimed he had not even meant to hurt her, let alone—

There was a picture of him in the papers beside Morgan's picture. Curtis Maye. Thin. Dull eyes. Weak mouth. *This?* Harriet remembers thinking. *This* was the dark Pluto who took Morgan down?

That first semester back at school after Morgan died, Jill lost her virginity to a married English professor, breaking her heart for the first of many times. Harriet decided to transfer to the University of Toronto, where she would meet Halvor.

Patrick pays a visit. Sits on Harriet's couch and eats most of a plate of cookies she puts in front of him. No wonder he's gaining weight. She can't help staring at his jiggly chins, even as she listens to him describing how emaciated Ranald has become. The chemo is especially harsh, because the cancer is especially aggressive.

"Why couldn't they just take the lump out?"

"It wasn't that simple. The lump—it has a root system. So it would be like picking the bloom off a weed. They have to try to kill it. And it's fighting back. It wants to live, too." He starts to cry. A piece of cookie falls from his mouth. Harriet embraces him.

This is how it was for Jill that time in the closet, she thinks, trying to reach round Patrick's plumpness. *This is how useless she felt.*

She has it wrapped up in waxed paper. It is warm—something that surprises her. But of course, why shouldn't it be warm?

She has just put a pot of water on to boil and has come back into the dining room where Morgan sits at one end of the big pine table. The summer house hasn't changed. Neither has Morgan. But something isn't right. Harriet feels embarrassed, as if she's committing a faux pas and being forgiven.

She gets all brisk and bustling to cover up. Assures Morgan that once the thing is boiled and chopped up and mixed with lemon and capers and a bit of mayonnaise, it'll taste like chicken. She'll see. Just like chicken.

Morgan looks down at the plate and cutlery that have been put in front of her. Says something about not being able to stay long. Harriet senses—no, not disapproval. Pity. For her.

It won't take long, she assures Morgan too heartily. Not long at all. The water will be coming to a boil any second now.

She knows she is imposing on Morgan. Has no right to ask what she's asking. It is the wrong thing to do. But what is the right thing? She has to do something.

Back in the kitchen, she hears the waxed paper crackling. Unfolding to reveal the thing it contains. She looks. There is a

sort of nucleus. The lump, she supposes. Like a little pink brain.
A long dark hair trails out from one of the folds. She gives it a
tug, and the surrounding flesh winces. She'll leave it alone for
now. Once it's cooked—

The roots—more like tentacles—are groping for the edges
of the waxed paper. Trying to fold them back over. The thing is
trying to hide. It wants to live, too. Who said that?

Morgan has come into the kitchen and is trying to tell her
something. It's hard for her, because she is becoming transparent.
Going back to wherever she has been all these years. The stove,
Harriet, she is saying through disappearing lips. Something is
burning on the stove. The stove. The—

Harriet wakes up to the smell of hot metal. She has
sleepwalked into her kitchen. Has put an empty pot on a
burner and turned the heat up to High.

"May I ask you something?" One of the Aqua Fit women.
Chinese. About Harriet's age.

Harriet nods. She has just pulled on her bathing suit. It
sags on her now. She should get a new one.

"Have you been losing weight? I'm sorry. I hope you
don't mind. It's just that I'm a retired nurse and I know that
weight loss is not always a good thing."

"No, that's okay. I've been dieting. On purpose. So it is
a good thing."

She has been preparing her meals the same as always.
Then she has been dividing every item on her plate in half.
Once she's eaten half her meat, half her vegetables and half
her dinner roll, she has gone to the kitchen and scraped the
other half into the organics bin.

The first time, she thought, *There. That's yours.* It took
her a while to understand who—what—she was addressing.

Now she talks to it matter-of-factly. *Feed yourself. Take from me. Leave Ranald alone.*

"You do look like you've lost quite a bit," the Chinese woman is saying. Other women in the change room have started to listen in. One says that she noticed too, and was worried that Harriet might be sick.

"No. I'm fine. I'm not sick. Not me." She hesitates. Then, "It's my son. He's the one who's sick."

The other women come round. They stay and listen to her, past the time they should be in the pool, as she goes on and on. *My son. My husband. My son. My son-in-law. My son. My son.*

"Go ahead and laugh at my hat. I know you want to."

"No. No." She can't stop smiling, is all. "It's just, you would *never* wear a baseball cap. Not even when you were a little boy."

"Believe me, you don't want to see what's under it."

They are back in the Rendezvous. Ranald is managing to get down a cup of soup and a small glass of juice. His chemo was successful. He has just come from his first three-month checkup. The cancer is still gone.

Harriet is having the soup-and-sandwich combo. Looking forward to eating every bit of it. When she arrived carrying her damp Aqua Fit bag, Ranald greeted her with a critical once-over and said, "So it appears we've both been on diets."

He's different. Not just physically. She can't put her finger on it, and doesn't want to push things. She wonders if he's different with Patrick, too.

Outside the restaurant when they're done, she asks him if he wants her to accompany him home. He's walking with a cane these days.

"No. I'm fine." Then he takes her by the shoulders, stoops and says, "You look good with the weight off. But don't go and disappear on me." Looking with Halvor's eyes into her own.

When Ranald is told he only needs to come back for check-ups every six months, Patrick's parents host a celebration barbecue on their deck.

Ranald is still wearing the baseball cap and probably will until his hair has completely grown back. "They give you these at the clinic when you do your last chemo session," he says. "And everybody claps. Jesus. As if it's some kind of achievement."

"Well, it is." Steve, Patrick's father. Harriet likes him, for all she can tell he has never liked Ranald. He puts his hand on Ranald's shoulder and says, "Well done. Son."

Marion, Patrick's mother, starts to cry. *Right on cue,* Harriet thinks, hoping her eye-roll went unnoticed. Marion is a quintessential my-my woman. When Patrick embraces his mother, Harriet slips away before she can be pulled into a group hug.

Unseen, she steps down off the deck into the shadows of the cedar trees. She goes to the back of the yard, past the koi pond, and stands where there is no light, where they can't see her, but she can see them. There's something she needs to do. Because there's something she's finally figured out.

She stands in the dark and looks at each person on the deck in turn. Raises one hand, exactly the way Morgan did. Says what she now knows Morgan was saying.

Cyclist and Crow, 1981.

In the Crow's Keeping

CLARISSA KNOWS SHE SHOULD THROW it all away. Just get rid of the stuff. After all, where is it going to go, once she's gone? She doubts even Morgan, had she lived, would have taken it. Ramsay's been dead five years, and she herself is ninety. So where will it all end up, when somebody gets stuck with having to clear out her apartment? Flea markets? Junk shops? Sidewalk sales? Strangers pouring over photographs of her daughter, her husband, herself. Saying *Who were these people,* and, *Look at the funny hats.* Landfill, more like. Well. Doesn't everything become landfill, eventually? Even people?

So she has to do it. This damned restlessness that's been plaguing her lately. Hard to be restless at ninety. There is a window of energy—just a few hours—that opens for her in the morning. If she has errands or tasks to do, she has to get them all done before that window closes.

When she was young, she thought old age would involve sitting serenely in a chair and watching a film of her own life as it looped round and round in her memory. Ha. A chair does not exist that will accommodate her joints comfortably for much more than half an hour. And living means moving. *Inability to move* was one item in a list of indications of death that appeared in her Biology 110 text-book all those years ago. Its obviousness made her laugh out loud.

All right. If she's going to start weeding her possessions, if that's what this is about, she'll start with Morgan's effects. The photographs. The certificates and prizes. Even the diaries. Well. Maybe she'll reread the diaries, one by one. But then she will dispose of them, one by one, as she finishes.

Five years ago, when Ramsay died, she discontinued the annual visits to Morgan's grave. She was eighty-five and the four-hour train trip to Ottawa had become impossible. The last time, she actually flew from Toronto, but even that almost did her in. The standing in line, the fuss over security, all for a flight of less than an hour. Then getting a cab to the hotel. Checking in. Unpacking. And then, when she was so exhausted she just wanted to crawl into bed and sleep through till her morning flight home, the trip to the graveyard.

She and Ramsay started meeting up for their annual vigil in 1975—two years after their daughter's death. It was his idea. Clarissa had begun divorce proceedings by then, and had moved to Toronto. Taken a small apartment she could afford while finally finishing the degree in biology and zoology she had started as a young, single woman. Ramsay's letter was one of the first pieces of mail she received at her new address.

She sighed when she saw his handwriting on the envelope. She half expected the first line to read, *Clarissa, there's a spider in the bathtub.* Their old running joke about why she must never leave him.

It still interests her that her first published book would have been one her ex-husband would not read. Could not read, in fact. Could not even pick up and thumb through, for fear of encountering any of the drawings or photographs it contained. His fear of spiders was so profound that he claimed to dislike seeing the word *spider* printed on a page or hearing it spoken, and could not tolerate calamari, crab, lobster, or anything else remotely spidery on his plate unless it had been rendered unrecognizable.

Still, Clarissa doesn't think her choice of topic had anything consciously to do with Ramsay. It was certainly not a gesture of meanness or revenge. From girlhood, long before she met her future husband, she had been fascinated by spiders—their grace and speed and creativity. Their ability to spin or dig a home, to trap, hunt, and even fish for their food. And their almost complete independence.

There. All right, maybe her choice of topic did have something to do with Ramsay. Leaving Ramsay. She had planned to wait till Morgan was through university. But the girl's death pulled the two of them—their bodies, at least—back together for a time. After years of a celibate marriage, she lay beneath Ramsay night after night while he pumped away, sometimes dropping tears on her forehead. It would have been cruel to refuse him. Even once he had stopped reaching for her in bed, there was the issue of how he would deal with spiders once she was gone. This was the story she told herself to explain her persisting inertia. Absurd as it was, it made sense.

"You do know that a spider is a clean and necessary creature of God, don't you?" Clarissa said to him once early in their marriage, when he was momentarily paralyzed because an occupied web stretched across one corner of a doorway. The look he gave her was so bruised that she resolved, as she swiped the creature into her cupped hands and carried it outside, never to say such a thing again.

The letter that arrived shortly after she moved to Toronto did not in fact begin with their old joke. Instead, it simply suggested an annual reunion in the graveyard where Morgan was buried. And so began a tradition spanning over forty years.

Ramsay would always be there ahead of her, sitting on the bench across from Morgan's headstone. Some years, it would be pouring rain. Others, there would still be snow on the ground. April, the month of their daughter's birth and death, was so unpredictable. Clarissa would sit down beside Ramsay and take his hand. Even the first time, when anger at her defection came off him like a smell and they sat without speaking, she did that much.

The following year, the fourth since Morgan's death, Ramsay breached the silence. He told Clarissa that when she first left him, he would wake up every morning trapped inside his combined anger and grief. He would spend the whole day inside it, as if inside a bubble. But in time, he started waking up by its side, as if it were in bed with him. It would dog him through his day, a constant presence. Now, however, it does not even do that much. Instead, he will come across it at random, when some sight or sound causes him to remember that his wife is gone and his daughter is dead.

Clarissa was so astonished at how close his experience was to her own that all she could do was squeeze his hand. It was like one of those moments in their courtship, years ago, when they discovered some small or big thing they had in common, and took it as a sign.

After that, they started greeting each other every year with smiles. In time, small talk felt natural. Queries as to each other's health and happiness. Was he as surprised as she was when happiness once again became possible?

In the last decade, they began going out for dinner together after their yearly vigil. A little bistro in the Byward

Market that they both liked. She would sit across from this shrunken, white-haired man she had slept beside for twenty-two years of her life, this man she had kissed and bitten and confided in and pummelled and screamed at, and feel nothing more than a slightly bored fondness. Each year she would look forward to their dinner. Then, not quite half way through it, she would start looking forward to its being over.

She did not attend Ramsay's funeral. It was held at Christ Church Cathedral in Ottawa, where he had been dean until Morgan died. There was a short article about it on the back page of the front section of the *Toronto Star*. Some of Ramsay's old church colleagues were there. A few from his CBC days, too. One or two minor politicians who had been fans of his show in the 1980s. Ramsay collected colleagues and fans. He did not have friends. And like her, he never remarried. She even retained the title *Mrs.*—perhaps out of some perversity, more likely because she could not abide the sound of *Ms.*

The news of his death gave her, yes she admits it, a pang. She would not call it grief. It was more a kind of pity. There was relief, too. Ramsay would be buried beside Morgan. And that somehow assured her she would never have to make that graveyard pilgrimage again.

Ramsay bought his own burial plot a year after Morgan was killed. He came home and informed her, coldly, that he had made the purchase. An identical plot was available on the other side of Morgan's grave. Should he purchase it for her?

That was when she knew it was time to go. Spiders be damned.

She has donated her own body to science. She's been told that once a cadaver has been used up, has taught all it possibly can to the ones doing the slicing and sawing and peeling and excavating, it is given some kind of respectful, vaguely spiritual send-off before being incinerated. She wonders if that's true. She doesn't really care.

She'll start with the pitching and tossing tomorrow. Morgan's diaries first, since they'll be the most difficult to deal with. It's too late to start in today.

March 6, 1963

I am so disgusted with myself. Not even a teenager yet—a month still to go—and already I've sold my soul. For a baby grand. Baby. Why couldn't he just have made it a grand piano? Still, it is a step up from the old upright I've been plunking away on.

In return for it, I will be confirmed this Easter. I will kneel down in front of the bishop, feel his hand (with its dirty fingernails!) on my head and listen to him praying for me to a God I don't believe in. At least, I'm pretty sure I don't. I should wear a sign on my back: I AM DOING THIS FOR A NEW PIANO. NO OTHER REASON. I'm not the only one in the confirmation class who's being bribed, either. Michael's getting a canoe. The twins are going to Europe in the summer. And Philippa—I still can't believe this—Philippa is getting a nose job.

When I was still fighting with Daddy, before he dropped the hint about the baby grand, Mummy took me aside and said, "Just think of being confirmed as a kindness to your father, Grace. Imagine how it will look in the eyes of his bishop. And do it out of kindness." Which of course made me feel like a complete brat. Peace in the family. That's what Mummy lives for. Keeping the peace, no matter what.

Honestly, does she even know it's 1963? Can't she see what Jackie Kennedy is wearing on every cover of every magazine in the house? Sunday morning after Sunday morning, I watch her putting her hat on in front of the mirror. Her flowered hat. Which she slides back then pushes forward so a couple of her poodle-permed curls can poke out from under the brim. Then she puts her purse over her arm, exactly like the Queen.

At least she's stopped making me wear a hat. But she won't even try to remember to call me Morgan. How many times have I told her and Daddy that I am going by my middle name now? If they would just look at me, they would see a Morgan. Grace is not me. Grace is all frilly and ladylike. Grace would not need to be bribed with a baby grand. Grace would have no trouble believing the garbage they teach us in confirmation class.

Grace would not have had the thoughts I did, last Thursday when I arrived early at the church after school and saw Daddy kneeling in the lady chapel. He was in his alb—no stole or robe—and had his back to me. I had the strangest feeling he knew that I—or just somebody—was there. Seeing him in his simple white alb, on his knees in the lady chapel. The Reverend Dean Doctor Ramsay Pettingill. At prayer.

Grace would never have thought that.

Grace would never have said what I came out with at supper last night either, about the bishop's nose hairs. About how last week, when he dropped in on our confirmation class, one of them—it was black and greasy-looking—was actually curling up the side of his nostril. And he has tufts of hair coming out of his ears, too.

Daddy cleared his throat the way he does when he's hearing something he'd rather not hear while eating. So

Mummy, typically, said that the poor man was a widower, and was just showing signs of needing a wife again. So I said, "Oh really? Is that a wife's duty? To clip hair out of her husband's orifices?" So Daddy said, "Grace, leave the table!" and I screamed back, "My name is Morgan!"

So now I don't know who I'm maddest at. Daddy. Mummy. Or myself. Morgan. Grace. Morgan. Grace. Morgan.

Clarissa has read that passage before, more than once. Now, for the first time, it makes her laugh.

It was a mistake, all those years ago, to read the diaries just six months after Morgan's death. As soon as she started, she knew it was a mistake but kept on anyway. The pain of it was fresh and sharp. She actually welcomed it, in the perverse way she imagined people who slash themselves welcome the sear of the blade.

That first time through the diaries, the description of Ramsay posing in prayer gave her a stab of nasty delight. The girl had put her finger on something, no doubt about it. But the business about herself smoothing her flowered hat over her poodle curls filled her with pointless regret. What if she had defied convention, thumbed her nose at the congregation with its notions of how a priest's wife should dress, and tried to follow Jackie Kennedy's example? Dared to appear on Sunday mornings in a sleek Chanel suit and smooth bouffant, topped by a plain little pillbox? Would Morgan have been less contemptuous of her? Less rebellious as a teenager? Less inclined, later, to fall into the arms of the man who killed her?

Ridiculous notion. But forgivable, as she can see now.

When she did her second read-through of the diaries—some time in the late '80s it would have been—the put-down of Ramsay and the flowered hat and poodle perm passage made her angry. Then guilty, for being angry with her poor dead girl. It wasn't Morgan's fault that she had lived long enough to discern her parents' shortcomings, but not long enough to forgive them. Still, had she ever at least suspected there might be more to her mother than a clergy wife adjusting her hat in the mirror on Sunday morning?

As a child, Clarissa would ask the adults around her, "What are you thinking?" Then be so disappointed by the banality of the replies. *I'm wondering where I put my glasses. I'm thinking a cup of tea would be nice.* She couldn't believe that was all there was to being a grown-up. She began to wonder if the banality was not in fact a baffle. Maybe growing up, for many people, was a process of gathering their more interesting thoughts and questions, a good part of their imagination, and almost all of their curiosity, then packing it into boxes, putting the boxes inside a closet at the back of their mind, and locking the closet door. Finally, in many cases, forgetting where they put the key.

This early hunch, that appearances were essentially disguises, drove her later writing. She chose as her topics creatures nobody wanted to look at and really see—spiders, bats, crows, octopuses. And she always started a book by saying to herself, *Imagine if this creature—tentacled, eight-legged, fanged, winged, whatever—were every bit as intellectually sophisticated and nuanced as I am, albeit in such a different way that I just can't see it yet.*

Ramsay Pettingill, when she met him, gave the impression of being an adult with the mind of a brilliant child. There would have been no packing up of his imagination and curiosity into boxes in a closet, she believed, and no losing the key. She never even had to ask him what he was thinking because he was forever telling her. *I'm thinking about the author of 'The Cloud of Unknowing.' Wondering why he remained anonymous. Was it humility or fear?* In Ramsay, she sometimes felt she had discovered a new species. A creature subtle and inexhaustible. Worthy of a lifetime's study.

She was two years married and three months pregnant before she finally admitted to herself that he did not see her this way. That her curiosity about him was not reciprocated.

Clarissa closes the 1963 diary. It is the first of ten. Morgan started keeping them when she was twelve, after reading the diary of Anne Frank. She wrote sporadically, recording the highs and lows of her teens and early twenties. And she began a fresh new volume every first of January, even if the previous year's was only half filled.

It is unreasonable, Clarissa decides, to set herself the task of rereading the entire set. This morning's single passage from 1963, with its associated memories, has exhausted her. Her narrow window of energy is closing for the day. Soon it will be time to fix her lunch, then follow that with a nap. Then the long slope of afternoon into evening, with its dipping into library books and television.

Library books. Almost time to return her latest batch. The weekly trip to the library has become something of an epic journey, but one she relishes. She doesn't even mind being addressed as *Miss Pettingill* by the increasingly younger staff. She stopped correcting them years ago, having decided that a perceived sexlessness, as if she had never been married and a mother, was part of old womanhood.

She still restricts herself to three books. A murder mystery, a biography, and a natural history. Now that she's using a wheeled walker—marvellous contraption, with its double basket, fold-down seat and handbrakes—she could allow herself more than three. But she established the three-book habit in her eighties, when, with her purse strapped over one shoulder, her book bag over the other, criss-crossed like a tin soldier and more or less balanced, she would cane-tap the two blocks to her local branch. Three books was what she could carry, and three books what she could get through in a week. What she can still get through.

She will not reopen the 1963 diary. Having sampled that year of her daughter's life, she will move on. Yes. Just a taste of each volume, then—

She drops the diary into a plastic bag and carries it down the hall to the garbage room, clutching the wooden rail jutting from the wall. She consults the posted chart as to how to dispose of books. Recycle. She pushes the appropriate button. Opens the chute. Closes it again.

All the way back down the hall, as she half drags herself along, still clutching the bag with the diary in it, she berates herself. *You've buried a daughter and left a husband. Surely you can do this.*

Apparently not.

July 10, 1968

Up at Lost Lake for three weeks. Stuck here without a piano, just when the Rachmaninoff is—literally—within reach. My hands are opening. They will manage to span those chords. But only if I practice, practice, practice. Not if I rest, as Mummy keeps insisting I do, or if I seek balance, as Daddy goes on about. What does achievement, or yes, I will say it—genius—have to do with rest and balance?

For some time now, I've had the feeling they're both jealous of me for being poised on the brink of such a brilliant future. Just one more year of high school. Then McGill. Then Juilliard. I will insist on McGill. I will not go to Carleton on the bus every day and come home every night like a good girl. It's bad enough not being allowed to go straight to New York. Having to waste four years getting a BA here first. I am old enough, damn it. No matter what Daddy says.

Even so, there's going to be a battle royal when I apply for McGill. It has already begun, in fact. Last April, on my seventeenth, when I came in from school, Mummy and Daddy were both waiting for me. Nothing suspicious about that. Daddy always comes home early from the church on my birthday. But then Mummy said, "Morgan, would you come with us into the music room?" And there it was. A Steinway Grand. Just dwarfing the place. I actually cried. I still can't forgive myself for that. Felt like such a dork. Then, after I had thanked and hugged them to death, I sat them down together on the loveseat while I played the Rachmaninoff. Not perfectly. A few of the chords were still out of reach. Still, the tears seemed to have opened something in me, so my playing was bigger and more passionate than it had ever been.

But then, when I had finished and spun around on the stool to face them, I saw—What? I swear, I had the feeling that I had hurt them. My playing had hurt them. Somehow. I don't know. They looked older. And smaller. And scared.

I think they're afraid of their own future. They see me poised to take flight, while they're stuck. They've been burrowing through their lives, deeper and deeper, in one direction. And now they realize they should have been going another way, but—

Is that why they're trying to keep me on the ground? I will not burrow. I will fly.

First the Steinway Grand. And now the way they're renovating the rec room—putting in a bathroom and a kitchenette. Even a private entrance out the back. They call it my apartment and claim it's to give me more independence. But I know a dungeon when I see one.

Meanwhile, I'm stuck at Lost Lake for three weeks. Though if I'm honest, I will admit that I love the place. The big old summer house that's come down through Mummy's family. Everything kind of creaky and stained with age. The old-fashioned kitchen. The pond out back. The lake, with its view of the bluffs. I would never admit this to anyone, but sometimes it all makes me wish I could forget about the piano for a while, and just be.

I came close yesterday, when I went out on my bike. I was pedalling along the path beside the meadow. All at once a crow was flying right beside me. He was following me. Or racing me. Anyway, we were together. Communing with each other.

I did a foolish thing. But it felt so necessary. For the longest time, until it flew up and away into a tree, I took my eyes off the path and fixed them on the crow. I did not look where I was going. I trusted the crow to guide me. I gave myself to the crow. I put my life in the crow's keeping.

Clarissa closes the 1968 diary. Doesn't even think about bagging it for the chute in the garbage room. No, whatever this needing and seeking are about, it is not about getting rid of things. This is the sixth volume she has dipped into. That phrase of Morgan's—*in the crow's keeping*—became the title of her third book. Her favourite, for all it proved to be the least successful.

Just now, when the 1968 volume fell open in her hands to that particular entry, her courage almost failed her. She wanted to close the diary and try again for an easier passage. But no. This one, which the first time through caused her to throw her head back and howl, would be the one she would reread now.

Hubris. Oh, yes. The three of them. Morgan with the forgivable hubris of youth. At that age, one *must* believe that everything is within one's reach, and despise the old for losing faith. Herself and Ramsay too, with their ridiculous conviction that they could contain their child and keep her safe. The irony is that they did manage to persuade Morgan to stay home and go to Carleton instead of McGill. After all, they coaxed, she would likely be off to New York soon enough, wouldn't she? To try out her wings?

In the crow's keeping.

Morgan was so very much alive. Did that make her death harder for her? At the time, Clarissa and Ramsay were assured that the crushing of her windpipe would likely have killed their daughter almost instantly. Though she tried to believe that, Clarissa had enough grasp of biology to know better. The body, the mind—it is just too intricate a machine to turn off in a second, like a lightbulb when a switch is flipped. And even a lightbulb has its afterglow.

She can only hope that Morgan lost consciousness immediately. Or if not, that she had one of those light-at-the-end-of-the-tunnel visions of an apparent afterlife that Ramsay threw himself into researching. A few years after Morgan was gone, he began interviewing people who had had near-death experiences. He drew some highly unscientific conclusions about the phenomenon and published them in a book that became a pop-science hit.

He had left the priesthood by then, and managed to work his crisis of faith into every interview the book garnered. It all added up to a CBC educational TV show in the 1980s called *What If.* As host, Ramsay welcomed experts on ESP, UFOs, crop circles, ghosts, and other paranormal phenomena. He began each show by asking his guest, "Do you have a question for me today?" The guest would respond—liturgically, Clarissa could not help thinking—"Yes, Ramsay, I do. What if the pyramids were in fact built by visiting extraterrestrials?" Ramsay's job was to play devil's advocate, voicing the doubts that would be going through a viewer's mind. But he did it with a twinkle, making it clear to his guest and the audience that he at least wanted to believe in whatever popular theory was being paraded that week.

Clarissa used to occasionally turn the show on. She and Ramsay were chatting by then during their annual graveside vigils, and he seemed to want her approval of his new career. Once, he confided to her that he only felt truly alive when the TV make-up was itching his neck and the studio lights warming his forehead.

Poor Ramsay. Though his show purported to probe mysterious depths, it was in fact such shallow junk. Early in their marriage, she concluded that what had drawn Ramsay to the priesthood were the splendid robes and the opportunity to chant ancient verses and elevate the host for all to see. His professional persona—benign, urbane—rested as lightly on him as his stole. If anyone ever came to him with a real problem, he was able to muster sixty minutes of apparent compassion, some sensible enough advice, and an appropriate prayer.

She never told him any of that, not even when she was trying to explain why she was leaving him. The truth was that she still loved Ramsay, but could no longer pretend to be part of the *one flesh* they had been deemed on their wedding day. Besides, she was willing to admit she might be wrong about his vocation. Who was she to say why anyone did anything?

Nor was it easy for him to leave the church. At first, Morgan's murder made him pull his priestly robes more tightly round himself. He recounted, in the introduction to his book about near-death experiences, how he actually approached his bishop for permission to conduct her funeral. (*I baptised her. In time, I would have performed her wedding.*) The bishop (*wisely, I now concede*) managed to dissuade him.

Clarissa concluded privately that Ramsay left the priesthood because it was threatening to get real. To reveal itself as a real something, or a real nothing. Either way, he did not want to be there for the revelation. He found his niche in television. Once more, he was being watched and admired. Once more, after sixty minutes, he could leave it all behind.

Why on earth had she married him? They were such opposites. Unlike Ramsay, Clarissa resented the spotlight that publication trained on her. She loved writing her books, delighted in the research that preceded writing them, would all but live at the library, seeking out references to her subject—ravens, for instance—in works of literature, philosophy, folklore, the Bible and other mythologies. First and foremost, though, she would ground her work in provable facts gleaned from experts—marine biologists, arachnologists, ornithologists. Her books, for all their scholarly discipline, were engaging and layman-friendly.

With the exception of *In the Crow's Keeping,* they sold better than books of natural science generally did. That alone would have been enough for her—just knowing that people were buying or borrowing her works and reading them with silent pleasure. But publication brought with it a degree of attention she could hardly stand. *What are you all doing here?* she would wonder at a group of people assembled to hear her read. And afterwards, as they lined up to get her autograph, she would want to say, *Oh, for God's sake. It's just a scribble. I could be anyone.*

She is not sure why her book about crows fell flat. Perhaps the topic lacked what the critics called the *ick*-factor, which had buoyed her other works. People might not like crows, with their drab plumage and squawking cry, but they didn't shudder at the thought of them. Or maybe the book simply appeared too soon after the one about bats, which did take off.

Echo Life came out in the early 1990s, concurrent with a glut of vampire novels and movies. For a short time Clarissa became the focus of radio interviewers and TV talk show hosts who wanted to add a pinch of science to their programs. Once, under hot studio lights, she found herself seated beside a vampirologist. Such people were actually being invited by accredited universities to teach courses in what they called their discipline. This one, in full gothic costume and makeup, argued vehemently for the existence of human vampires, then went on to plump for their rights as a marginalized community.

When it was Clarissa's turn to talk, she began by saying she did not know what she was doing there. Only three out of dozens of species of bat in fact sucked blood for a living. The rest ate fruit and insects and so on—not unlike birds. As for

the existence of the likes of Dracula, well, did her esteemed colleague also believe in Sasquatch and Nessie and the Windigo?
If not, why not? Did these creatures not also deserve our
respect and support? Perhaps, even, the right to vote?

Her next book, about ravens, crows, and other cor-
vids, did not do well. For a few years before she got started
on *Octopus Heart,* Clarissa was at loose ends. She read
Morgan's diaries for the second time. And she would sometimes indulge an odd fantasy of sneaking onto Ramsay's
TV show. Just imagine the look on his face as the spotlight
hit the interviewee's chair and—it was her! Unexpected.
Unscripted. His ex-wife. The mother of his dead child.

She would follow the format. Even if Ramsay sat there
in shock, failing to introduce her or to ask the ritual, "Do
you have a question for me today?" she would still say to
him, "What if Morgan had not been killed?"

Impossible, of course. There was no way that she could
pull it off. CBC's security was tight, and she knew no one on
the inside who would risk their job to get her into that spotlit
chair. Impossible morally, too. Indefensibly cruel thing to do
to Ramsay. So why did she keep imagining it? What was she
hoping to accomplish? What would it get her?

Focus, perhaps? The way he paid attention to his *What
If* guests, never looking away from them, barely blinking.
And the sense of intimacy he achieved, as if the two of them
were making love instead of speculating that what we think
of as ghosts might actually be evidence that time is not lin-
ear, that the past and future are instead concurrent with the
present. She never got even the appearance of such interest
from him.

She went straight from her girlhood bed to Ramsay's.
He punctured her on their wedding night. That's how it

felt—push, push, then *stab*. It made her think of the word *compunction*. Once she was home from her honeymoon, she looked the word up. *To prick severely* was the first definition. *Remorse for wrongdoing* was the second. It was her first inkling that her marriage might have been a mistake.

But something good did come of it all. Morgan. That's what she told herself through the dry years, the years of silent contempt. *We had Morgan together.*

Clarissa remembers sitting beside her virtually estranged husband on the loveseat in the music room that day in 1968, listening to Morgan play the Rachmaninoff for them on her new Steinway grand. Though of course, Morgan was not playing for them. Morgan never played for anyone but herself.

What the girl would have seen on her mother's face that day when she finished the piece and spun round on the piano stool was indeed fear. Clarissa had just realized how close she was to extinction. Her husband had not touched her in years. His affairs were discreet enough. He would never do anything that might impede his chosen path to the bishopric. But she knew the other women existed, perhaps even glancing her way on Sunday mornings with eyes full of smug pity. She still wore a hat to church, for God's sake. When she looked around, the only other hatted women were the elderly widows.

She knew, that day, as she listened to her daughter play, that she was dwindling. Less and less noticed. In time, transparent. In a little more time, not there at all.

Once she has finished with the 1968 diary, Clarissa goes out to buy meat. She cannot transport a full load of groceries home all at once, not even with the aid of her walker, so she compartmentalizes. Monday, enough meat, fish, and cheese for the week. Wednesday, fruit and vegetables. Friday, bread, cereal, crackers, and so on. Though she eats less, she is still blessed with appetite and the ability to cook for herself. Her horror of *assisted living* has largely to do with the very thing the pamphlets play up—*our well-appointed dining room and varied cuisine.* She especially likes to grill a bit of chicken or beef for her supper. She is contemptuous of vegetarians, considers them elitist. A good part of the world's population would sell its soul for a scrap of meat to eat. She also considers them morally naïve, the way they go on about the cruelty of slaughterhouses. Have they no grasp of the immense, pervasive cruelty of nature, the way a raptor lifts a shrieking baby rabbit into the air, for example, then feeds it, still living, to its young? Has it never occurred to them that they are not in fact at the top of the food chain, but somewhere in the middle? That all kinds of creatures would happily have their attached and quivering entrails for lunch?

Clarissa stops for breath half way to the grocery store. She sets the handbrakes on her walker, pulls down the seat, and sits. As she looks around, she spots yet another change in the neighbourhood. What for decades was the Melville Staines Funeral Home is now something called *Valé.* She stands up, gets her walker rolling, and approaches the front entrance. After reading the brief description on the plaque beside the door, she turns the knob and goes in.

The place smells of eucalyptus. The walls are done in pale shades of ochre and sage, and there is music of a sort playing—an all but tuneless humming. A woman of about forty rises from a chair behind a desk. "Hello," she says. "I'm Felicity Staines. May I ask what brings you to *Valé?*"

"Nosiness." Clarissa leans on her walker, declining the offer of a chair. "This place used to be a funeral parlour. What happened?"

"We still do offer funeral services," Felicity Staines says. Her voice is pitched to such a soothing tone that Clarissa can barely hear it. Her hair is uniformly gray, pulled back smoothly into a chignon. She wears a cream-coloured robe that reaches the floor. "However, in our new incarnation as *Valé*, we have begun to move forward, heeding the wisdom of recent legislation and anticipating our clients' additional future needs."

It takes Clarissa a minute. "Are you talking about assisted suicide? Isn't that already on the books?"

"It is and it isn't, Ms …?"

"Pettingill. Mrs."

"Mrs. Pettingill. The present situation is legally very restrictive and, we believe, depressingly clinical. The peaceful, painless, even joyful culmination we plan to offer our clients, entirely on their terms and only when the time is right for them, remains a vision. However, we are compiling a waiting list, and it is our hope that, as legislation evolves—"

"Why the accent?"

"I'm sorry?"

"Why the acute accent on the *e* of *Valé?* Doesn't any-body actually get that it's Latin for farewell? Or do they think it's about the valley of the shadow? Or departing this vale of tears, maybe? Sorry. I'm a writer. Words interest me."

Felicity Staines smiles. "May I give you some literature to take away, Mrs. Pettingill? I would love to talk to you about our mission. Unfortunately, I have a funeral to over-see in just a few minutes. Please feel free to call or drop in at any time."

Once home with her meat, Clarissa has a read of the folder she took away from *Valé*. It begins by complimenting her for doing just that—for having the wisdom to look ahead and realize that the independent and active life she enjoys now may well become significantly less so, with the passage of time. It goes on to drop little verbal bombs—*Disabled. Disoriented. Dependent. Burden.* ("You left out *incontinent*," Clarissa mutters at this point.) Ah, but there is a way to avoid all that unpleasantness. And that is where *Valé* comes in.

It seems a client can indeed sign up for services that have yet to be legalized. But once it is within the law to let the *Valé* people kill them, they'll be able to choose their day, then check into the place as they would into a luxury hotel. There, they will enjoy spa services, excellent cuisine, films of their choice—the list goes on. Of course, before they start in on all that, they will have had a painless, almost undetectable chemical patch fitted someplace on their person that will, over the next twelve hours, release sufficient endorphins that by the time the needle enters their skin they will greet it as they would an old friend.

"Drugged to the gills, in other words," Clarissa thinks. She goes to recycle the folder. Hesitates. Puts it instead into the mail caddy beside the phone.

April 6, 1973

Curtis wants me to marry him. Actually, after last night he might never want to see me again. But he did ask. We were in bed at his place and he laid it all out. Our entire future, as Mr. and Mrs. Curtis Maye. The house. The kids. And—this is the part I could hardly believe I was hearing—how if I wanted to, once the kids were in school, I could give piano lessons!

I really think I tried to be respectful. I did not conde-scend. So I don't think he was justified in losing his cool the way he did and saying the things he did. The facts are just the facts, as I tried to explain. Again. In September I will be in New York, fighting every minute to keep my place in the most prestigious music school in the world. After that, if all goes according to plan—my plan, that is—I will be travelling and performing. That is the life I want.

Besides—okay, this is maybe when I took it a step too far. But that fruity smell was coming off him, and he had that glassy-eyed look he gets when he's had one too many.

He didn't want to hear anything I had to say, though, especially about his drinking. He got out of bed and yanked his clothes on—just about put his foot through his jeans—all the while going on about the snot-nosed attitude people like me have toward people like him. And how I was going to be a very lonely person some day. Then he said he was going out and that he wanted me gone by the time he got back.

I've never been thrown out of anywhere. I felt so ashamed, the whole time I was getting dressed, even though I knew I was right. I stayed for a while, just in case he might turn around and come back in and we could maybe make up. At least not leave things like this.

I had always known it wasn't going to last between us, and I thought he did too. No. I'm lying. I knew from the first that he wanted more of me than I did of him. And that's why I feel—well, it must be compunction. The thing Daddy goes on about during Lent, even though I doubt he's ever felt it in his life.

I can't believe I just wrote that. Maybe the things Curtis said are right. Maybe I am cold and unnatural. Maybe I do use people. Maybe I will be very lonely someday.

But I've always been lonely. Even though I've always been surrounded by admirers, starting with Mummy and Daddy, I've always been essentially alone. The only time I feel really connected, really a part of anything else, is when I'm playing the piano.

And yet. I did say yes to sex with Curtis. I'd said no to so many other guys—some of them brilliant. Artistic. Then along came Curtis. Older than me. Rough around the edges. A guy who did a general BA then took the first campus admin job he applied for. On our first date, when I tried to describe what playing the piano did for me, he barked a laugh and said it sounded like what a couple of scotches did for him.

Still, there was something cozy about him. Comfortable. I felt as If I could show him sides of myself I'd never shown anyone else—not even Mummy and Daddy. Especially not them.

Maybe that's what this is all about. I am just so sick of being Mummy and Daddy's little girl. Living at home for four years when I could have been—should have been—in New York.

Am I punishing them? Hoping they somehow find out about Curtis? Sometimes I imagine the looks on their faces and feel the most appalling glee.

Oh, Mummy and Daddy. I have a suspicion they're going to break up once I leave for New York. And I think Mummy will actually make the first move. And that just blows my mind.

But Mummy has changed. There's something about her now—I don't know—it's as if after years of quietly drowning, she's fighting to get to the surface. She's sharp with Daddy now in a way she never was before. And she's actually arguing with him about female ordination. Daddy, as always, is opposed. He lays out the same old ridiculous arguments against it in the same infuriatingly calm way he's always done. But Mummy, for once, is not even pretending to support him in public.

Sometimes I think I should stay home and try to keep those two together. And I have to admit that, for just a moment, I was almost seduced by the comfy domestic scene Curtis was painting for the two of us. It would be so easy.

The diary ends there. A week later, Morgan was dead.

Clarissa closes that final volume. Puts it back with the others. Then goes searching for a certain book on her shelves. There it is. *Suffering Fools*, by Phoebe Stang.

She weeds her bookshelves every five years or so. Each time, this particular book has stopped her in her tracks. Not because she thinks she ever will reread it. She could barely get through it the first time, decades ago, when her book club chose it for discussion. She suspects that if she were to restart it now, or even if it were to fall open in her hand—

It falls open in her hand. What she sees is the epigraph that begins the chapter on wives: *"Pity the wife, whose life is not doubled but halved. Envy the widow, at last free of the cleaver."*

Phoebe Stang published the book in 1972, then, to Clarissa's knowledge, never published again. *Suffering Fools* was one of those incendiary works that light everything up for a brief time before burning out. It attacked traditional women, calling them masochistic idiots. Psychological and sexual slaves of men. Accused them of having no self-respect. In the face of global overpopulation, Stang called upon women to seal themselves off. To reclaim their virgin autonomy. *"This is not about revenge,"* Stang wrote. *"Revenge is petty. Small. You, Woman, are neither. It is about the achievement of self. Medea compromised her autonomy with Jason. Those children were collateral damage. When Jason left her, she caught a glimpse of the freedom she had given up. Getting rid of the children was no more or less than a case of widening the view."*

This was the very passage Clarissa had been reading, that night in 1973, while she waited for Ramsay to come home with Morgan. Whenever the girl studied late in the campus library, as she was doing that night, her father insisted on waiting for her in the parking lot and driving her home. There had been the usual fight about that, but Morgan had finally acquiesced. It was likely a small concession on her part, given that she knew by then she had been accepted by Juilliard and would be on her own in New York in just a few months. Clarissa remembers being nervous while she waited. She had decided to tell Ramsay, that night, that she was leaving him. Even if Morgan overheard, it would be better than prolonging this hypocritical farce of a marriage.

At the inquest—there was no trial, for Curtis Maye pleaded guilty—it came out that the man had been drinking heavily when he confronted Morgan outside the library. She rebuffed him, but he followed her into a laneway and, in his own words, "tried to shake some sense into her." The shaking became choking. When he realized he had gone too far, he panicked and ran.

Clarissa never resented Ramsay's being the one to hold their daughter as she finished dying. When Morgan failed to show, he had gotten out of his car to go and look for her. He told Clarissa that as he held her he looked into her dimming eyes, not letting himself blink, all the while murmuring, "I see you. I see you." Clarissa did, deeply and terribly, resent the fact of that death—the wrongness and absurdity of their child leaving life before they did. But after a year or so, when her grief was less of an open wound though not yet the aching scar it would become, she saw a degree of rightness and balance in the father witnessing the mystery of death. After all, she, the mother, had experienced in her body the mysteries of conception, gestation, and birth.

That night, as Clarissa waited for her family to come home, she heard a knock. She put her copy of *Suffering Fools* down and opened the door. Two police officers were on the porch. Between them was an old man, barely able to stand. He looked like Ramsay.

Once she has gone through Morgan's scrapbooks, report cards, and diplomas, again putting each item back where it was, Clarissa feels at loose ends. That restlessness, the nagging conviction that there is something she should be doing, some project she should take on—her age notwithstanding—will not let her alone. On a whim, as a distraction, she takes herself out to dinner. She can still do that, once a month or so, as her wallet and digestion allow.

In the Rendezvous, she is led to a dark table near the washrooms. "Why are you putting me here?" she asks the young hostess. "I'd rather sit near the window." The place is not even half full.

"Oh! Well, I thought—" The girl is flustered. Clarissa, leaning on her walker, does not blink. The girl stumbles on. "I thought this would be—maybe—more comfortable? For you?"

"I walked two blocks to get here. I am capable of crossing a room, should the need arise."

She gets her window seat. Studies the menu. When the waiter arrives, he says, "And what can I get for you, young lady?"

"I beg your pardon?"

He leans down. Speaks louder and more slowly. "I said. What—"

"I heard you the first time. I was giving you a chance to redeem yourself." Then, into the young man's blank-faced confusion, she says, "I am neither young nor a lady. You may address me as Ma'am. And you may bring me a martini. Gin. Dry. Straight up. Twist."

She decides on a Caesar salad and a steak, because she knows what that is, doesn't have to think about it or ask about it and can take half of it home with her afterwards. Her drink comes. As she sips the cold, fiery gin, she thinks again about *Suffering Fools*. Why did she go looking for it? And why, instead of getting rid of it, did she carefully slide it back into its slot on the S shelf, between Muriel Spark and John Steinbeck?

It is a hateful, almost psychotic book. She knew that as soon as she started reading it all those decades ago for her book club. She never actually made it to that book club meeting. Never went back, either. She had become a bereaved parent, soon to be a divorcee. She no longer fit in with the mothers and wives.

Still, she hung on to *Suffering Fools*. Even packed it up and moved it with her to Toronto. And now, though she could easily justify getting rid of it, she still can't let it go. There is something talismanic about it. It is a solid, sensual reminder of the moment in her life when everything changed.

What if Morgan had not died? Had instead come home that night with her father and as usual retreated downstairs to her private quarters? Would Clarissa in fact have had the talk she had planned to have with Ramsay, or would her courage have failed her? Inertia is such a strong force. Almost irresistible.

That talismanic business is a thing of the imagination, though, projected by her onto an inanimate object. Once more, she envies the animals she has studied. Their only external effects—nest, web, perhaps a sparkly stone to present to a prospective mate—are purely useful. Discarded or abandoned the second they outlive their usefulness. No sentiment involved.

What if she had been able to bring herself to get rid of Morgan's effects? Then had started in on her own? Beginning with her books—donating them to libraries and hospitals and so on. Calling up some service like *Got Stuff?* and having her clothes and furniture and pictures and knick-knacks hauled away. What then? Would she have ended up sitting naked on a bare floor, waiting for death to find her? Even making it easy for death—pulling that *Valé* pamphlet out of the mail caddy by the phone and making a single call?

Her Caesar salad arrives. As she crunches down on romaine, Clarissa finally recognizes her state of mind for what it is. The restlessness. The distracting activity. Yes. She is on the brink of something. For the first time in years.

It would be so easy.

Morgan's last written words. Too easy indeed. Too damned easy. *Thank you, Morgan,* she thinks as her steak arrives, blood-rare and sizzling.

"Fresh-ground pepper, Ma'am?"

When she gets home she strips naked and stands in front of her full-length mirror. Takes inventory. Skin hanging in folds. Texture less like crêpe now, more like tree bark. Breasts concave and hanging. Pubis almost bald. She fetches a hand mirror, stands with her back to the full-length. Spine bowed and knobbed. Buttocks gone. She turns. Neck forward-swaying like a vulture's. Nose sharp-ridged. Shape of skull visible through thin fluff of hair.

Perfect. Perfect specimen. Another creature no one looks at because they do not want to see it. Specifically, they do not want to see anything about it that might remind them of themselves. *Crone Alone*. All right. She has a title.

"Mrs. Pettingill! How lovely to see you again."

Clarissa gives Felicity Staines full marks for remembering her name. Her robe today is peacock-blue, but other than that all is the same at *Valé*. The same waft of eucalyptus met Clarissa as she came through the door. And she wonders what it must be like to have to listen all day to that ethereal humming.

"I just wanted to bring this back," she says, laying the promotional folder on Felicity's desk. "I won't be needing it."

Felicity's smile remains serene. "You know, Mrs. Pettingill, putting one's name on *Valé's* waiting list is in no way binding. Again, we are attendant on evolving legislation. But even once we are free to proceed, any client of ours will be correspondingly free to opt out of the program. Even during the course of the actual chosen day."

"Provided they still have their wits about them."

"I'm sorry?"

Clarissa sets the brakes on her walker. Flips the seat down. Sits. "What got you into this business, Ms. Staines?"

"Thanatology? Well, my father—"

"Yes, I remember Melville Staines. Forgive me for interrupting, but time gets precious when you're my age. I meant the assisted-suicide business. And please don't call it culmination or any of the other euphemisms you come out with in that thing." She stabs a finger at the promotional folder.

Felicity's gaze cools, and for once her voice assumes an edge. "A few years ago," she begins, "I had to retrieve the remains of a woman who committed suicide. She had gotten into a hot bath and slit her wrists. I knew this woman. Had grown up with her, more or less. She had been my father's receptionist for decades. That's why I did the job myself instead of delegating it to my staff. The bath water was dark red. Almost opaque. Her body was bone white. And her expression—"

Felicity pauses. Resumes. "All I could think about was how hurt and frightened and alone she must have felt, in those last minutes."

"Not to mention alive," Clarissa says.

"Pardon?"

"I'm assuming she wasn't wearing one of those happy-patches you're going to slap on people to make them think they're just drifting off for a nice nap. So she'd have known full well what she was doing. Maybe, before she lost consciousness, she would have been filled with regret, too. Wishing with all her heart that she hadn't gotten into that tub with that razor blade."

"Mrs. Pettingill, I don't understand where this is going. Surely you're not suggesting that what happened to Miranda—that was her name—was preferable to—"

"My daughter was killed. She was young. Healthy. Brilliant. With what would have been a wonderful life ahead of her. When she died, all I could think was, *I hope it happened instantly. I hope she had no idea what hit her.* My husband, her father, went the other way. Dreamed up all these visions of a heavenly afterlife and projected them onto her. To hear him tell it, her last minutes would have been the most glorious thing that ever happened to her. Neither of us could face the truth. Which was that at some point, however fleetingly, our daughter would have known that her life was ending. It would have been a terrifying and awful knowledge. But it would have been hers."

Clarissa stands up. Flips the seat of her walker back and releases the brakes. "I won't take up any more of your time, Ms. Staines. I'm sorry if I sounded overly critical of your enterprise."

"Not at all, Mrs. Pettingill. And while I respect your views, please understand that if there is ever anything *Valé* can do for you—"

"Goodbye."

Clarissa turns and wheels her walker as fast as she can toward the door. She needs to get out of there. Needs to stop breathing that cloying eucalyptus and hearing that damned music. She has a book to write. And she'll write it, too. If it kills her.

Acknowledgements

THE FOLLOWING STORIES WERE PUBLISHED previously: "Late Breaking" in *The New Quarterly* Number 136 Fall 2015; "Witness" in *The Walrus* May 2016; "The Last Trumpet" in *Canadian Notes & Queries* Number 98 Winter 2017 and *Best Canadian Stories 2017*; "Olly Olly Oxen Free" in *The New Quarterly* Number 141 Winter 2017.

I am grateful to Biblioasis, Mansfield Press, *The New Quarterly*, and the Canada Council for the Arts for grants that greatly aided in the completion of this book.

My thanks to Kim Aubrey, Elaine Batcher, and Andrew Macrae, my thoughtful and generous first readers.

I am indebted to Gemey Kelly and Patrick Allaby of the Owens Art Gallery, Mount Allison University, for allowing me access to Colville House.

For their interest and support, I owe thanks to Allan and Holly Briesmaster, Leslie Deane, Marvyne Jenoff, the Literary Lobsters, and Judith Watkins.

And as always, I am grateful to John Metcalf and Dan Wells, editor and publisher of Biblioasis, for their diligence, faith, and friendship.